The guard came at me, using the rifle as a club.

I let him. Lowering my center of balance and shifting to the balls of my feet was an immediate survival reaction. At the last moment of the charge, I turned and twisted, like a feather riding the energy off him. He stumbled past, as surprised as if I really had vanished, and I was out the door.

Tai Chi. It's more than just a funny dance.

I ducked the second guard. Spun past the third. Began to run. When I heard a rifle being cocked behind me, I lengthened my stride and tried to sense everything around me as I ran.

You hear legends in the martial arts, including the idea that masters can dodge bullets. I'd never tried it. But I was about to learn whether I could escape tranquilizer darts....

Dear Reader,

I'm sitting at my computer in August '06 and just got some sad news. The Silhouette Bombshell line, which has been my writing home for two years, will be ending with the publication of the January '07 books—including this one. Wow. A line and an individual series, both closing at the same time.

THE MADONNA KEY has been a learning experience in the worst and best possible ways. I've made friendships I hadn't dreamed of, developed skills I hadn't guessed at and grown up in ways someone in her forties doesn't expect. And beyond all of that, I watched what was almost nothing—just a flitting of thought—gather in talented writers, agents, editors and readers and become *real*. Thank you, dear readers, for your role in this surprising creation.

And as for the Silhouette Bombshell line? This unique line of action-adventure stories featuring kick-butt heroines has been opportunity incarnate, from start to finish. It gave many of us a place to push the envelope with our writing, and has rewarded us in unexpected ways. I am honored and humbled to have been a part of it.

Best wishes, and farewell!

Evelyn Vaughn

P.S. Check out www.madonnakey.com and www.grailkeepers.com for more about, well, everything!

Evelyn Vaughn

SEVENTH KEY

Published by Silhouette Books

America's Publisher of Contemporary Romance

The MADONNA KEY series was cocreated by
Yvonne Jocks, Vicki Hinze and Lorna Tedder.

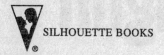 SILHOUETTE BOOKS

ISBN-13: 978-0-373-51435-9
ISBN-10: 0-373-51435-2

SEVENTH KEY

Copyright © 2007 by Yvonne Jocks

Visit Silhouette Books at www.eHarlequin.com

Printed in U.S.A.

Books by Evelyn Vaughn

EVELYN VAUGHN

has written stories since she learned to make letters. But during the two years that she lived on a Navajo reservation in Arizona—while in second and third grade—she dreamed of becoming not a writer, but a barrel racer in the rodeo. Before she actually got her own horse, her family moved to Louisiana. There, to avoid the humidity, she channeled more of her adventures into stories instead.

Since then, Evelyn has canoed in the east Texas swamps, rafted a white-water river in the Austrian Alps, rappelled barefoot down a three-story building, talked her way onto a ship to Greece without her passport, sailed in the Mediterranean and spent several weeks in Europe with little more than a backpack and a train pass. While she enjoys channeling the more powerful "travel Vaughn" on a regular basis, she also loves the fact that she can write about adventures with far less physical discomfort. Since she now lives in Texas, where she teaches English at a local community college, air-conditioning still remains an important factor.

In 2005, Evelyn won the prestigious RITA® Award from the Romance Writers of America for her first Bombshell novel, A.K.A. Goddess. Feel free to contact Evelyn through her Web site, www.evelynvaughn.com, or by writing to: P.O. Box 6, Euless, TX, 76039.

The Silhouette Bombshell line and THE MADONNA KEY series are about strong women, and this book would not be possible without more strong women than I can count—so my apologies to any of you I might leave out! I'm increasingly grateful to my readers, for that moment of magical kinship when I realize you see what I see. To my fellow Madonna authors, for playing story with me. To the kick-butt Bombshell authors, who made this line such an honor to write for. To the people at Harlequin/Silhouette Books for taking a chance with us. To my agent and her staff at Folio Literary Management, for their keen support. I'm grateful to my family, for their patience. My colleagues, for their approval. My chapter-mates and critique-mates and book-club-mates, for their rapport. Even my pets, for their fidelity.

Moving into coed thanks, I'm grateful to brilliant nonfiction authors, from Margaret Starbird to Antonia Fraser, without whose brilliance I could never make these fictional journeys; and to numerous imaginary friends, of my own creation and the creation of others, who remind me when I'm flagging why stories may be the best magic in existence. I do not mean to lessen the importance of any one individual by counting so many. But THE MADONNA KEY series took two years, from initial idea to final page, and I'm just that grateful.

So this book is dedicated to all of you, in no particular order: Jenna, Paige, Juliet, Cindy, Karmela, Tashya, Sadhbh, Sharron, Charles, Helen, Toni, Kelly, Penn, Georgette, Carol, Kermit, Judith, Roberta, Pattie, Isabel, Rae, Lorie, Jayne, Cady, Lorna, MOM!, Carolyn, Meg, Gracie, Lisa, Kathy, Ramses, Simone, Maggi, Lex, Rhys, Catrina, Scarlet, Vicki, both Henrys, Clare and Diane, Laura, Deb, Pam, Karen, Mo, Angel, Paula, JaninieBean, Frenchie and so many, many more I'm sure I'll remember too late.

And it is dedicated to the faithful authors and readers of the Silhouette Bombshell line.

Thank you for helping me to write, and thus to exist.

Chapter 1

Once, not long after the Romans crucified a prophet and kindled a religious revolution, a handful of woman refugees arrived in Southern Gaul. Their leadership revived an ancient tradition of priestesses, spreading good news and wisdom while guarding against the rise of patriarchal fears, in hopes that their descendents would survive and someday save the world.

I regained consciousness slowly. For a while, I hung in grayness, almost able to believe this was only a nightmare.

Then I tasted the very real gag in my mouth—folded silk against my tongue—and I knew better. Fear hit me, the reality of my situation almost too awful to face through the disorientation of the drugs. Yet despite the temptation to drift back into that painless place, even my addled brain knew there was one precious thing that made facing reality worth any price.

I concentrated on finding my hands. I had trouble with even that, through the haze. Fingers. I had fingers, right?

Pretty basic thought processes for someone with a Ph.D., but a struggle. A memory of baby talk flirted with me: *Are those* your *fingers? Whose fingers are those…?*

No, Maggi. Concentrate. I'd been in tight spots before, hadn't I? My fingers curled at my command.

A mechanical purr surrounded me. An engine. Was I in a truck? A plane? I fought all distractions, even the memory of how I might have gotten here or who had taken me. Freedom first. Now that I'd established fingers, I focused on my tied hands. I began to flex my wrists, just a bit. If I figured out the bonds, maybe I could slip them. Once I freed my hands, *then* I could consider—

"She's moving," said a male voice, nearby.

A sharp pinch in my shoulder—*crap!*—and I slid back into memory….

And motherhood.

Having a baby is life altering—and I don't just mean the leaky breasts, time off work or baby-proofed house. I mean, it changes you. Me at least. I was still Magdalene Sanger-Stuart, a comparative mythology instructor for a small northeastern college, still somewhat tall, still brown-haired. I was still a grailkeeper, intent on finding the sacred cups of ancient goddess worshippers for the empowerment of women. I was still very much in love with my new husband, Lex Stuart.

Yes, that one. Billionaire Alexander Rothschild Stuart III, and you don't know the half of it.

But all of that, *all* of it, was now filtered through the ever-present awareness of my baby daughter, Kestrel.

One of the many ways this manifested was that I now kept track of time by how old Kestrel was.

I first learned about the Black Madonnas after getting home from the hospital with my two-weeks-early redheaded offspring. Of course I'd *heard* about Black Madonnas— comparative mythologist, remember? "Black Madonnas" are black-skinned representations of the Virgin Mary. Usually the term refers to older works—they were the big thing during the Middle Ages, at the same time that a record number of cathedrals were named Notre Dame and subversive trouba- dours sang of a divine and unattainable lady. I've always believed there was something pagany about that gothic fad— see above: goddess grails.

But the Black Madonnas that my friend Rhys Pritchard called about from Paris sounded different from the norm.

"You should be with your baby," he insisted, once I told him the good news. Considering that we'd once flirted at a romance ourselves, barely a year earlier, Rhys's congratulations sounded remarkably heartfelt. "I can call at a better time."

"This is a perfect time," I insisted. Actually, I had uncom- fortably engorged porn-star breasts and was wearing a sanitary napkin manufactured for a race of giants. But I'd dropped into a comfortable chair in my embarrassingly fine new Connec- ticut home when I answered the phone. Compared to other ad- ventures I'd had—like being thrown in front of a subway train in France, scuba diving in storm conditions off Egypt and more than one real sword fight—this was bearable.

And I couldn't help but think that maybe, just maybe, I ought to spend a few minutes focusing on something other than the timbre of my baby's cry or the color of her poo. "Kestrel's asleep with her daddy. So tell me about these Black Madonnas."

"The iconography's unique. She's wearing a sword, and

holding not just the child but a key. She has a white jug or jar at her feet, similar to—"

"Mary Magdalene," I finished for him, about the jar. Intriguing! Having had that name my whole life, it was good to see the Magdalene finally getting some good press and losing the trumped-up prostitute image. But despite recent rumors about her own motherhood…a Madonna? I wasn't quite ready to go that far. Rhys and I talked for a few minutes about the similarity of Madonnas to Isis statuary—Isis had been popular for thousands of years before Mary. She held a child, and was often represented as black. We speculated on the possibility of her blackness being symbolic—a mix of all colors, or the absence of all colors. Then Rhys mentioned a more disturbing bit of information. "The relics are Catrina's, actually. Catrina Dauvergne's. She found them. We're…together now."

There'd been bad blood between me and that museum curator.

"Ah," I said, and shifted with lingering discomfort. Just afterpains and muscle soreness, I think. Catrina Dauvergne seemed surprisingly unimportant just then. "Good for her."

That's when my husband, Lex, made his entrance, wearing only pajama pants, cradling our tiny darling against his bare, scar-etched chest. Lex's hair was a ginger brown, though it had been red in his childhood, and he carried himself like royalty. Kestrel's head was pointy, her eyes barely focused and her little mouth hung open, as if to taste the world around her.

They were beautiful together.

Their presence seemed easily as important as Rhys saying, "You heard about the earthquakes here in France? We suspect they may have been induced, and that they're somehow related to the Black Madonnas Catrina and I found."

"Are you okay?" I thought to ask, but when Rhys assured

me that they needed nothing more than my mythological expertise, I let it go.

See what I mean?

Changed.

Moisture in my mouth. That's what pulled me back toward consciousness the second time. The gag had been shifted, replaced by a cool, wet cloth. I sucked greedily on it out of pure instinct, like an infant myself, before I even remembered.

I'd been kidnapped. I was being held against my will.

And something worse...

I tried to protest, tried to form my cracked lips around words while I could. "You...you have to let us go. My husband—"

Rough hands slid the gag back into place, muffling my cry of protest. I began to thrash then, my hands and feet still tied. I had to escape. I had something precious—

Again, the sharp stab of a hypodermic needle slowed me.

My husband. Was this because of Lex? His wealth had always made me uncomfortable. But I couldn't concentrate anymore.

My second-to-last thought as I faded to oblivion was to notice the pressure in my ears. We *were* on an airplane.

Kestrel was about three months old when I heard from Ana Reisner Fraser, an art specialist for Interpol's Cultural Property Division, with questions about ley lines.

"I hope you don't mind," she said over our speaker phone. "Rhys Pritchard gave me your name. He said you specialize in mythology of the, er, feminine persuasion?"

"Goddesses." I grinned as I turned down the radio in the midst of a newscast about the second big storm to hit Europe in a week. I'd been moving around the spacious kitchen, chopping and storing snack vegetables. In the adjacent dining nook Kestrel lay on her tummy, on a quilt, lifting her head to look at the dog. Our huge Irish wolfhound lay three feet away with his nose on his paws, watching her right back. "Yes, he said you might call."

"I'll get right to the point, then. Are you aware of any connections between the divine feminine and ley lines?"

That was an interesting question, and for a while we happily discussed all the possibilities. Supposedly, ley lines are channels of power just below the surface of the earth. Imagine a topographic map of the world. Then imagine a huge, rough net of string. Imagine laying the net over the map, and the earth sort of…soaking it up, to hide it. And now imagine currents of energy, running through those threads like underground rivers. That's what ley lines are.

"The main connection to goddesses would be an Earth Mothery Gaia consciousness," I suggested. "If the earth is a woman, the ley lines are her circulatory system. Or maybe her nerve network. Iffy analogy. So…is this connected to the Black Madonnas Rhys mentioned?"

I hadn't been actively involved in any goddess quests since the week of my wedding—long story, that. I'd been four months pregnant at the time, so that adventure hadn't been on purpose. A few months later I'd given financial assistance to a nurse from Chicago who was doing the work I'd temporarily abandoned, and we'd kept in touch. Other than that, I'd been on a sabbatical.

Ana confirmed my guess. She and a group of friends, including Rhys, Catrina and Ana's new husband, Robert, were pursuing proof that a cult of women they called "Marians" had worshipped an unorthodox version of the Mary figure. The movement seemed to have existed since the Middle Ages, and even included queens such as Elizabeth I of England and her rival, Mary Stuart of Scotland—a distant ancestor of my husband's and thus my baby's.

That explained the sixteenth-century embroidery of a Black Madonna that Catrina Dauvergne had unexpectedly given us for Kestrel, done by the hand of Mary Queen of Scots herself. It was now in the Cloisters museum, being worth millions, and had gone a long way toward easing the bad blood between us.

Now I felt the oddest twinge of…envy? My baby was related to these Marians, but I wasn't. This wasn't my adventure.

Kestrel chose the middle of my conversation with Ana to roll over, all by herself, onto her back. She began chortling and blowing raspberries at this accomplishment—a huge milestone for a three-month-old. So she wasn't just Gerber-ad adorable, but quite accomplished, and I knelt to quietly tell her so.

"You've got a baby?" asked Ana, no slouch as an investigator. "How wonderful! Boy or girl?"

As it turned out, Ana had recently discovered she was pregnant, after being told she couldn't conceive. To say our conversation "degenerated" from there would buy into the societal denigration of feminine power. Having a baby is about creating and protecting *life,* thank you very much—if you think it's easy or unimportant, let's see the guys give it a go!

But I'll admit we got distracted by the benefits of breast-feeding, our preference for the word *mother* over *mom* from anyone but that mother's child, and our distaste for women telling labor-and-delivery horror stories to first-time mothers.

"Big surprise—it hurt," I admitted, though I didn't know Ana enough to share that even making love had hurt afterward, the first few times after we'd passed the six-week prohibition. It had been nothing we couldn't overcome. "But some things are worth the hurting. My husband survived childhood leukemia, and later a knife attack that left him in the hospital for a week. He never complained, through either one. I wanted to show that women can be just as tough."

"So did you?" Ana asked.

"Damn right I did. Not always quiet—" I grinned "—but tough. Nature can be a bitch sometimes, but she usually knows what she's doing."

"Which brings us to…" she said, in reluctant segue, and we were back to ley lines. She feared they were somehow being manipulated to threaten Western Europe. There had been the earthquakes that spring. Then power outages. We could only wonder if the strange weather of late had any connection.

"If only we knew who was doing it," Ana sighed. "And how!"

I considered suggesting an ancient, secret society of powerful men, but decided not to go there. When Lex got home from work that night, he vetoed the idea, as well.

"Dominant powers prefer the status quo," he reminded me, using a bottle to feed pumped breast milk to Kes. He enjoyed his father–daughter time. "People who want more power, or who fear they're losing power—they're the ones who go for desperate measures."

And my husband knew from dominant powers. He was still very much involved with a few of them—maybe too involved—even as I stayed home with our child in our perfect new life.

Third time's a charm. This time, when I found myself swooping back into tenuous consciousness, I didn't move. I controlled my breath, trying to keep it as slow and deep as if I were still out cold.

This time I remembered my own particular strengths.

It's like with Tai Chi. Or childbirth. You have far more power when you go with the flow than when you fight against it.

We were still moving, the hum of a motor constant. But my ears were no longer popping. Had the plane landed? A shifting of my center of gravity felt more like a truck on a winding road. Good. Much easier to escape from a truck than an airplane.

But first I had to know what was going on.

My throat wasn't overly dry, despite the gag in my mouth; my captors must have been giving me water on a regular basis. The main abuse to my body came from being tied up for so long. How long? Had we left the Northeast? The USA?

Someone up front called an announcement in Italian. Crap! I don't speak Italian. The words *nostra destinazione* I understood, though. Our destination. Had we reached it? Were we nearing it?

I couldn't wait any longer. I had to know. I risked slitting my eyes, tried to see through my lashes and got only a view of the roof. It *was* a van, carpeted and padded inside. No windows. I would have to turn my head to see if anybody else was with me. I tried to do so as if in my sleep.

Immediately, someone shouted in Italian. I got only a glimpse of the person beside me—also bound, her coiled black braids sagging loose—before the sting of the damned hypodermic took me yet again. *Olga*, I thought. *Just Olga. But where…?*

The winter had passed with several more calls from Rhys and Ana. We discussed the earth's shift from the dualistic Age of Pisces to the more egalitarian Age of Aquarius—and whether this worldwide change threatened someone dangerous. We discussed the power outages and a deadly flu outbreak that seemed like certain terrorism, and the droughts, hurricanes and freak blizzards that, amazingly enough, also seemed deliberate.

And we discussed the mysterious Adriano family of Naples. They, too, seemed to be after the Black Madonnas. Their fingerprints were on the earthquakes and a recent outbreak of the Spanish flu.

Was it possible the Adrianos were using ley lines and astrological influences to cause natural disasters?

Could they cause worse?

The modern-day Marians set up headquarters of a sort in southern France. More women joined their ranks—an antiquities thief, a photographer, an epidemiologist and someone who understood geomancy. One of them was brutally murdered.

I helped them with whatever information I could find, sent sympathy cards and contributed to relief organizations. But I remained distracted. Kestrel was four months old when I went back to teaching, part-time, for the fall semester. She was eight months old for my first wedding anniversary and for baby's first Christmas. I'd planned on teaching full-time for spring term, starting in January, but decided that two classes were more than enough for now. Every time I nursed my baby or took her out in the stroller, I felt so relieved not to be in Europe, not to have *her* there, that my need to protect her overrode my guilt and envy. Mostly.

Kestrel was almost ten months old when little Alexandria Bishop, age two and a half, came from England to stay with us.

On a day's notice.

"Nadia wouldn't ask, if she weren't really worried," Lex had insisted about his friend as we drove to JFK to fetch the child and her adopted grandmother. Grandmother Bishop would only stay a few days. Lexie, as the girl was suspiciously nicknamed, would be with us indefinitely.

Lex glanced in the round baby-view mirror almost as often as the rearview, at Kestrel asleep in her car seat behind us, but he also glanced at me. He rarely avoids people's gazes, even if he feels guilty. It's part of that noble posture I mentioned.

"I know," I said, about Nadia's worries for her daughter.

"Lexie's my goddaughter." One consequence of his wealth was regular paternity suits. He'd always demanded testing. It had always cleared him. But the Bishop girl had never been tested. My husband's answer to questions about her parentage—when someone got rude enough to ask—was a mysterious and uncharacteristic, "No comment."

He'd told me about the child early in our engagement, to explain why we shouldn't name *our* daughter Alexandria. Maybe I'd had to work to believe him, at first, especially with a British cousin of mine buying into the whole scandal. But I'd known Nadia already, if from a distance, and met Lexie at our wedding in New York. The reality of them had soothed away suspicions that determined faith in my lover couldn't.

Her real father mustn't know she exists, Nadia had explained. *He is dangerous. You can't know the favor Lex has done me, with those "no-comments."*

Besides, Lexie's long, silky hair was darker than both her mother's and Lex's. The girl looked nothing like my husband.

I reached across the stick shift and laid my hand on Lex's tight forearm. Nadia, some sort of covert agent, had just begun investigating the murder of Rhys and Ana's Marian friend. That was why she wanted her daughter safely out of Europe. "I know she's your goddaughter. I know you care. And this is something we can both do to help the Marians."

As traffic forced us to stop, Lex looked over at me and mouthed, *Love you.* Since I hadn't been raised with upper-class reserve, I just said it. "I love you, too, Your Highness."

That gave him a smile, as beautiful as his daughter's.

After that, I had *two* little girls in the house. Kestrel practically weaned herself in her hurry to embrace the sippy cup the way Lexie had. Considering that my daughter was teething, I wasn't as heartbroken to get my breasts back as I'd initially feared. Kestrel learned to stand, with something to hold on to, and to play pat-a-cake—or, as my family called it, circle-to-circle—and to wave bye-bye. She could even say "Mama" and "Dada," usually to the dog.

Lexie was as helpful as a two-year-old could be, when she wasn't ignoring the baby completely. She only made one trip home to visit, accompanied by Lex. It turns out her birth father *was* dangerous—he was one of the Adrianos, whose involvement in Europe's latest crises had increasingly concerned the Marians. But he wasn't dangerous to his daughter or her mother. Joshua Adriano was now helping the Marians work against his family. Because of the growing threat of "natural" disasters in Europe—not to mention the human threat—Lex brought the child back to Connecticut. This time he also brought her nanny, Olga, who had been in Nadia's family forever and was recovering from an Adriano beating.

When you hear *Nanny* you don't think of a woman in her midfifties, competent and in surprisingly good shape. Olga and I clicked immediately, like some women just do. It's not as if the house wasn't big enough for her.

Not long after that, Kes turned eleven months old. I had the Friday before spring break off.

And Olga and I decided to take the girls into the city.

I regained consciousness very slowly, my mouth gagged, my hands and feet bound, drifting in and out of memory like a piece of driftwood in a tidal basin.

We'd been window shopping in New York.

"This is the place," I'd said, looking from the brochure one of my students had given me to the sign in the window. My bodyguard, Frank—Lex was big on bodyguards for us—went in, checked things out, then stationed himself inconspicuously outside the gallery.

No, I thought now, with the power of hindsight. *Don't...*

Reliquary, the little Manhattan gallery was called. It specialized in items salvaged from demolished churches and monasteries, which is why my student had thought I'd like it—one person's religion is another person's mythology. The girls had enjoyed pointing at the statues, crawling under the carved pews, watching sunlight through stained glass play across their pudgy hands. I didn't expect to find any Black Madonna images, not in the States. Instead, I was studying the different versions of the Virgin Mary, looking for anything that might key in an idea.

Considering the Marians' tenuous connection to goddesses, and the absolute absence of sacred cups in the mix, I felt at something of a loss. The Marians' quest wasn't really mine.

We had a potty-and-diaper break in the shiny facilities at the back of the gallery. Kestrel was safely back in her almost too small Snugli, all wiggles and the scent of baby powder, when my throat began to tighten painfully. That's how my subconscious warns me of danger. Call it a gift of the goddess—one of the few gifts that still lingered in me, low-key, after over a year out of the game. Sure enough, a glance around the gallery revealed three large, black-suited men pushing through the front entrance.

I couldn't see Frank.

Throw a statue through the window! Make a scene for passersby! Attract attention! But those desperate suggestions came in hindsight as I lay wherever I was, the drug wearing off, the world swooping around me. They didn't arrive in the gallery.

At the time, Olga and I had exchanged dark looks. She'd seen them, too. She didn't trust them, either.

"Back entrance?" I'd suggested, hooking Kestrel's diaper bag more firmly over my shoulder.

"Let's play a game," the older woman had said, picking up Lexie. "It's called Emergency Exit. Where is it? No, look!"

Lexie pointed at the glowing red sign, then grudgingly covered her ears as instructed. I pulled Kes's head against my bosom to muffle the sound and pushed through the heavy metal door into a back room.

Noooo...

Alarms screamed—this was an art gallery, after all. The police would be a positive development. Kestrel wailed. Olga and I wove our way across the back room toward the second Exit sign, which Lexie kindly pointed out for us.

Before we reached it, we were surrounded.

More men in black suits—men with guns—emerged from behind cubicle partitions and stacks of boxes, dressed much like the men up front...who had apparently been there to flush us into the privacy of the back rooms.

I had the awful thought that this was my husband's fault. He had enemies far more current than mine. He was so rich we made great targets. The bodyguard he'd hired—

But I'd fought the idea of a bodyguard. I'd believed the student with the brochure. I had my own eyes, and my own good sense. It was my fault, too.

Lexie started to cry, either from the whoop of klaxons or the tension pouring off her caretakers. Olga and I shifted to stand back-to-back, instinctively. But the girls... Almost immediately we made it side by side, Olga facing ahead and me facing behind so that Lexie, on Olga's hip, sat safely between us. I wished I risked dragging Kes out of her Snugli to do the same. Instead I had to pray that my arms and the carrier would cushion her from harm.

Please, nooooo…

I bent my knees, sank into a basic Tai Chi pose. It really can be used for more than relaxation. On a good day, I might have managed to use these brutes' strength against them. I would let them come at me, spin out of their way, use balance and flow to "become invisible." I hadn't given up the practice. I'd sometimes worn Kestrel in her Snugli while doing my daily forms if she was fussing.

But that had been mostly for exercise and meditation, this last year. This was combat. If I attempted to slip between our attackers, Kes might get hit. Besides, me moving would leave Lexie Bishop exposed.

Nadia had left her in Lex's safekeeping. Lex had left her in mine.

Crap.

"So let's negotiate," I said boldly, over the alarm and the children's screams.

The *crack* of a gun and a stabbing pain in my thigh ended my dilemma. I looked down in surprise at a bright orange blossom of plastic fringe. Tranquilizer dart? I dropped to my knees, fast. The drug almost beat me there. I barely had time to wrap my arms around my baby and force myself to fall backward so that I wouldn't crush her, before everything—

Everything….

With an audible gasp I now opened my eyes and my mouth, dragging in more clarifying air. I wasn't gagged anymore. I lay on a narrow bed in some kind of high-ceilinged bunker. My hands weren't tied. My feet weren't tied. I had to pee something awful but didn't care. I was able to push myself up, despite someone's cry of, "Maggi, don't overdo it, you—"

The room swooped around me from the lingering effects of the drug, and with it swooped children's faces. Two. Four. I noticed them only long enough to dismiss them, seeking out the one precious thing for which I'd had to stay sane. If I were lucky, the thugs who'd kidnapped me had left her unharmed in the gallery. If—

But there she sat, held by nanny Olga, scowling at me through fussy blue eyes.

"Kes," I croaked—and Olga was smart enough to give her to me, sinking onto the cot beside me as if to catch the baby should I drop her in my weakened state. I didn't drop her. I held Kestrel so tightly that she squeaked. I inhaled the scent of baby shampoo off her red curls. I kissed her head, and her pudgy hands, as if just touching her completed a necessary circuit…completed me.

I felt so relieved she was unharmed that only eventually, reluctantly, could I make myself face how bad this was.

Kidnapped alone, I might have stood a fighting chance.

Kidnapped with my eleven-month-old daughter, I could be forced to do anything. *Anything.* And so might her father.

We could be used as hostages to bring about Lex's downfall, even his death. The fact that people existed who wanted just that had been a sour note to our otherwise wonderful marriage. But now…

Now, after my long, drug-induced trail of thoughts, I had to suspect something just as bad. Some might say worse. The thugs had spoken Italian. And they'd taken Lexie Bishop, too.

This wasn't about Lex or his money. It was about the Black Madonna.

If Adrianos held us, we hostages could secure their plans to destroy all of Europe.

Chapter 2

Lifting my gaze from Kestrel's precious head, I took stock of the large, echoing room with its children and cots and two Porta Potti...no, one was a port-a-shower. There were toys, even a plastic play gym. There were colorful tables and chairs, a stack of books and board games, a gerbil cage with its little rodent racing around its wheel—and none of those diminished the harsh sterility of the white walls and industrial lighting.

Lexie Bishop had climbed onto Olga's lap beside me, almost as soon as Kestrel had emptied it. One other adult, a handsome woman with silver-blond hair, held an infant no larger than a newborn. That made one, two, three...

At least five children. Six, counting Kes.

Six innocents being held against their will.

The blond woman, about my age, came to me with her child. A pink onesie proclaimed the newborn to be a little girl.

"Maggi Sanger-Stuart, right?" the blonde asked in a

familiar voice, and offered her hand. "I'd say 'pleased to meet you,' but under these circumstances, let's stick with hi. I'm Ana Fraser. We've spoken before."

Since Kestrel was standing on my lap, pushing back against the brace of my arm, I could take the woman's hand. "What...?"

She slid a gaze toward the children who'd followed her like ducklings—I had an idea which mother figure had been here the longest—and she forced a smile.

"First, let me introduce several friends of mine. These two—" Ana gestured the two oldest forward "—are Laurel and Phillipe Fouquet. You may know their guardian, Eve St. Giles Petter, who works for the CDC in Europe."

"The epidemiologist." She'd almost single-handedly stopped a freak outbreak of the Spanish flu the previous winter. "Hello, Laurel. Hello, Phillipe."

"I want my Aunt Eve," announced Laurel, dark-haired and solemn. About ten, she held a doll tight in her arms like a smaller girl might, and who could blame her? "My father died, and then my mother died, and I want my Aunt Eve, please."

"And Uncle Nick," added her smaller brother, as fair-haired as she was dark. "Uncle Nick will make the bad guys let us go."

"I'm sure he will," soothed Ana, touching Phillipe's shoulder and then stroking her free hand over Laurel's dark curls. "We'll get you two home as soon as we can.

"You already know Lexie Bishop, of course, with her nanny Olga," Ana continued, to me.

Lexie had condescended to play with Kestrel—from the safety of Olga's lap—by trying to catch Kes's flailing hands.

"Thank you for letting Olga hold Kestrel until I woke up, Lexie," I said. "That was very generous of you."

"*My* baby," Lexie announced. They'd been together almost two months. But then she added, as if in warning, "*My* nanna."

"This little bundle of joy is Maralise Fraser," Ana continued, about her own infant. "'Mara' fits her better for now, though. And that handsome young man over there—come closer, honey—this, Maggi, is Benny Adriano."

My smile faltered for a split second, before I recovered it. The lost little boy with his dark brown hair and olive skin and puppy-dog eyes certainly didn't *look* like the spawn of evil. But…*Adriano?*

"Hello, Benny," I said. He couldn't be over five years old. Surely he was too young to be here as a spy, much less as any kind of guard.

Scowling, the child said nothing.

"Benny is Joshua Adriano's son," clarified Ana, as smoothly as if each word didn't carry volumes of back story. Nadia Bishop's lover. Lexie's long-lost daddy. Was it possible his son was being punished for his defection? "By his former marriage."

Now I could see a distinct resemblance to his half sister Lexie. But if nobody else had mentioned that to the children, I sure wouldn't.

"Pleased to meet you, Benny," I said. "This is Kestrel."

"That is a stupid name," he accused, with a thick Italian accent.

"She's named after a kind of bird, a falcon. Aren't you?" I didn't go into detail about the Isis-Osirus-Horus legend that had prompted us to get so creative. At the moment, Kes might easily have been trying to take flight, twisting around in general protest of the last—how long had it been?

And I really needed to use the facilities, so I made my excuses. Awkward or not, I took my baby with me. When I got back, Olga and young Mlle Fouquet were leading the other children across the room in a kind of marching game, leaving Ana and me some privacy. Benny Adriano went with them, but he seemed somehow separate from the others.

"So where are we?" I demanded of Ana, relieved to drop the smiles.

"I think," Ana said, "we're under the Adriano compound, outside Naples."

Oh…goddess. Naples, *Italy?*

The story didn't take long. Ana and baby Mara had been taken from the park, outside her summer home in St. Tropez. When she came to, the Fouquets were already in the bunker with her, snatched from a field trip. But since they'd been left conscious, perhaps since doses for children can be so dangerous, they'd described the trip and terrain very well.

"Phillipe is Geography-guy," Ana explained with a grin. "He was giving me 'west' and 'south,' and how long in each direction, like an eight-year-old scientist. He thinks he glimpsed Mount Vesuvius across the water when they got out of the van. Apparently his class is studying volcanoes, because…well, you know."

Because of the increasing likelihood that more volcanoes than that one in Greece would soon blow. We were now at ground zero for Europe's building apocalypse….

If the Adrianos meant to do what the Marians suspected, for reasons I didn't yet know.

And if we didn't stop them.

Benny had arrived after Ana woke. He kept asking for his Poppi and a man named Eric—"one of the guards," said Ana—but to no avail. "Benny says we're downstairs, 'in the basement.' We've heard there's an extensive network of tunnels and bunkers under the compound, so I assume that's what he means, although this one seems new."

She was right. I could smell the fresh paint and sealant.

"Along with the toys, there are plenty of supplies—diapers, baby food, snacks. Obviously they mean to keep us alive, probably as better leverage. But there are no windows. No electrical outlets. No vents wider than ten inches. No way to communicate with our loved ones."

"Their parents must be…" There weren't even words for what these children's parents were going through. And Lex…

Lex had always maintained a reserved control—except when it came to my safety. Now to have no word of either me or Kestrel, or Lexie for that matter…what kind of hell was he in?

I had no doubt he was turning the world over to find us by now. He had the connections to do just that. But did he have any idea where to look? What if he assumed we'd been taken by enemies other than the Adrianos?

"Exactly," agreed Ana darkly. "Robert must be going crazy."

"How many guards?" I put Kes down on the floor so that she could pull herself up using my hands, then plop down onto her butt again. Her diaper was dry, so she'd been changed recently. She must have eaten at some point since our abduction, probably more than once.

"The few times the doors have opened there were three guards, all armed, plus the man Benny calls Eric. I think he was Benny's bodyguard before this. Eric's the only one who comes more than a step or two into the room, usually to bring food, take out trash, make sure we've got everything we need. He seems like a good enough guy."

Ana stared at me intently as she said that last part, which made me think she knew even more about this Eric person—and reminded me that we couldn't be wholly candid with each other, even now. Was there the slightest chance the Adrianos weren't listening in on our conversations?

"Anyway, he's not armed, so it wouldn't do us a lot of good to jump him," she continued. "I doubt he'd have any value as a hostage."

So he had more value as a guard. Got it. "Weapons?" I asked. Our captors had to expect I'd ask things like this.

Mara was squirming now, and making little mewing noises. With an unnecessary apology, Ana unbuttoned her shirt, unfastened her nursing bra and eased her fussy daughter to her breast. She used a sheet from the cot as a drape, so that the other children were unlikely to see anything. In a moment, the infant was suckling away. Kes reached upward, fascinated.

I suddenly missed breastfeeding.

"No actual weapons, of course," Ana said, readjusting her hold on Mara. "The baby food is in plastic bottles, with plastic utensils. So's the juice and the water. Our meals are brought in on paper plates. The cots are bolted down. There's nothing in the toilet or shower that we can use."

My gaze had settled on the sheet over her shoulder—sheets can become ropes, and ropes could be used as weapons. She winked in understanding, but said, "Nothing at all. And anyway…"

Ana inclined her head toward something above us. A silver half sphere was embedded in the ceiling.

"They've got a camera on us," I guessed.

"Bingo," she said.

So whatever we did, we had to do without speaking of it or being seen by the eye in the sky. *Crap*.

There went any obvious plotting. Instead we had to make ourselves go along, doing nothing toward our release at all, which I don't think sat any better with Ana than it did with me.

At least the children gave us something to concentrate on

other than our anger and fears. They gave us a reason to hold our temper, to pretend everything would turn out fine.

And of course, pretending something empowers it.

We had story time—I told the kids my own family fairy-tale about a great queen who gives her nine beautiful daughters magic cups. We supervised some playtime with Buster, the gerbil. We had lunchtime, and got the children to help us clean up afterward in some little way or another. Diapers were changed, temper tantrums were averted and naps were decreed.

And then the thick metal door opened, and a new visitor arrived—flanked by three guards, each armed with rifles.

Against *children!*

Our visitor was a small woman, painfully slim and fragile. Her honeyed highlights were expensive, her doe eyes large and her face a frozen mask of displeasure. Before she could even speak, Benny hurled himself at her. "Mama! Mama!"

Her quick back-step couldn't avoid his hurtling body, and she stumbled slightly under the impact, snapping something in Italian that probably meant "Careful!" or, to judge by her continued scowl, "Don't!"

"Hello, Pauline," greeted Ana, with narrow-eyed distaste.

Pauline ignored her in that deliberate way women have. "I am to bring Magdalene Stuart to see Duke Adriano. Come."

I slowly stood, Kestrel in my arms. Benny continued to babble in Italian, reaching up for his mother. Beside me, Olga quietly translated, "Mama, why am I here? I want to go up to my rooms. I want Eric and Papa."

Pauline's response got translated as, "Poppi says you must be here with the other traitors. Stop crying. Do not be such a baby. You are embarrassing me."

Benny backed away, trying valiantly to stop the tears. The

Pauline hatred coming off the rest of us was so thick, I'm surprised she didn't collapse under its force.

"Not," she commanded in English, as I approached her, "with the brat."

My protective arms tightened around my daughter. "Then, Duke Adriano can bring his high-handed butt down here to talk to me."

Pauline's chin came up, and she practically stamped the ground in her ire. "No, you are coming to him."

I raised my eyebrows and didn't move. If they thought they would separate me from my baby...

"Duke Simon!" she called, loudly—

A dangerously smooth voice floated down to us from an intercom system. "Do not be such a baby, Pauline," it purred in barely accented English. "You are embarrassing me."

For a moment I almost liked him.

"Poppi?" called Benny, his face lighting with recognition as he looked up and around him, as if seeking God. "Poppi!"

Then the voice—Simon Adriano's voice, I assume—said, "I am too busy to wait for Mrs. Stuart to regain consciousness. Sergio, shoot the older girl. She might survive the adult dose."

And just that quick, one of the guards stepped forward.

I surged toward him, only fully understanding what was happening after I'd begun to move.

He shouldered his rifle, aimed it at Laurel Fouquet—

"No!" I tightened my hold on Kestrel with one arm and struck out with the other, shielding her body as I knocked the rifle barrel—

The crack of the shot, so near her head, made my daughter scream. With an Italian curse, Sergio swung at us. I ducked, body-checked him, knocked him back with my free shoulder.

But I saw that he would clip Kestrel if not me on that trajectory, so I stopped and took the full blow myself.

It knocked us backward onto the concrete floor. Backward because I practice balance and, with my baby in my arms, I refused to land any other way. I barely caught hold of her with my free hand before she could be thrown from me by the impact.

And nothing else happened.

Kestrel's screams became gasping and frantic. Baby Mara had stuttered awake into a full-out wail, and Lexie quickly joined them.

Ten-year-old Laurel just stood there, terrified.

Perhaps three feet behind her and two inches over her head, a tranquilizer dart had embedded itself deep in the industrial white wall.

A piece of orange fringe had stuck in her curly hair, as the dart passed through it.

"I'm sorry," I whispered to my daughter, rocking her there where I knelt on the floor. I was terrified I'd deafened her, terrified I'd shaken her in our fall, so damned terrified to face what women must have recognized for millennia, since the days of cavewomen.

No matter how tough you are, it's hard to fight effectively with a baby in your arms.

That's why some part of us still needed strong, dependable cavemen as mates. Damn it, damn it, *damn it!* And I didn't even know where mine was just now. Where the hell was he?

"Oh, Kes," I murmured. "Mommy's so sorry to scare you like that." Actually she didn't look scared so much as righteously pissed off. That's my girl.

"I have proffered an invitation, Mrs. Stuart," announced Simon Adriano's voice. "Adults only. Do not be rude again."

The other guards aimed their rifles at me while Sergio, who'd stepped back behind them with Pauline, reloaded.

I stopped looking into Kestrel's eyes and lifted my gaze to Olga's. She'd come forward—to take my baby. I glanced quickly to Ana, and saw confirmation. I had to go.

With more strength than I'd known I possessed, I rolled to my feet and leaned close to Olga as I passed Kestrel into her competent grip. "Someday," I whispered to her, "I'm going to kill him."

"I go first," Olga whispered grimly back.

Intriguing.

"Come," said Pauline, with a jerk of her chin. As if she were still in charge.

Simon's voice hissed, *"The dart,* Pauline."

Crap. I'd hoped they'd miss that. Or…had she only pretended to forget? The eye in the sky was looking at her, too.

Pauline walked slowly, and had to use both hands to yank the tranquilizer dart out of the wall, wincing as if recovering from an injury. By the time she returned to sweep past me, her fragile face was quite flushed—but, I thought, from more than effort. Hidden wounds? Embarrassment?

She completely ignored the big eyes with which Benny hopefully, futilely watched her progress, in both directions.

"Come," she snapped, sweeping through the heavy doorway to take me to Duke Simon Adriano.

Oh, I still hated her. But I had to hope there might be some motherly instincts hidden deep within that slim breast, instincts she just wasn't letting any of us see. Womanly instincts are a fairly powerful force.

And she wasn't the only one walking away from her child.

Chapter 3

To my surprise, I was led not into a corridor but a walkway through another, older room. After the sterility of the bunker, this place—which had the look of a WWII bomb shelter—felt ancient. But that wasn't the most surprising part.

No, that was the artifacts.

It was like stepping out of a gulag and into the Louvre. The artifacts weren't just stacked around—they were on display, on pedestals or in lit glass cases, many with engraved nameplates. I was only close enough to read the ones on the wall beside me as we walked. They labeled a Donatello bas-relief. A da Vinci painting! Beyond us ranged treasures whose details I could only guess at. A beautiful Black Madonna statue. An old alabaster jar—

Something shifted subtly inside me at the sight of that jar, its semitransparent whiteness glowing in the soft display light. Suddenly, what had been mere surprise at this hidden gallery—vague past more immediate concerns—became a flash of true interest.

It felt like that first deep breath you take when waking up in the morning.

The alabaster jar was one of the symbols of the Marians' Black Madonna. But like I've said, it often represents Mary Magdalene as well. The Bible holds that the Magdalene was on her way to anoint the body of Jesus when she found the empty tomb and then saw him, resurrected. An argument can be made that she is the woman who anointed Jesus's feet, too. Sacred oils were often kept in alabaster jars like that. I've got my own theories about why a powerful woman would anoint the feet of a figurative king, but that's not what suddenly held me.

The ancient jar in the display case looked easily two thousand years old. Could that be *the* alabaster jar?

Holy—

One of the guards gave me a hard shove, forcing me to keep walking. The one in front banged on a round metal door. I realized we were inside a vault, with no way out other than by whoever was on the other side swinging the door open.

I filed that information away to share with Ana and Olga when I returned. We wouldn't get out until someone let us out.

Pauline exited the vault door first, letting the guards focus on me as she led the way up two full flights of stairs, then down a marble-floored hallway to a bookshelf-lined, first-floor office. Only glass doors onto a rainy patio and the room's breadth gave the office any sense of openness...but I noticed the electric lock on the French door, and I wondered if the glass was bulletproof. A large desk dominated the room, with a smaller computer desk and a large, flat-panel monitor to one side. A high-backed chair was situated to work with either one...the kind of chair you half expected to turn and reveal the bad guy sitting in it. But this bad guy already stood to the side, by the bar.

He was maybe sixty and clean shaven, with a strong profile and a hawkish nose. His thick hair, a tawny shade of brown for an Italian, was lightened further by impending gray. He wore a deliciously expensive gray suit that could have made up for any number of sins, but his perfect posture and broad shoulders didn't really need the help.

"Sit," he commanded—and Pauline gingerly sank onto one of the two lesser chairs, in front of the desk. *Simon says.* "Would you care for a drink, Mrs. Stuart?"

For the record? My legal last name was Sanger-Stuart. I loved my husband desperately, but I was a liberal intellectual and, yes, I hyphenated. I usually didn't make a fuss about people dropping the Sanger part when there was a decent reason—such as a kindly older person who never considered otherwise, or at a function for my husband's business, when I was basically there to make him look good. Lex never protested at the occasional "Mr. Sanger," when we were at a school event, so it all worked out. This man might be older, but he was not kindly. Anyone who knew me well enough to track my movements into the city and take out my bodyguard knew what I preferred to be called.

The presence of Sergio and his tranquilizer gun, in the doorway, urged me to hold my tongue on that subject. But I did say, "No, I would not care for a drink. You're Simon Adriano, right?"

Simon laughed, and I had to bite back my answering smile—that's how charming the bastard was. "You women watch too much cinema," he mused, pouring himself a brandy and coming back to the desk. "Always you imagine poison in the drinks."

His English had the clipped edge of a British education and a seductive, sinuous quality that was all him. Power came off him in waves.

"Maybe I said no because drinking with someone is a social nicety," I suggested. "And I don't feel either social or nice about you."

"You will still sit," he insisted, with less charm. And he turned the large, flat-panel monitor to give me a better view of what was on his computer.

It was an overhead shot of the bunker playroom, with Olga singing to the children as they lay on mats for a nap. Baby Mara lay asleep in a crib, and Ana was bouncing Kestrel, my Kes, to keep her from fussing. In the corner—the monitor had a glorious 24-inch screen—red numbers, an inch high, counted down. 10:02. 10:01. 10:00. 9:59.

My knees weak, I sank onto the chair Simon had indicated. "What does the timer mean?"

"If you behave *nicely,* perhaps I will tell you." He took a cultured sip of his brandy, studying me. "How do such useless creatures as women cause so much trouble?"

If you can't say something nice… I said nothing.

He made a rude noise. "Americans," he muttered dismissively. "Then business it shall be. You are here to do three things, Mrs. Stuart. And you have exactly one week to accomplish them."

I didn't like the sound of this. Only someone really stupid would imagine he'd let her take her baby on whatever quest he'd thought up. "And my mission, if I choose to accept it?"

8:17.

"First, you are to have the ladies outside Lys send the mosaic, with full diagrams and photographs to facilitate reassembly, to me. You will be the courier, once it is dismantled."

That was one of the weirder requests I've heard. "A mosaic?"

"You really aren't in the inner circle, are you?" It shouldn't have bothered me—especially since he said it *especially* to bother me. I couldn't be at the center of every adventure. I didn't want to be, this time. When it came to collecting goddess grails, I *was* the inner circle. Wasn't that enough?

"Isn't that why you chose me, instead of Ana or Olga?" I asked, as if I felt as unaffected as I should have. "Because I'm not a Marian myself?"

Simon studied me. "I do not fear Marians. Your deadline for delivering the mosaic—every single tile of it, mind you—is midday on Saturday, or there will be consequences."

"Worse consequences than the total destruction of Europe?"

"Let us just say…more *personal* consequences." He slid a satisfied glance toward his monitor. 7:05. "And do not be naive. Surely an educated woman such as yourself is aware that any manipulation of the electromagnetic fields across Europe, particularly with drastic results in geological and atmospheric stability, will have long-term, worldwide consequences. It is called, I believe, a chain reaction?"

I said nothing. It was hard for me to pay attention to him and not the tiny, fish-eye-lens view of my daughter—or the clock. Head games, I warned myself, despite the panic in my throat. Why bother with toys and food and clean diapers, just to hurt or kill the children?

"This brings us to your second duty. While your friends are dismantling the mosaic, you must find the last tiles. My men have been monitoring the ladies' progress in Lys, for the most part without detection, and the Marians are missing just over a dozen of their tiles. I know where they are."

I waited. 5:48.

"They were likely taken from France to Scotland by Queen

Mary Stuart," explained Simon. "They are your daughter's ancestral tiles. You will reclaim them for her."

My daughter's tiles. Kestrel really was a Marian.

Through Lex.

Like that poor child didn't have enough on her eleven-month-old shoulders, between my goddessy lineage and the power-drenched bloodline of her father.

"Is that all? And where should I look, beyond Scotland?"

Simon shrugged a shoulder, as if to say that such details were my problem. 4:51. I looked at Pauline, to see if she also watched the monitor and Benny as closely as I was watching Kes. But as she fingered her simple, amber-stoned necklace, her gaze on Simon's face.

Either she was the best actress in the world, or the woman really didn't care a thing about her son—and everything about her father-in-law. *Yech.*

"Third?" I prompted, turning back to Simon.

"Your third task is to explain the final key."

I blinked at him. "The what?"

"The prophecies which my family has extracted across the centuries, both from Marians and from other sources, continue to challenge us in this. They insist that to bring the mosaic to its ultimate power, the presence of seven Marians are key. We must know why before dawn on Monday. I am told you make a living explaining ancient mysteries. This gives you a week to explain this one."

My mind was already racing in a different—but obvious—direction. I might not understand the importance of this mosaic yet, but I could count. Ana, Mara, Olga, Lexie, Laurel, Kestrel…and Phillipe? Unlike with grailkeepers, I'd had no indication that men counted as Marians. Then again, this latest revelation about Kestrel made it clear that they could be carriers.

Only one person could directly answer that. "You only have six Marians, unless you count boys."

Simon's gaze, moving to Pauline, was one of disgust. "I have seven."

Holy crap. His daughter-in-law was a Marian, too? She looked none too proud of it, either, her big brown eyes glistening with tears of shame and entreaty. At him, I mean. Always at him.

Poor Benny. Both his parents had managed to betray his Poppi, hadn't they?

I was having to fight for clarity, with that damned timer working away. 3:23. Despite that this was probably his intention. Despite the fact that, if he needed seven Marians, he couldn't risk losing any of them.

As if reading my thoughts, Simon said, "If you think we cannot get more, you are sadly mistaken. We paid your student to entice you to Reliquary. We traced the final tiles to your husband's family and to Scotland. And speaking of your husband…"

He opened a bright cardboard box on his desk. I don't read Italian, but the language is close enough to French—and even more to Latin—that I got the impression this was a prepaid cell phone.

"Your authorities have kept the kidnapping quiet, but I've no doubt they will soon see past the false trail we planted, especially once your husband knows of the other Marian abductions. You must convince him that any attempt to rescue you or your daughter will result in dire consequences. He is not to contact European authorities. He is not to arrive in Italy with the kind of mercenaries I am sure he can afford. You must believe that I have informants in all levels of the government, and that I will learn of such efforts. And when I do…"

He shook his head with a tsk-tsk noise, as if the consequences he had planned were so dire, even *he* was disturbed by them.

The threats of a bully, I thought—but I also realized I was going to talk to Lex. I needed that so badly, I almost forgot to watch the clock on the screen beside Simon. Almost. 1:33.

"I am sure your husband has an unlisted number that even the police and FBI are not monitoring," continued the duke in that sinuous way of his. "What is it?"

I hesitated only for a moment. Sure, I could have given him Lex's regular cell phone number. Heaven knew the authorities would be poised to trace calls and capture communications. But until I knew exactly what those dire consequences were…

I wouldn't have erred on the side of safety for myself. But back in the bunker, on its fish-eye lens, Ana had finally gotten Kestrel to sleep. I couldn't take chances with my daughter or the other hostages.

1:12.

I recited the number to Lex's secret, emergency-only mobile phone. Simon dialed it, pressed the speaker-phone button on the prepaid cell, and laid it on the desk between us.

0:58.

Lex picked up on the second ring, indicating his level of worry. Usually the secret second phone lived in his briefcase. "Stuart here."

Just that, two words in the familiar voice I loved, felt like a homecoming, a salvation. I almost lost it, then and there. "Lex. It's—"

"Christ, Maggi!" His voice came out in a rush, almost a sob. At least I'd known we were still alive. What kind of hell had he been in? "Mag, where—"

Simon narrowed his eyes in warning. Beyond him, I could still read the screen. 0:32.

It had to be a hoax, that damned countdown. It had to be a kind of psychological torture. It's not like Adriano would set off a bomb or something, not directly beneath his own home. With a great amount of effort, I made my voice calm, even casual, as I interrupted my husband.

"I've been told to instruct you that any attempt to rescue Kestrel and me will have—" what other words were there? "—dire consequences."

"But she's all right? *You're all right?*"

0:00 read the clock. It continued to flash, as if it were some great alarm. 0:00. 0:00. But nothing happened.

Nothing happened!

I could have laughed with relief. Instead, I continued with my instructions, though less frightened than I'd been since I'd reached Adriano's office.

"We're okay. You aren't to contact the authorities. You aren't to bring any kind of manpower to Italy. Our captors will know if you do, and I'm told you don't want to risk it."

"I don't," repeated Lex slowly, more aware of my halfhearted effort than anybody. Because he knew me better than anybody.

"That's what I'm—" Which is when I saw movement on the computer screen. Ana stood, her head cocked, at full alert. Olga suddenly began moving from mat to mat, waking the children. What…?

Only then did I see it, the faint yellow mist beginning to pour from the ventilation grates into the bunker like filmy waterfalls, pooling on the floor in ankle-high clouds beneath, heavier than the air. The misty puddles spread.

I was on my feet even as understanding dawned.

He was gassing the children.

"Stop it," I commanded.

"Maggi, what's wrong?" asked Lex, his voice deadly soft.

"You wish me to key in the appropriate code, then?" asked Simon softly, at the same time, with a smile.

"Yes!"

"Who is that? What's going on?"

On the screen Ana and Olga were trying to get the older children as high as they could, on top of the Porta Potti and port-a-shower shells. Phillipe was handed Lexie to hang on to. Benny ran away from Olga, shaking his head.

Ana turned back to the cribs, but the yellow was spreading too quickly, it would rise too quickly, no matter what Simon Adriano did now. Holy Mother…

"Just take him seriously, Lex!" I ordered, at a shout—

And I bolted straight at Sergio, who stood blocking the office doorway with his tranquilizer gun.

I had to save my daughter.

Chapter 4

Sergio came at me, using the rifle as a club.

I let him. Lowering my center of balance and shifting to the balls of my feet was an immediate survival reaction. At the last moment of Sergio's charge, I turned and twisted, like a feather riding the energy off him. He stumbled past, as surprised as if I really had vanished, and I was out the door.

Tai Chi. It's more than just a funny dance.

I ducked the second guard. Spun past the third. Began to run. When I heard a rifle being cocked behind me, I lengthened my stride and tried to sense everything around me as I ran.

You hear legends in the martial arts, including the idea that masters can dodge bullets. I'd never tried it. But I was about to learn if I could dodge tranquilizer darts.

"No!" Simon's command spurred me to almost inhuman speed. "We know where she is—"

By then I'd swung around the corner, my body at a fifty-degree angle, one hand brushing the marble floor to keep my balance at that speed—and like that, I was free of the first group of guards. I took the stairs two, three at a time, hit the bottom and charged for the vault door.

This time I was ready to take some guards out. I doubted even a Tai Chi master, which I'm not, could have evaded them while turning the wheel that latched that monster of a door. To my unnerved relief, the vault door stood open.

Yeah. By now I'd guessed Simon was letting me get away with this. As long as it got me to my daughter, and got her and the others out of the gas, I didn't care.

I pounded through the door and past priceless treasures of antiquity to the open door into the bunker. This time there were guards. They weren't facing me, but instead covered the hostages.

Open door. That meant they were getting fresh air....

The temptation to grab a tranquilizer rifle and crack one of them over the head was strong. The need to take advantage of Simon Adriano's lenience and get into the room was stronger.

One of the guards swore in Italian as I twirled between him and his partner. I looked around, saw that Laurel—still on top of the Porta Potti's shell—held a screaming Kestrel.

Only then did I stop. Only then did the driving need in me ease. It's a lesson many parents learn, me included, at our first child's first breath.

Screaming means she's breathing.

I still wanted to snatch my baby from the ten-year-old, and from the possibility of a six-foot drop to the concrete floor. Instead, I made myself take in the aftermath of Simon's little demonstration—and it didn't look good. The yellow of the gas had receded to ankle height as it slid slowly away, into two floor-level ventilation holes. The gerbil cage sat ominously silent.

Three adults—Olga, Ana and the guard called Eric—had circled around the snack table. Eric held a coughing Benny against his side and proffered a small oxygen tank with his free hand. And Olga...

Olga held the too-large oxygen mask over the bluing face of tiny baby Mara, who lay deathly still while a white-faced, short-breathed Ana massaged her baby's chest, murmuring pleas.

Oh, no. *No!*

As I came closer, Olga moved the mask. Eric took it from her, holding it to Benny's face, while Ana bent closer to her infant. She breathed into her baby's mouth, then pushed at her tiny, terry-covered chest to force the air back out. Again she tried it—and Mara coughed, a tiny hiccough of sound. Olga took the mask back from Benny, who obligingly hid his face in Eric's side, and they held the mask over Mara's face again.

The baby was breathing now, but not well. You could hear it, the raspy struggle of an inhalation, like the purr of a dying kitten. A whimper of exhalation. Every muscle in me tensed, wanting to breathe for her, as I joined the other adults. Mara didn't seem to have the strength to cough again or open her eyes, much less to cry.

I reached slowly out, stroked her tiny head and imagined it was Kes. I'd once had the ability to heal people—not like miracles, but to help mundane efforts. It had been a gift from the Goddess Isis, after I drank from one of Her sacred cups. Her other gift to me—the ability to sense where Lex was, at any time—had vanished after the birth of Kestrel. I assumed my healing touch had, as well. It had been well over a year since my last grail quest, after all. Now that I thought about it, my throat had barely tightened before Simon's sadistic "demonstration" began. What had happened to my prophetic scream, another goddess-given ability?

And yet if even a remnant of my healing skills remained...

Kestrel's and Lexie's wails, from where Laurel and Phillipe Fouquet held them high above the floor, seemed muffled by the horror of what had happened to the smallest of us.

"Let me try," I suggested to Ana, who was having trouble getting a deep breath herself. Of course anything the baby inhaled, her mother would have inhaled first. It just affected the baby faster.

With the quiet acceptance of one barely clinging to sanity, Ana hesitated, and I tried breathing for baby Mara. *In the name of Isis, Sacred Mother, Goddess of a Thousand Names...*

Olga moved away to help the other children back down, now that the gas was gone. I hoped she wouldn't let Kestrel crawl until the floor had been wiped clean. I tried not to get distracted. *Goddess of Medicine, She who could breathe life...*

She had to hear me. If anyone could understand taking time off for the miracle of a baby, it would be a goddess. Patriarchal religions had historically made childbirth unclean. For centuries, postpartum women weren't allowed back into churches for weeks—forty days after the birth of a boy, double that after the birth of a girl. But childbirth was the *center* of many matriarchal religions.

Children were everything.

Please, Mother. Please....

Only Simon's voice over the intercom had the nerve to interrupt our vigil. "I chose to be lenient and to input the appropriate code, Mrs. Stuart," he announced. "This time. Just be aware—and tell your allies—that only I know when the next incident will occur. Only I know the code to stop it when it does. If something happens to me, everyone in this little playroom could die. Of course, I cannot help that the youngest are the most vulnerable."

After my breath inflated Mara's tiny chest, Ana's soft pressure eased it back down. In with the good air. Out with the bad air. The infant's tiny, congested cough sounded a touch stronger.

"If I get word of an attack being planned on my compound," Simon continued, "everyone in the playroom dies. If the Marians do not send the tiles to me—every tile, just as I told you—by Saturday, everyone in the playroom dies. If the authorities are pointed in my direction—"

"I get it!" I screamed upward, at the futile nothingness of him. *"Shut up!"*

We were scaring the children. Laurel and Phillipe, now safely down, held tight to each other. Lexie strained upward to be held, but Olga already had Kestrel.

"I am merely stressing that all players must understand the consequence of false heroics," Simon's voice insisted, as I pinched Mara's tiny nose shut and inhaled again into her mouth. "Eric, put that dirty-blooded brat down and secure the room. Take the oxygen with you. I tire of this diversion."

"Sir," called the handsome guard Ana had described as "a good enough guy." "The infant should be in a hospital. If the others would promise to—"

"Are you questioning my judgment?"

We all jumped—Simon's sinuous voice tended to ease you into the belief that he never shouted. Benny cringed into Eric's side. Laurel curled protectively over Phillipe.

And under the gentle pressure of her mother's hand, baby Mara's cough turned into a weak cry. Thank heavens. *Thank you, Isis.*

"No, sir," called Eric immediately, crouching to lower Benny to the ground. "I apologize. My previous position—"

"The brat no longer needs a bodyguard. He can take his chances with the other troublemakers."

"Yes, sir."

I stepped to block the overhead camera as Eric chucked Benny under the chin with a gentle finger and gave him a wink, to comfort the child he let go. Then Eric was heading for the door. He didn't look back when Benny, sounding younger than since I'd gotten here, called, "Eh-wic!"

"Mrs. Stuart," warned Simon. "You must go, as well."

Olga's and Ana's heads came up in dual surprise. We hadn't had a chance to debrief about my surprise assignment. And now we wouldn't.

"Not yet!" I insisted. Mara was still crying, and I'd waited long enough. I turned and took Kestrel from Olga. Again, I felt a soothing sense of completion, to know my baby's weight in my arms, to smell her soft skin against my face as I held her tight. Kestrel had stopped crying. She said, "Dadadada," like a mantra, and looked ridiculously proud of herself for it.

"Daddy is coming," I whispered into her perfect little ear as if she'd really meant Lex. Saying it soothed me, too. Even as I went to her diaper bag and dug out my wallet, I kept talking. "As soon as it's safe for you, he and I will come and get you. Promise. We love you, Kes. Mommy and Daddy love you more than life itself."

"Dadadadada," she sang. Sort of.

"*Now,* Mrs. Stuart," commanded Simon, and the guards at the door raised their rifles—again, at poor little Laurel Fouquet.

Olga reached for Kes.

"Olga and Ana will take care of you until Daddy and I can come," I breathed quickly into Kestrel's hair, and landed three kisses on her head before we'd finished the exchange.

Olga gave me a quick hug, which gave me one more hug with my baby, too.

"Clean the floor before—" I whispered.

"Of course. Get this tested," she whispered back, and I felt something slide into my slacks pocket.

One look at Ana, and I almost didn't hug her goodbye. She looked so calm, so remorseless that I suddenly feared what she might do. In her place, I might forget all reason, too. Because of that, I *had* to hug her.

It was the only way for me to whisper, "Patience," without anyone overhearing.

"When I get in the same room with this guy," she announced against my cheek, still with deathly calm, "I will rip his face off. Starting at the hairline, so he survives as long as possible. But not yet, Maggi. Not at the cost of our babies."

"Five," announced Simon sharply. "Four."

Another fucking countdown.

I stroked my hand over Kestrel's red curls once more—and I couldn't do this. I had never left her overnight, not even safely at home with Lex or with my parents.

Now I had to go for a *week?* Leave her with near *strangers?*

"Three."

But I had to. I backed away, staring at her for as long as possible.

"Two," counted Simon, even as I walked. He sounded amused.

At a demonstration from Olga, Kes lifted a pudgy hand and curled her fingers in bye-bye—

And I spun and walked past the damned guards, and out of the room, just as Simon said, "One."

But nobody fired. The door shut behind me.

Coldly, I glanced again at the alabaster jar on display as I passed it, still not close enough to read the title card. Ahead of me, the guard named Eric banged on the closed vault door. After a delay long enough to reawaken mild claustrophobia, I heard the wheel being turned on the other side.

I met Eric's gaze. He met mine and, just barely, nodded.

I could only hope he was agreeing to what I'd hoped, to keep them as safe as he possibly could until I got back.

Because I *would* be back.

And when I got here, I seriously hoped to hold Simon Adriano down while Ana Fraser cut his face off.

The guards who took me out of the compound insisted on wrapping me in a tarpaulin first. I had a split second to decide whether to keep a hand near my pocket—not the one Olga had accessed but the other, where I'd put the prepaid cell they gave me—or up around my head before I was held immobile by the heavy canvas. I chose my head, which meant no telephone calls for help until I was back out. But at least this way I could still breathe.

Mostly.

They swung me none too gently onto a surface that felt familiar—the floor of a van. I heard the engine start, felt us roll into motion.

Almost immediately I heard the drumming of heavy rainfall on the roof. Occasionally the van swayed, as if buffeted by heavy winds. I thought of Ana's claims—now Simon's—that the Adrianos could affect the electromagnetic stability of the earth. Did he really plan some kind of an apocalypse? Why?

People who fear they're losing power, Lex had said, *they're the ones who take desperate measures.* I thought of Simon Adriano's son deserting him, of him discovering his grandson was of Marian blood—but that couldn't be all of it. That had happened too recently.

My mind was a cacophony. Kestrel, Lex, the Marians, all those frightened children. Poor, struggling baby Mara. My identity as college teacher, as mother, as wife, as grail-keeper…and now as gofer for Simon Adriano. I didn't want to help him. But I wanted to endanger his hostages even less.

The drumming on the roof got louder. Was that hail? Then I felt the van slowing, heard the men guarding me call to each other in Italian. I heard the cargo door slide open and smelled salty sea air, probably the Bay of Naples.

Then I felt my tarp lifted—and swung out the door of the still-moving van!

For one awful, airborne moment, I could only duck my head closer beneath my raised arms and try not to imagine plunging over the rocky cliffs of the Amalfi Coast. My common sense knew I couldn't follow Simon's orders if I was dead, but my sense of survival wailed my fear until, with a heavy thud, the roll of canvas hit rocky ground and began to tumble.

Gravity and ground aren't a great mix. I bounced, rolled and skidded blindly, every impact a blow to my hip or elbow that several layers of tarp couldn't absorb. I felt my descent accelerating, like it might right before the steep mountainside became a sheer drop to the sea. *Kestrel,* I thought.

Lex.

Then, hard enough to shake every bone in me, I struck an immovable object with enough force to make you question Newton's first law. For a moment I couldn't even breathe.

Although some of that was being wrapped like a burrito.

Unsure where I was—on a cliff's edge? In the middle of a rainy road? I struggled to free myself. I tried to remember which direction Adriano's thugs had wrapped the tarp, so that

I could reverse the direction to roll out of it. That's some pretty tough thought processing when you're alone and hurting and scared…and a really solid rainfall is pelting over you.

I was starting to make progress when I heard more, closer shouts. Heavy hands grabbed my swathes of canvas, rolled me sharply to one side and began tearing the tarpaulin back. In only moments rain began to hit my face. Gulping air, I stared up at a man in a black rain poncho, its hood fallen back so that his dark hair was plastered to his head, his expression a mixture of concerned wariness. Despite his upset, he was remarkably handsome. He looked Italian.

Before I could say anything, the beam of a halogen light hit me full in the face, blinding me to almost everything— except the pistol barrel being held just under the flashlight, inches from my nose.

You always think the frying pan's bad, until the fire shows up.

Chapter 5

Then a woman's voice exclaimed, "Bloody hell. *Maggi?*"

It was Nadia Bishop, Lexie's mother and my husband's very good friend.

"Lexie's all right!" I said immediately, as she holstered her pistol while the man with her continued to wrench wet canvas off me. "I just left her with Olga and—"

Damn it, my voice broke. But I got it out over the rush of rainfall around us. "And Kestrel. Nadia, they have Kes, too!"

"She isn't hurt?" Nadia exclaimed at the same time, holding my arm. "Is Lexie frightened?"

I was still babbling. "And Ana Fraser and her newborn, and Laurel and Phillipe Fouquet, and Benny Adriano's in there—"

The rugged Italian who'd just managed to free my legs bit back a curse, white-faced. I realized this must be Nadia's lover, Joshua Adriano. Father of Lexie and Benny. Pauline's ex-husband.

That last part was a mystery for another time.

"We can't make any rescue attempts," I continued, trying to cover the information as fast as I could, like a student anxious to take the quiz within seconds of closing the book. "I know kidnappers always say that, but he's set things up so that he can gas the hostages at any time—and if we take him out, nobody can stop the gas. The smaller children are most susceptible. Little Mara Fraser—she's breathing again, but…"

To my relief, they obviously believed me.

"We need to fall back," Nadia said grimly. She was a lovely woman, slimmer than me, with sleek brown hair and the kind of delicate bone structure that shouldn't host such dark determination. "Simon knows exactly where we are, or he wouldn't have tossed you out of that lorry right at our feet. He probably knows we've been looking for the tunnels. Under the compound," she explained for me. "So far, we haven't found an entrance."

With her and Joshua holding my elbows to help me back up the hill—not necessary, but not unwelcome—we made our way to a grove of twisted olive trees where they had hidden a dark Saab sedan. Nadia bundled me into the back seat with several towels—some muddy, some clean and folded. She shut out the rain behind me before I could ask for what I needed most. Not that I minded the towels! I dragged one immediately over my shoulders, between my neck and my dripping hair. Then she climbed into the passenger seat up front and shut out the rush of the storm again. Kneeling to better face me, she quickly poured a cup of what smelled like hot tea from a thermos.

"Thanks," I said—and meant it. My hands shook as I accepted the foam cup, both from the chill of the sheeting rain and the stress of the last how-many hours. At least an hour to get from the gallery to some kind of airfield. About eight from New York to Naples. Maybe another hour unconscious, two? About two hours with Kestrel and the other hostages, before I was called to Simon. How long, since my perfect life had been abruptly violated? I'd done okay, but… "But, Nadia, what I really need—"

She handed me her cell phone before I'd even finished asking. "I've already dialed his private number. Just hit Send."

Our eyes met with a moment of complete, feminine understanding as I took the phone and did just that, stealing two more quick gulps of soothing tea as the line connected. The car dipped as Joshua closed the trunk—I think he'd stowed the tarp. He handed a blanket back to me as he climbed into the driver's seat, while one of the two most important voices in the world answered with, "Have you found something?"

For a moment my own voice deserted me.

"Nadia?" The panic that infused that one question said much about what my husband had been through, these last hours.

"Lex," I managed, my voice rougher than usual. "I'm out."

And then, over the rush of his own sigh of recognition, the hardest thing I'd ever had to say in my life:

"Kes isn't."

Nadia and Joshua turned on the stereo up front to give me a little extra privacy. Lex was wonderful, insisting that I'd done what I had to do, agreeing that Kestrel should be as safe—almost as safe—with Olga and Ana as she could have been with me, glad I'd bought us time to get her and the others out. Me, I still felt awful.

It was the second time he promised, "We'll get her out,"

that I realized my aching-stomach, tight-throated fear wasn't just guilt or my previous, already red-level concern.

"You can't try to get them out, Lex. Didn't you get what I said, about the cameras and the gas and the code?"

"There are always options," Lex reassured me. Or he thought it was reassurance. He hadn't been down there. He hadn't seen the blue pallor to baby Mara's face.

"If you try to bring in troops, you could kill them!"

Nadia and Joshua *had* to have heard that. They pretended not to.

"And if we don't keep all our options open, then *he will!*" Lex insisted right back. "Maybe not while they're useful to him, not until he has what he needs. But after that? We need backup plans! We…" His voice trailed off. "I'm sorry, goddess," he said then, more quietly, using his pet name for me. "You've been through something awful, and I'm not making it any easier. We don't have to talk about this right now."

"I'm not a fragile flower, Lex. I deserve to be in on any plans you have for going after our daughter." Even if it was so I could veto them. "So do Nadia and Joshua, for that matter, and the Marians back in France."

"And I'll do my best to keep everyone in the loop. But sometimes these things have to go down quickly—"

"No. Not quickly. We have a week."

"To do Simon Adriano's bidding."

"As long as he's got Kestrel's life in his hands? Damn right!" I felt like crying. The last thing I wanted was to fight with my husband. I wanted to share our grief, and our hope that grief was temporary. I wanted to let him comfort me. But every time he pushed the swoop-in-and-rescue-them gambit, comforted is the *last* thing I felt. He was so used to getting his own way….

There was a long moment of silence, just the rain on the roof, the whisper of the windshield wipers and the soft stereo.

"We'll talk about this later," said Lex finally. "When we're together. The important thing for now is that he let you go. You're safe with Nadia. That's more than we could have hoped for, at this stage."

And still far less than was acceptable. But he didn't have to say that part.

"You're on your way to Europe?" I asked, surprised by how badly I needed that. I felt a primal desperation for him, like for air or water. As though if we were together, everything really could be fixed.

Scary emotions, for a feminist.

"I'm in the Hawker right now, over the Atlantic. I'm coming as fast as I can."

It didn't surprise me. Even during the times in our rocky courtship when we'd been "off-again," I'd somehow known that Lex Stuart would move mountains if I needed him to. Now that I was his wife, now that someone had taken our baby…

This was the good side to his possessive streak. "I love you," I said, which didn't come close to expressing what I felt, but was the best I had at the moment. If I apologized, he would deny I was responsible, but I knew better.

If we hadn't gone to the city. If I hadn't been duped by that student. If I hadn't consulted with the Marians.

"Me, too, Maggi. Christ, me, too. But I—" He sounded guilty now. "I haven't told your parents anything. The authorities said we shouldn't let it hit the news, but that's not why."

"You didn't want to worry them until you knew something," I guessed, and could only imagine his single nod. Then a darker reason. "And you didn't want them asking questions."

About what kind of enemies he had. About his possible involvement. About whether their ungodly rich son-in-law had proven untrustworthy, at that. The Cinderella story does have a dark side.

"That, too. I'm sorry. I never thought I'd be such a coward."

"No. I'm glad. If they knew, I'd have to call and say I'm all right, and I don't know…" Maybe I was a coward, too. I couldn't imagine trying to relate any of this to my mother without dissolving into tears, and tears were the last thing I needed. "Thank you."

For a long moment we just listened to each other breathe. Then he asked, "I'm sorry to have to ask, Mag, but…could you put Nadia on?"

He knew I was on her phone because of the caller ID.

With a wrench of irrational jealousy, I passed the cell phone back between the seats to his oldest, closest friend. Then I leaned back, sipped my lukewarm tea and closed my eyes. Up front, Nadia seemed to be reassuring Lex that I really was in one piece, but I deliberately didn't listen in. Heavens, I was exhausted. But now I had hope, too.

Lex was coming.

As long as I could keep him from doing anything stupid and privileged and *patriarchal*, that was an excellent turn of events.

Then I remembered what Olga had secreted into my pocket, before I left. *Get this tested.* Oh…goddess.

The dead gerbil hadn't made it through our tumble as well as I had.

By the time Nadia and I boarded a small, private airplane— a six-seater about the size of Lex's Piper Saratoga—I was wearing a dry change of clothes, some hers and some

Joshua's. Also, the worse-for-wear remains of poor little Buster had been safely ensconced in a zipped baggie, and that in a small ice chest. With it, there was a chance that the Marians could figure out what kind of gas Simon had used against the hostages, giving us the possibility of counteracting it when I went back in.

All commercial flights out of Naples had been grounded because of the bad weather. Nadia had found a pilot willing to chance the storms only through exorbitant payment. It hurt, in my chest, to watch her and Joshua embrace one last time on the rainy tarmac. A mix of envy, sympathy and guilt made me uncomfortable, so I busied myself fastening my seat belt. From what I already knew of their story, they'd been apart for so long already. They'd sent their own daughter away, to keep her safe—and I hadn't managed even that for them.

Nadia had to want to be with her child's father now, as desperately as I did. But someone had to keep an eye on the Adriano compound—who better than an Adriano, even one who'd defected? And Nadia felt it important that I be brought to the Marian headquarters by someone they trusted—since Ana was being held hostage and Rhys apparently had left on some mission—as well as someone who simply knew the way.

Especially since I currently had no purse or passport, and my credit cards were probably being watched. After barely a year and a half of being Mrs. Lex Stuart, it's surprising how my sudden poverty and anonymity unsettled me. Bad habits, Maggi. Bad habits.

Besides, Nadia had to fill me in on exactly what I'd landed in here. In a minute she was climbing into the plane, then shutting and fastening the door behind her. The benefit of a six-seater was that she and I could fly facing forward, with the rear-facing seats situated between us and Geno, the young pilot.

Geno spoke to the tower, then to us—both in Italian—as we taxied onto the runway. With a laugh, he gestured to the barf bags in a basket at our feet. Then, crossing himself, he accelerated into the storm. I normally don't mind flying, although private planes give me unpleasant thoughts about Buddy Holly and JFK Jr. But this! The wind shook us even before we lifted. Water washed across the windshield, reducing visibility to almost nothing. Once we were airborne, it felt like some great god tossed us from hand to hand, just for kicks. But the plane continued to climb.

Eventually we must have reached altitude. To say we leveled off, considering the way our plane kept randomly dropping or leaping upward, would be overstating it.

We kept our seat belts on. I already regretted the cheese and warm rolls Joshua had fed me at his apartment in Old Napoli. But at least we were flying.

Only as Nadia drew her hand from mine did I realize we'd entwined fingers, as if the power of sisterhood would get us off the ground. I've dealt with goddess energy enough to believe it.

"This is part of it, you know," she told me then, as low as she could over the sound of the engine and the storm. "The bloody vicious weather. Just like the earthquakes and the power outages, the outbreak, the volcanoes."

We'd had not only food but news at Joshua's, while I cleaned up and Nadia arranged for our flight. The television reported that the island of Santorini, in Greece, was being evacuated against growing signs that their long-active volcano was readying for a blow. Now even Vesuvius concerned the scientific community. Considering that the Adriano compound, where our children were being kept, sat across the Bay of Naples, that concerned us, too.

"Because of the ley lines," I admitted, knowing that much from my conversations with Ana. "But I don't understand how a natural energy grid in the earth can be responsible for so much damage. Or for this!"

I gestured toward the water-combed window beside me, clouds pulsing with veiled lightning.

"It's being manipulated, that's how. Usually the energy that runs through ley lines is positive, regenerative. But long ago—millennia, actually—the Adrianos discovered how to abuse them. They learned to make the energy go sour, to lower the immune systems of the people living over them, or to intensify bursts of energy through the ley lines, to cause earthquakes. The more their ancestors manipulated the earth's electromagnetic system, or at least the European portion of it, the more this affected storms, tides. That's in part what the early Marians created the mosaic to protect against."

"The mosaic," I repeated. "Simon spoke of tiles."

Nadia drew some photographs out of her satchel and handed them to me. They showed an intricate mosaic, in the style of those found in ancient Roman ruins, depicting the same beautiful Black Madonna Rhys had initially called me about. Sword. Key. Alabaster jug. Babe in arms.

My own arms felt empty, just looking at her.

"The early Marians learned just what could happen with the destruction of Pompeii…" Her voice trailed off for a moment as if she'd temporarily gone someplace else. "Likely that's what brought the Adrianos into power…and what showed them the benefits of shaking up the status quo. Recognizing the danger, the Marians built this mosaic, not just as a symbol of their Madonna—whoever she was—but as an intricate filter of gems and metals. They knew it would be most needed when the earth transitioned out of the Age of Pisces."

I'd heard this, too. "To the Age of Aquarius. Like the song."

"The world is in transition. My sister Scarlet—the one the Adrianos killed—she had the right of it all along. In the same way certain sun signs can affect individuals, the earth itself passes backward through zodiac signs. But instead of lasting for a month, these ecliptics last for over two-thousand years."

I was nowhere near as surprised by the idea of zodiac signs for time periods as I was by the fact that Scarlet, the murdered Marian, had been her sister!

"Goddess worship was particularly strong during the Age of Taurus, a real earth-mother sign." I said it casually. But I hoped my sympathy was in my gaze.

Nadia nodded. "But Taurus was replaced by the Age of Aries. Warlike. Patriarchal. And Aries was replaced by the Age of Pisces. In some ways it was an improvement, but it was also divisive. Suddenly everything became two-sided— masculine versus feminine, wrong versus right, the weak versus the strong. Winners. Losers."

"False dichotomies," I agreed. The plane lurched, and I closed my eyes for a long moment. "Either-or thinking."

"It was the downside of the time of Pisces," agreed Nadia. "And the reason the Marians thought they stood a better chance in the Age of Aquarius. So they destroyed their mosaic and sent the tiles and their priestesses into hiding."

A lightning bolt zapped ungodly light through the plane. A simultaneous crash of thunder drowned out Geno's excited whoop. The plane shuddered.

I handed back the photographs, not wanting to get airsick all over them.

"So Simon Adriano plans to bring on an apocalypse as what…some kind of power grab?" I remembered what Lex had said, so many months ago, about the kind of men who took such desperate measures. Not those in charge, like him. Those who felt they were no longer in charge. "Because he fears he's losing control as we move into a new age?"

"Something like that. We're well into the cusp, but change is naturally volatile. Like labor pains. He's capitalizing on that. If he can throw Europe into chaos, he can be the one who steps in and takes charge in the midst of the confusion, and emerge as a leader for the new age. First Simon planned on his oldest son being the leader, then Joshua." Nadia's bitter tone showed me just how much she hated her lover's father for such assumptions. "But he's fully capable of doing it himself."

"I hate power-hungry men," I muttered.

"But that's not the only reason," she assured me, digging out more papers. "There's a timing issue, as well. The cusp between the Age of Pisces and the Age of Aquarius has lasted almost a century already. If Simon can send this blast of energy at the exact moment of transition, when we move from Pisces colored by Aquarius to Aquarius colored by Pisces, he can do more damage than has been possible for two thousand years, or will be possible for two thousand more. Give or take a century."

"Which is why he doesn't want the Marians finishing the mosaic," I realized. "Making his efforts…impotent?"

Nadia smiled at my word choice. "That, and worse. The mosaic was created in a dualistic time, so even it was affected. The same tiles that can neutralize destructive energy one direction can amplify it if reversed."

I stared at her.

"Exponentially," she insisted.

"Holy crap." I was supposed to deliver this weapon myself? And yet…*Kestrel.*

I could only do this one step at a time.

"We've got inside information," Nadia continued. "And if it's correct, the exact time of transition for Europe is next Monday around dawn. Everything seems to be falling into place—the planetary alignments, the comet, the lunar eclipse."

Of all the reasons to hate Mondays, I'd never imagined apocalypse to be one of them. More volcanoes. Worse earthquakes. The resulting tidal waves, fires, injuries. Death.

"That would explain why Simon wants me back by Saturday," I muttered. "He's not leaving a lot of wiggle room, is he?"

"No. Nor is…" But Nadia's voice trailed off again, her expression one of growing incredulity.

I followed her gaze and saw that Geno, our pilot, was climbing between the seats facing us. He lounged into one, spreading his arms, like a king surveying his kingdom. Or maybe just a crown prince. He couldn't be over twenty-two. He was the usual Italian handsome, his hair black, his teeth bright against his olive complexion.

My expression must have mimicked Nadia's, because he laughed. "It is, how you say, automatic pilot," he assured us.

"In *this* weather?" I demanded.

"The plane, she knows how to fly, yes?" His grin widened. "But she no know how to land. This flight, it is crazy. I be brave, to fly it. But I deserve, *come dite*…bonus, *si?*"

My mouth must have been hanging open, even before another jolt of turbulence made me gasp. This *was* a crazy flight, crazy dangerous, but it was necessary. My daughter's life was at stake. Nadia's daughter's life. The other children. Ana. Olga.

"We don't have time for this crap," I warned. If my voice was unsteady, it was from fear of what was at stake more than of him.

"You'll get no more money with such games," Nadia said, almost in unison with me.

"If you want we land where you said?" Geno's hands went to the buttons of his jeans. "I deserve bonus. S'okay. You like."

He wasn't talking about more money.

Chapter 6

"How *dare* you?" I began to lecture, sitting up into my full height despite the lingering turbulence, and Geno went white.

I think that had a lot more to do with Nadia's 9mm, now aimed at his forehead, than with my harsh tone of voice.

Well, we certainly had his attention.

"You will get your skanky butt back up into that pilot's seat," I continued, unlatching my seat belt and—with some effort at balance—shifting across to the facing seats.

"Line of fire," warned Nadia, deadly soft.

"Watching it," I assured her, just as low.

Geno's mouth opened wordlessly. Worked. Closed. His long-lashed eyes were liquid with fear.

"Oh, and don't play the poor naughty-boy card." I grabbed the beltline of his jeans and hauled upward. To judge by Geno's gasp, that caused the seam of his jeans to do just what I'd hoped it would. This way I didn't need to be able to lift his weight—he was lifting it immediately, following my guidance with his whole body, just to relieve the pressure. "You're not a boy, and this isn't just naughty. This is attempted rape."

He all but dove back into his appropriate seat. I let go so that he could. But he did glance over his shoulder, wide-eyed. *"Rape?"*

"Crossing over," I warned Nadia softly.

"Check." She levered the barrel of her 9mm toward the plane roof long enough for me to vault into the copilot's seat, slide into position and buckle in.

Then I turned on Geno, now beside me. "You demanded sexual favors in return for a safe landing."

"Safe? Of course you get safe landing. God willing." He crossed himself.

"But someplace other than where we hired you to go— that's less than safe, especially for women alone in a foreign country. How often have you tried this, huh? How often have you assumed—"

And on I went, for the rest of the flight, glad of my marginal familiarity with a cockpit panel and my fluent ability to speak French so that, as we approached the small airport at Lezignan-Corbieres over an hour later, I knew that Geno had done exactly as we'd commanded him.

By then Nadia had holstered her pistol, and I took full credit for his ashen pallor and the spread of dampness on his shirt, under his arms and neckline. Normally I don't relish moralizing quite that thoroughly. But I'd just had perhaps the worst day ever, and my child's life and the lives of several others—or millions, depending on the Adrianos' success— were on the line. And I believed everything I was telling him. Just because he was cute, and even if some of the younger female tourists may have thought his demands a sexy adventure, didn't lessen his crime. *And* it was a great distraction from the lurching, jolting flight, the endless sluice of water across the windshield, and the occasional blasts of lightning or thunder.

Not to mention I'm a college instructor. I can go for a full three-hour lecture at full volume, if necessary.

"Please," begged Geno, as he started our descent toward Lezignan-Corbieres. "Please to sit in back. I land us safe. I promise. Please, no more about Mama."

One of the best attitude checks against sexual harassment is the old "What if I were your sister, mother or daughter, how would you feel about it then?" line.

Since it seemed just as well not to distract the boy during his landing, I unlatched my seat belt and made my awkward way over the seat backs.

I only fell against the cabin wall twice before dragging myself back into my seat and strapping myself down.

"Feel better?" asked Nadia, forcing amusement past her obvious concerns.

"I will once we report him and get his charter license revoked," I returned, though quietly—no need to toss those kinds of threats at the pilot himself while we were still airborne. "And once we get the girls back. And save Europe."

The world seemed to rise and dip and lurch around us. The plane wiggled from side to side, nose down, then nose up.

I felt sick from more than that. "Nadia, I'm so sorry—"

A stern shake of her head interrupted me. "You can't think I blame you. Your own child is being held with mine. I know just how dangerous Simon can be."

We dropped, hard. Nadia bit back a curse. I began to eye the barf bags.

"Your bodyguard." Nadia paused, significantly, until I met her gaze. "He didn't make it."

That provided sufficient distraction. "Frank?"

"Lex asked me not to tell you—he imagined you would feel responsible—but I think you're smarter than that. Bodyguards earn good money for a reason, Maggi."

Frank had been a nice man, soft-spoken, very low-key. Although I'd argued against the need for him, I hadn't resented the man himself. But Nadia was right. He'd understood what he was getting into when Lex hired him. "How?"

"It looks like a bump-and-dump. One of the Adrianos' men probably ran into him on the street and hit him with a hypodermic of something so powerful he couldn't hit the panic button before he was down. Then they probably dragged his body into a car on the excuse of getting him help, and dumped his body. It's only because he had a tracking chip under his skin that the police found him."

"I'm familiar with the technology." It's called RFID, for radio-frequency identification. Lex had suggested it for Kestrel once. So far he was biding by my resistance to the idea. Apparently the same didn't go for our protectors.

"I mention it as more proof that you did everything you could for Lexie—and still are doing so."

I covered her hand with mine, and we entwined fingers. Through the rain-streaked windows and the roiling clouds, in the occasional pulse of lightning, I caught the briefest glimpse of the Pyrenees to the north and the Mediterranean to the south. We were close. Another lurch of the plane knocked my head back against the headrest.

Geno was swearing—I assumed—in Italian. But he managed enough English to say, "I die? You fault. You murder me."

I still wasn't caring enough about Geno to overworry his fate. Me and Nadia, though…

We had to survive in order to save our daughters. Besides, it would be doubly hard on Lex to lose two of his "best girls" at once.

The snide edge to that thought surprised me, and I squeezed Nadia's hand as if to make up for it. The plane bucked and rolled. I couldn't even hear what Geno and the tower were saying to each other, over the boom of the storm. Suddenly the mountains were *right there,* just to our north, and the sea was too far off to glimpse, and I shut my eyes and clenched my teeth in time for the private plane to slam onto the runway, bounce back up, waggle, then hit again.

Then we were down, rushing across the flood-drenched tarmac in the airport spotlights. I opened my eyes in time to see Geno cross himself, then recognized something out the window beside me and immediately unhooked my harness-like seatbelt.

"Maggi?" asked Nadia, since we hadn't even finished braking when I stood and grabbed the handle near the roof. I rotated the door latch, high beside it, counterclockwise. "What…?"

But then she must have seen what I did.

Geno drew the plane around. As it came to a stop, I was shouldering the door open and swinging myself out—

Into Lex's embrace. It was his company jet, a Raytheon Hawker 800XP, that I'd seen waiting for us.

His arms closed hard around me as he caught my weight, swung my feet to the tarmac, buried his face in my hair. "Maggi. Oh, Christ—Mag."

For a long, suspended moment, he just held me tight, and I clung hard to him, and it was enough. How long had really passed since he'd left for work Friday morning—teasing pillow talk, steam from the shower, breakfast, goodbye kisses? I couldn't do the math in my head, not hours, not time zones. I just knew it had been too long, and this moment was a miracle.

"I thought I'd lost you," he mumbled at last, drawing back just enough to kiss me, there in the sheeting rain. I responded completely, loved him totally. "Oh, Mag."

But he'd thought he lost someone else, too. That was enough to make *me* reluctantly draw back. "Kestrel—"

"We'll get her back." My husband stood about six-two. Partly in response to a childhood illness, he was doggedly fit, with shoulders just broad enough to carry the weight of the world. He had neatly cut ginger-brown hair, hazel eyes and the classic face of a nobleman, probably because his blue blood-line came straight from exiled English and Scottish royalty.

All of which I note because: one, he was damned sexy; and two, when Lex said something like, *We'll get her back,* I believed him. For a moment I even felt comforted. How could the world *not* submit to the wishes of someone like him? Except…

Except it already hadn't. Kestrel was gone. And I'd seen what could happen if we didn't play by Simon Adriano's rules, at least for now.

Luckily, before I could ruin our reunion by protesting, Geno ruined it for me.

"Outta my plane!" he was commanding Nadia. "Go! Scary women. *Go!*"

Lex bit back a curse at his own rudeness, reaching even as Nadia climbed out beside us. Lex hugged his friend, hard, and kissed her cheek…but he didn't breathe her hair. Then he drew back, his usual composure lost. "Nadia, I—"

"Don't," she warned. "I will not have the two of you taking responsibility for Simon Adriano's actions. If Lexie hadn't been with you, perhaps you wouldn't—"

She swallowed, hard. Did she think this was her fault, through Lexie? True, I wasn't a Marian, but— "It can't be that simple, Nadia!" I protested.

"We don't know what it is," Lex intervened, taking her satchel and shouldering its strap. "But at least we can get out of the rain to figure it out. This way."

While Nadia carried the cooler, he led us both toward a town car, one woman on each side of him. That's how we ended up sitting in the back seat, too. The driver, Lex explained, had been to the Marian headquarters once before, when he brought little Lexie to meet her father.

"He was one of the guards," he explained. "So, ladies… what don't I know?"

I told him about the kidnapping, Simon's instructions and his demonstration, which turned Lex's expression to stony neutrality—a dangerous sign. While Nadia repeated much of what she'd explained on the plane, I rested my head on Lex's shoulder and closed my eyes, just for a minute. According to him, the airport wasn't twenty miles from the Marian headquarters, although much of that was back roads.

One minute, Nadia was saying something about "Wrong versus right. Winners. Losers."

The next, Lex was kissing me awake. For the briefest, happiest moment, I imagined everything had been a nightmare—we were in our home in Connecticut, Kes was safe in her nursery, and all was well.

Then I heard the rain through the open door, saw light washing out the front door of a centuries-old farmhouse and saw—

I had to be dreaming. Was the usually reserved Catrina Dauvergne giving Nadia a tenuous hug of welcome? It looked like her—sleek and honey-haired—but Nadia must be hugging Cat. Mist from the rain tickled my skin, and Lex drew back. "We're here."

No dream. Our normal, happy family life was the dream now.

I let Lex help me out of the town car and into the sanctuary of the farmhouse. The main room, which took up most of the large first floor, was surprisingly cozy for someplace belonging to Catrina—but, I reminded myself, my friend Rhys also lived here. Dark beams across the white ceiling gave the whole place a Tudor feel. The mismatched furniture had apparently been chosen for its comfort, and a fire in the large fireplace warded away the chill.

"I will get coffee," announced Catrina stiffly, and vanished into what must be the kitchen. In the meantime Nadia greeted another couple, already inside, and led them forward. The woman had dark, curly hair and a no-nonsense attitude. The dark-haired man with her had a military build and the faintest limp. The tightness with which they held each other's hands and the hard set of their mouths were all too familiar to me.

"Maggi Sanger and Lex Stuart, meet Eve St. Giles and Nick Petter," said Nadia, understandably leaving out the hyphenates for convenience despite everyone's wedding rings.

Now I saw the resemblance to Laurel in the dark hair. "Laurel and Phillipe are fine," I hurried to assure them.

This led to another refrain of what had happened, what had been threatened, where the children were now. Halfway through, Lex kissed my hand and drew away from me to pace. By the time I finished, Eve had gone white-lipped with fury. Nick and Lex, to judge by their restlessness, were bonding over their need to kill something.

Catrina had slowly brought in not just coffee but bowls of thick, hot stew and slices of baguette. The two of us exchanged a wary greeting mainly consisting of each others' names: "Magdalene." "Catrina." Otherwise, she sat back as if resting, petting her cat and absorbing the story.

By then, another rain-soaked couple arrived out front, setting off a high-pitched alarm that Nick reset after giving the all-clear. These were Tru Palmer, an athletic woman with shoulder-length, sun-bleached hair, and Griffin Sinclair, equally tanned and darker haired, who had the same kind of military bearing as Eve's husband, Nick. My husband had military *school* posture, but with an aristocratic, Fortune 500 polish. These guys were more along the lines of basic-training, automatic-weapons military.

Tru helped herself to some stew and dropped onto the sofa beside Catrina. Griffin joined the guys, now stationed around a thick-planked dining room table. Weird, how easily that split happens. Nadia passed the cooler containing the dead gerbil to Eve, who promised a full necropsy.

"So you're supposed to bring all the tiles back to Simon?" challenged Tru. "The mosaic I've spent *the past three months* putting back together?"

"If not, he could kill the children," I repeated, and then had to counter her mixed expression of doubt and annoyance. "And, yes, of *course* I know we can't count on him to keep that promise. But we have to try, don't we?"

Finally Catrina spoke, her French drawl cool. "If he has the mosaic, and it works as predicted, he could hurt many, many more children than yours."

"Kes is the one I'm responsible for!"

Catrina quirked an eyebrow. "Which is why you ought not be the one making the decision."

Luckily I'd already finished my stew; otherwise I might have thrown it at her. I was overtired, I knew that. Over-stressed. Overwhelmed. But damn, that woman rubbed me the wrong way. How she and my friend Rhys could have ended up together…

Speaking of which. "Where is Rhys?" I asked. I could count on Rhys to see sense.

"He is in Rome," said Catrina tightly. "With Ana's Robert. Trying to get the Vatican to help retrieve *your children.*"

"Enough." Nadia rose gracefully between us. "Nobody can do anything tonight. Lex?"

Lex looked up on command, and I had to stomp back dark suspicions about what he, Nick and Griffin had been discussing so intently around the table. Not rescue efforts, surely. "Bedtime?" he asked.

"If the northwest bedroom is still free. Catrina?" At the Frenchwoman's nod, Nadia continued. "I can sleep on the sofa tonight. I suggest that everybody get some rest. Tomorrow morning is soon enough to make what decisions need making, after we show Maggi the temple and the mosaic. Agreed?"

"Lex and I have to go on to Scotland tomorrow," I argued. "We have less than a week to figure out—"

"Lex has the jet," Nadia interrupted, gently but firmly. "Toulouse to Edinburgh is just over two hours flying time, and that with a stopover in London. We can give them the morning, Maggi. Especially considering how much we're asking."

We're asking. Nadia was good—I had to give her that. I found myself nodding.

"I'll get the luggage," Lex offered, heading for the door with Nick behind him. "I brought some of your essentials, Mag."

"I'll get the dishes," offered Tru, making no effort to mask her true feelings about housework. "Griffin can dry."

"Hey," protested her boyfriend, good-naturedly.

"Better than helping with the dead rat," Tru reminded him, nodding at Eve, who'd picked up the cooler.

They all seemed such good friends, the Marians. Over the past year they'd come together, celebrated victories, mourned losses, grieved one of their own. All in their struggle toward a goal that Simon had entrusted me, the outsider, with destroying. I hated it.

But that wouldn't keep me from doing anything I had to. *Anything.*

Chapter 7

I don't think I've ever needed Lex—as in, needed to have him in bed, to have him in me—as much as I did that night. Yes, I was beyond exhausted. But even more than sleep, I needed to *not be alone* with all this. The loss of our daughter, even temporary, was too vast to face alone.

Almost as soon as Lex closed the bedroom door, I turned, wrapped my arms up over his neck and kissed him. It wasn't just passion, though our bodies knew the other's so well, the passion came almost instinctively.

This was essential. Basic.

Primal.

I felt it in Lex, too—in the desperation with which his mouth covered mine. One hard arm wrenched me against him. I barely noticed the click of the door lock turning, even the sudden darkness as he switched off the overhead lamp, before his embrace doubled in strength. My fingers dug furrows into his thick hair. He fisted mine into a ponytail, using it to draw my head back, to lift my face more firmly to his while his kisses turned as fierce as mine became greedy. In a moment we'd fallen onto the quilt, bouncing slightly on the bedsprings. Our clothes were efficiently disposed of through months, years of practice, his shirt shoved down his arms and off his wrists, mine rolled up over my head, his slacks unbelted, unbuckled, kicked down his legs in the kind of treatment that would make his tailor weep.

The last person on my mind was Lex's tailor.

My jeans went the same way. So did our underwear.

Only when Lex gasped did I realize how deeply I was dragging my nails down his back. I almost didn't care. He nipped the side of my breast amidst his kisses. I gloried in that twinge of discomfort, both fighting and welcoming him. Anything to let off steam. Anything not to think. Anything to feel something other than the guilt and the fear and the impotence—

"Mag," Lex protested finally, his lips muffled against my skin, after a forever of winding together, holding on to each other as we couldn't with anybody else. "MaggiMaggiMaggiMaggi—"

He knew that would finally get through to me, and I made a noise of disapproval. Talking was too close to thinking. Too close to remembering. But he went on.

"Do you want…?"

For a suspended moment, he could have been speaking Chinese. Then I understood, and with the return of my wits, everything else crashed down on me too.

I had only recently gone back to birth control pills, because I'd only recently weaned Kestrel. Lex was asking if we were still using condoms.

A horrible jumble of contradictory responses hurt my head,

stuck in my throat. Everything from wishing he were less responsible, and so hadn't even thought of it, to a profane
moment of wondering if he meant to get started on Kestrel's
replacement already. I heard in my head, echoing like a
scream, the protest I could never, never have spoken.

She isn't dead yet!

It was the *yet* that broke me. I fell from sexual predator to
lost mother in one long, collapsing sob. Suddenly Lex wasn't
holding me preparatory to any kind of mating dance. He was
holding me as a far deeper kind of mate. The person I could dare
be weak in front of, even at the most inauspicious moment.

Stroking my hair, kissing my cheeks, as gentle now as he'd
been aggressive moments before, pretending not to tremble
with his own needs until he got them under control. He always
had everything under control, my Lex. Almost always.

"We'll get her back," he promised as he held me. I lost
count of how often he repeated it. When I stiffened, he quickly
added, "Your way. Safely. But we'll get her back, goddess.
We've got to."

When we did finally make love—and oh, we did—it was
tender. Slow. Poignant.

And Lex wore a condom, without asking again.

After all that, and the deep sleep that followed, it kind of
sucked to wake up alone. Especially to an unfamiliar ring
tone. Lex's private phone?

I reached out from the delicious weight of the quilt, to
nudge him awake, but Lex wasn't there…just his scent
clinging to the pillow. Rain against the window warned of
another dark morning, but I could make out the dark beams
against the slanted ceiling. If dawn hadn't already passed us,
it wasn't far away. The room had been furnished inexpen-

sively: a battered old chest of drawers with a freestanding mirror stood alone with the bed. The whole house felt…safe. Despite a lingering, vaguely smoky scent.

And the phone rang again. Suddenly figuring it out, I lunged out of bed, looked for my clothes. Another ring drew my eyes to my borrowed jeans. Before he left, Lex must have picked up my discarded clothes and left them, folded, on the bureau.

Nude, I dug the prepaid cell phone out of its denim prison and thumbed the green button, sure it would roll over to voice mail before—

"Yes?" I demanded.

Only one person had this phone number. "Good morning, Mrs. Stuart," greeted Simon Adriano's smooth voice.

"How is she?"

"You cannot honestly expect updates? You, Mrs. Stuart, report to me. I trust you made it safely to Lys?"

"Tell me how my daughter is, and maybe I'll tell you my progress." Negotiation 101, as Lex would say. Quid pro quo.

This time it didn't work. "Do not think to play me. Do you believe I've not kept watch on that pathetic nest of Marians? You are there. So is your husband. So is the witch who seduced—"

He must have been extra angry, because he bit back the rest of that.

"Then why did you ask?" I demanded.

"To test your reliability. I'm afraid you failed. Perhaps you need a reminder—"

"No!" Part of me longed for Lex, for someone to hang on to through this. The larger part felt relief that he wasn't here to snatch the phone away, maybe say something we would both regret. "I'm sorry," I added quickly. If Adriano wanted to believe himself in control, how did it hurt me to let him?

For now.

"I'm sorry," I repeated, just to be thorough.

"That is better," purred my daughter's captor. "I trust you have warned everyone involved of the futility of a rescue attempt?"

"Yes, I have. Several times."

"Good," he said, and I could have sworn I heard a smile. "And you have convinced them to dismantle the mosaic?"

I almost lied. But he was no fool…and I had no idea just how close a watch his men were, in fact, keeping. Could they have bugged the farmhouse? Be using parabolic microphones?

I played a hunch. "I'm still working on that part."

For a moment silence stretched between us. Then Simon all but purred, "Very good, Mrs. Stuart. See how easy that was? But do persuade them. I shall see you in five days."

And he hung up.

The bastard.

After collecting myself, I pulled my borrowed clothes back on and padded down the wooden stairway to the near-silent kitchen. I say *near* silent because Lex and Nadia were there, sipping coffee and speaking in low voices across a smaller table than that in the main room. My husband—and the woman who'd named her daughter after him. The woman whom I strongly suspected had been his first time, just as Lex had been mine. She'd grown up as a part of his privileged world, a world of ski trips and sailing and polo that, even married to him, I rarely visited.

Of my own choosing.

I forced myself into the kitchen, exchanged a smile with Nadia, happily took and returned a kiss when Lex lifted his face to me and went to help myself to some coffee. "Do either of you want a warm-up?"

"We're good," Lex assured me. "Nadia was just telling me about this Joshua character."

Nadia narrowed her eyes at him. He didn't grin—Lex isn't that free with the smiles—but his eyes warmed in return.

"The Joshua whose underwear I'm wearing?" I asked, sinking into a chair beside him.

Lex's eyes widened, Nadia laughed and I claimed the dead-gerbil defense. It felt good, all three of us being friends.

Soon the others were wandering in, breakfast was started, conversations branched away.

"I already made reservations for us tonight at the Balmoral in Edinburgh," Lex murmured to me. His gaze met mine with golden understanding. He shared my need to be doing something, and I loved him for it.

Still, I chose not to mention Simon Adriano's wake-up call until later. Away from the Marians Simon wanted me to betray.

First, though, came our visit to the Marian Temple.

I warned myself to stay indifferent. It was the only way I could do what Simon was requiring. The cave lay amidst the rocky foothills of the Pyrenees, not an hour's stormy hike from the farmhouse. Several of our men were armed, trying to keep an eye out for danger through the downpour. The cave entrance had been barred and locked; very recently, to judge by the shine of the metal.

"We only cleared this entrance in the last month," Nadia confirmed, as Nick Petter unlocked the gate and punched in a security code behind it. Nick, as it turned out, was a security specialist. "Before that, we got in through an underground river, behind a waterfall to the west."

I was just as glad to avoid the underground river. Not that we were much less wet. But as we entered the cave, it defined the word *shelter*. Things were dryer in here, out of the wind and rain. Quieter. Safe...in the arms of Mother Earth.

No, I warned myself. Indifferent, remember?

It didn't really help. This was absolutely a goddess place.

The first goddess temple I ever found on my own had been underground, but not very—it had lain hidden under an abbey and shared its Romanesque details. In contrast, the Marian "temple" had been formed by nature. While the men stayed near the entrance to discuss its defense, Nadia, Tru, Eve and Catrina led me deeper into its womb.

Tru explained how she'd first sensed the temple's presence through her dowsing skills. But it was Nadia's past-life visions that had revealed the secret route inside. None of that seemed as fantastic as the caverns themselves. As we wound our way lower, then lower still, crystal deposits shimmied across the rock walls and across the rising ceiling, to spiral up stalagmites, down stalactites and along the full length of rock columns. Even by battery-powered lanterns, the effect sparkled like stars in the sky. What would it be like to see it by open flame?

I could easily imagine prehistoric humans finding these caves and seeing in them warmth, shelter, magic and yet more proof of the divinity of Mother Earth.

This place was dark, echoing, damp, ancient…and powerful enough to make me shiver. The Marians had posted Danger signs on several passageways that branched off. "Some of them are pretty treacherous," warned Tru, who seemed to have spent the most time spelunking. According to Nadia, they'd buried the bodies of a half-dozen fleeing Marians who had not quite escaped invading troops, almost seven centuries before.

"We should stop to rest here," said Eve, her whisper echoing. "Catrina's tired."

Catrina scowled, but did not argue—and I was missing something. When I turned my questioning gaze on the others, it was Nadia who admitted, "Catrina was shot last month, by an Adriano sniper. She's still recovering."

"She *what?*"

"I am fine," Catrina protested, sounding embarrassed.

But I didn't buy it. Even I was tired after the hike out here. So we sat. When I glanced toward Catrina, concerned, she glared. I looked away. Somewhere in the depths of the caverns, beckoning to us, I could make out a strange, rhythmic thumping, like a heartbeat.

"From what we've pieced together," Nadia explained, "the Marians here were well-established goddess worshippers by the first century AD. Only the priestesses knew of the caves, though. Most people worshipped at a huge temple network outside, complete with stone circles, dwellings, even a hospital where they supposedly worked miracles. Because of the powerful ley lines that intersect here—"

"It's a major nexus point," Tru clarified.

"—when they decided to create the mosaic, they chose to put it underground, as a filter to ensure that the energy remained positive and healthful throughout the Age of Pisces."

"It took forever to finish," added Tru, the humor of her exaggeration tinged by unexpected sadness. "Like, three centuries or so, anyway. Most of the tiles have a ceramic base, but they have certain ingredients mixed in. The priestesses traveled across the world to find specific stones and metals. Petrified wood from the American southwest. Ivory from Africa. Larimar, which can only be found in the Dominican Republic…or possibly Atlantis. Even I would have trouble identifying some of them, if Nadia hadn't found a copy of the Marians' key and Rhys hadn't translated it."

"Latin." Catrina wasted no syllables, but it was impossible to tell if that was because she was in pain, or just obnoxious.

"Tru means the Madonna Key," Nadia explained. "It's a key in the same way a map's legend is a key. It explains which tiles should go where, so that the mosaic works correctly."

I repeated, "Like a filter."

"Almost like a computer chip." Tru spread her arms, and the lantern she held made the crystal formations around us sparkle. "The intricacy with which the power is channeled through the various elements—it really is mind boggling. By the time the mosaic was finished, maybe around the fourth century? The world had seriously changed. Rome had gone Christian, and pagan temples were being taken over by churches. That seems to be when the Adrianos first noticed just how well established the Marian priestesses were. The then-head of the Adriano family kidnapped some of the Marian children—"

She stopped.

"Like now," I said tightly. History repeats itself. I couldn't just sit here. I stood to go on, with a final glance at Catrina to see if she was up to it or perhaps wished to wait. Raising her chin, she stood, as well.

So we walked.

"Um, yeah," said Tru. "Back then, it was to force the women to convert to the One True Faith. But apparently the Marians weren't just healers. The children survived to tell the story. And their mothers sent the Adriano's body back with a message that they weren't to be bothered again."

And now I wasn't just admiring their temple. Or the fact that they were goddess worshippers. I was admiring the Marians' chutzpah. *Damn it.*

"Still, they could see the writing on the wall." Eve picked up the tale from where she was spotting Catrina, to Catrina's obvious annoyance. "They took their worship underground, literally. Eventually they pretended to convert. But they still worked as healers and midwives for centuries. It was only during the Cathar Inquisition, in the thirteenth century, that they were forced to stop even that."

So far, this was paralleling the history of most goddess worship—except for the personal vendetta.

"Adrianos again," said Nadia. "Working with the pope, and carrying a grudge."

"The Marians saw it was coming," Eve continued. "The entire culture of southern France was being systematically destroyed—how could they not? They decided to dismantle the mosaic and send its pieces away with different priestesses, until it would be safe to restore the Black Madonna. They would have gotten away unscathed, except that one of their proselytes was seduced by that period's Duke Adriano into revealing the entrance to the caves."

"We think she must be Pauline's ancestress," added Tru. "But that might just be because *we hate her.*"

"Pauline *Adriano?*" I asked. "Joshua's...?" Oops.

"*Ex*-wife," Nadia clarified for me. "Benny's mother. Apparently Simon didn't know, until recently. Between Joshua's allying himself with us and Pauline's dirty secret, perhaps it's not that surprising Simon put the poor child in with the hostages."

Bastard. Son of a bitch. It was at moments like that when I wished there were more insults for men like him that didn't attack their poor mothers. "Prick."

Tru grinned. Even Catrina looked momentarily amused, though that could have been a trick of the light.

"It was during the Adrianos' invasion of the temple that the Marians whose skeletons we found must have been killed," Eve continued. "The Adrianos collapsed the entrance, to make sure nobody would return...and apparently they didn't."

"Not even through there." Nadia pointed. Not only was the rhythmic thudding louder, so was the sound of running water. I now saw the underground river through which she had originally found the temple. "If they had, they would have taken care of the bodies."

For some reason, she, Eve and Tru were all looking at Catrina now. Scowling—as usual—Catrina finally said, "In the centuries since then, some of the Marian descendents still remembered their origins. More of them forgot, generation after generation. Especially since the Adrianos were systematically hunting them down during the Inquisition and the witch hunts. The knowledge became too dangerous. Finally, even the handful that remembered did not do so very well."

She shrugged as if to say, *finis.*

"Like the Sisters of Mary," clarified Nadia, putting a hand on Cat's shoulder. To my surprise, Cat did not pull away. Or bite her. "They were the women during the French Revolution who hid the cache of Black Madonna relics that Catrina found last year."

"With Rhys," Catrina clarified. "And Scarlet." Scarlet, Nadia's sister. The one the Adrianos had murdered.

Catrina had sent us an embroidery from that cache, done by the hand of no less a personage than Mary Queen of Scots, as a gift for Kestrel. Its monetary value exceeded even that of the chalice Catrina had once stolen from me.

"Thank you," I said, both because it was the right thing to do and because I suddenly sensed that she and Scarlet had been close, suddenly recognized how fresh her grief must be. "For the embroidery."

Catrina stiffly said, *"De rien."* It was nothing.

I suspected she meant it that way, too. "So even people as powerful as the Queen of Scotland—"

"And France," she interrupted. "Mary Stuart lived in France from childhood until the death of François II."

"—and France were Marians?"

"And Joan of Arc," said Nadia. "Perhaps even Elizabeth I."

And it had all started here.

Tru lifted the halogen lantern to reveal three sweeping archways, fanning out in the shape of a crescent. Once we passed through the center one, into the echoing temple itself, art interlaced itself with nature in ways I'd never have imagined. Columns had been fluted by ancient craftswomen, just enough to bring out their glitter of amethyst and quartz. Stalagmites had been carved into images of women—mother and child, woman kneeling, woman raising her arms in fulfillment and joy. Stalactites became angels overhead.

The firm thudding drew my gaze to the side of the room, where a hollowed stone tube sat balanced to catch a trickle of water. As it filled, it tipped over, striking another rock on its way down and then, after spilling its contents, striking rock as it righted itself.

For centuries, this simple metronome, the virtual heartbeat of the lost Marians, had continued. Waiting.

In the center of the circular chamber stood an intricately carved altar, against a backdrop of curving white flowstone that made me think of mother's milk. Carved pomegranates sat on the altar, a bouquet of fresh flowers that one of these Marians must have brought in—

And a cup. An ancient stone cup that I knew on a gut level had come with the temple itself. Slowly I approached it, the earth's heartbeat in my ears, the earth's sanctuary sheltering me from the storm outside.

A goddess cup.

There went my last hope of staying indifferent.

Chapter 8

As I've said before—I'm a grailkeeper. That means I find and collect chalices used in the worship of ancient goddesses. It's a family mission. Legend holds that when enough cups are collected, their combined presence will significantly improve the situation of women worldwide—a goal that nicely paralleled that of the Marians.

I'd collected three such chalices, now carefully hidden in England, before I had Kestrel. But then…I got distracted. After all, who leaves an infant behind to go on adventures?

To suddenly come across an ancient cup, smack in the heart of the oldest goddess temple I'd ever seen, made me feel marginally less excluded. As if I had more reason for being here than my husband's bloodline.

My heartbeat sped. Perhaps I could ascertain exactly which goddess the Marians had worshipped.

Perhaps I could enlist Her help!

"And here," breathed Tru with pride, "is the mosaic."

It took everything I had to turn away from the goblet, to look over my shoulder at the work for which these women had been fighting for so long.

But She was worth it.

The mosaic glowed in its flattened niche on a natural pillar, a rock formation greater than any mere meeting of stalactite and stalagmite. The life-sized woman revealed in the intricate arrangement of small tiles stood glorious, powerful. She could be called nothing other than a Madonna. She held Her child protectively in Her arms, like the standard depictions of the Virgin Mary with Jesus or Isis with Horus or Ceres or Devi. Like standard Black Madonnas, Her skin was jet—this time literal, shiny jet, radiant in Her blackness and absolutely striking against Her lighter eyes. The sweep of Her robes was blue—Tru explained that those tiles were mixed with ground lapis lazuli, using sapphire in the shadows and celestine in the highlights—with an underdress of red.

"Carnelian and garnet," Tru continued to explain. "The key on her belt is overlaid with copper—a natural energy conductor—and mixed with iron from a meteorite, in the shadows."

"And this is all that's missing?" I asked, not quite touching an expanse of dull background near the bottom, where something—presumably the jug—wasn't beside the Madonna's feet.

"Almost," Tru said. "I've been using the key—the legend, I mean—to re-create some of the tiles that are missing or damaged, but this area's a challenge. We can use pearl and opal to help make the jug, but chunks of it are supposed to be pure alabaster. Wherever the original pieces were quarried doesn't exist anymore."

"Which is why I have to find the Stuart tiles," I said. "The ones Queen Mary took to Scotland."

"We're also missing the stone from her headdress." Tru indicated the pendant that hung across the lady's forehead, in the location of Her mythic third eye. Sure enough, a hole gaped where some sort of ornamental jewel should sit. "This isn't supposed to be a tile, either. It's a gem of some kind. But even using the key, we can't figure out what kind of gem it should be. Worse, it's the one piece that seems to change colors in the different representations—the murals, the statues, all that. So I can't even narrow it down to being red or green or orange. We're so close, so very close…"

She hadn't just put months of work into this. It had become her mission, as sure as grails were mine. And I'd put the unpleasantness off long enough. If I had to request something this heinous, the least I could do was be up front about it.

"I hate to ask you to tear it down again."

Tru said nothing, having already heard this the previous night, but she looked ill.

Catrina folded her arms. "And we hate to say no."

Immediately my hackles rose. But before I could retort, Eve stepped in. "We should consider *all* our options, don't you think? We owe it to our children to make the best possible decision."

That decision must be to keep Simon happy—mustn't it? But I was too stressed; I was forgetting my Tai Chi training. Running head-on into a problem is far less useful than finding a way to work with it, or to go around it. There were four women here, besides me. If they made the decision to dismantle the mosaic on their own, that would make things easier on all of us.

And if they decided against it?

Then I would have to find a way to go around.

"How's this? Catrina—" I had to swallow hard to get it out. "Catrina's right about one thing, anyway. I'm too close to this. Maybe even more than Eve and Nadia, because while all of us have children at risk, I'm the one who's supposed to bring the tiles back to Naples. That definitely makes me biased. You four have been working at this the longest. Talk it out among yourselves, and…and then we'll see what happens."

"I have already drunk from the goblet," Catrina said. "Nothing happened. But you are welcome to try."

"What?" But even as I asked, my eyes returned to the cup on the altar, and I understood. She was right. I absolutely wanted to drink from it. But, "That's not what I meant."

"I missed something," said Tru.

"It is a long story," said Catrina, leaving the immediate chamber and just assuming they would follow her. With final, confused glances back toward me, they did. Eve left one of the halogen lanterns behind with me.

Thanks for making me feel selfish and manipulative, Cat.

But what she didn't get was, if that *was* a goddess grail, it was a direct line to divine energy. Like a rosary to a Catholic, or a Bible to a Baptist. I hadn't suggested that they work it out just to get some quiet time with the cup.

But now that I had the chance, I wouldn't feel guilty about it.

The goblet was made of intricately carved stone—marble, to judge by the weight and texture. When I lifted it, I sensed…something. Not the tangible buzz of power I'd gotten off other grails, but *something*.

I carried it carefully to the stream of water that fed the temple's percussive heartbeat, and almost placed the cup under the initial stream of water before it reached the tube. Concern over stopping the regularity of the rhythm, even a little, changed my mind. The stone tube filled with underground spring water. Sufficiently weighted, it tipped on its fulcrum and landed, with a solid beat, on the second rock. But instead of pouring into the continuing stream, I made sure it poured into the Marian Chalice.

Then, with a lighter thump, the tube tipped back into place and began to refill.

I carried the chalice back toward the flower-strewn altar, but at the last minute I kneeled before the mosaic itself. Goddess, it was beautiful. The way She was looking at the baby in Her arms. The mix of the colors, the tangible bounce-back of the tile energy…how could I destroy it?

But how else could I save my baby?

Well…this was why I needed help, wasn't it?

"Lady," I whispered. "Please, share your wisdom. What's the right direction? And…what's your name?"

Then I lifted the marble goblet to my lips, closed my eyes…and drank.

The water tasted cool and refreshing. But other than that? Nothing happened.

My heart almost broke. Wasn't this a goddess cup? Or, worse, much worse…had I somehow abdicated my ability to commune with the feminine divine?

"Please," I whispered, meeting the deep gaze of the mosaic's Madonna. I willed the connection to happen, as hard as I could. "I need your help. *Please.*"

Again I drank, this time holding Her gaze.

And this time the cave seemed to shift around me. Suddenly, instead of a mosaic, I stared at a natural stone pillar, lit only by torchlight. Other than the missing Madonna, the heart of the Marian temple seemed almost identical.

Well…except for the two priestesses arranging altar tools.

One woman is perhaps my mother's age, the other closer to mine. Both wear the ancient garb of the Roman

Empire, stola draped over palla draped over chiton. Ancient women were big on layering. These two also wear head cloths over their hair, but I can see that the older priestess has the olive complexion of the Middle East.

The younger woman is darker still. "Mother, they will listen to you." *I cannot tell if she means that the older woman is her biological mother or her superior. Perhaps both.*

"No doubt they will," *agrees her elder.* "But not for the right reasons."

"They have faith in your wisdom!"

"They are distracted by my fame. The more people esteem me as a saint, the less they hear our message." *Capturing water from the same stream I used, into the same marble cup from which I drank, the older woman sets it onto the altar.* "They have begun to call themselves after me. Have you heard?"

"'Marians.'" *The younger one smiles.* "Does it bother you?"

The older woman shakes her head. "The name is only a label. Once I am gone, they will forget."

But her daughter seems troubled, and not just by the idea of "Mother's" *death.* "The stars worry me. Pisces is a spiritual age. Several great religions will dominate for as long as it lasts, including that of your rabbi."

Her mother smiles sadly, fondly. "Good. His message is one of peace and love."

"But many men will corrupt it. The two fish of Pisces swim in opposite directions. The great religions will war with each other. Too many people will believe the illusion of opposites. And in the struggle of man against woman, man will win. For almost two thousand years, he will dominate. Mother, I am uncertain if we can survive it."

*The older woman is unconvinced. "Surely men will
continue to love their wives, mothers, daughters, sisters."*

*"As individuals, perhaps. But they will see them as the
exceptions. The dark energies that will come of this
continuing war—we must guard against them. And we
cannot lose time."*

*Her mother considers this. "When I was part of the
ministry," she slowly says, "other apostles resented me, in
part because I was a woman."*

"Then you believe the threat?"

"I do. But, Sarah—" The woman I now suspect is Mary
Magdalene—*the* Mary Magdalene—puts a comforting
hand on the shoulder of the younger woman. Is this her
daughter? If so, is it the daughter, the apocryphal child
of Jesus Christ? *"We must never abdicate our powers
completely, even to the most competent defenders. It is
your task to make the others believe."*

Then, like that, I was staring at the mosaic, by the light of
a twenty-first-century halogen lantern.

Holy crap! I brought the chalice back to the altar, dizzy
with the implications. This wasn't a goddess grail, or if so, it
wasn't like others I'd drunk from. I'd had no communion with
the divine. Instead, I'd experienced a moment of postcogni-
tion, to another priestess entirely. And what a priestess!

One person's religion is another person's myth. As a comparative mythologist, I knew that the rumors of Jesus Christ
marrying Mary Madgalene were neither new nor verifiable.
I also knew that every time they came up, people were
shocked all over again. So let me clarify, here and now: I was
fascinated with them as a mythic possibility. But I had no
great need to prove what probably could never be proven,
even if it were true, and I'm not saying it was.

How's *that* for a qualifier?

So why did I automatically assume that a goddess worshipper from ancient Gaul named Mary, with a dark-skinned daughter named Sarah, was the Magdalene? One reason is because of things that are *not* speculative. She was an apostle, whether or not she is given the official title—all four gospels in the New Testament show Mary Magdalene traveling with and supporting the ministry of Jesus Christ. In most places in the Bible, when the women with Jesus are listed, the Magdalene is named even before his mother, implying importance. And the risen Christ appeared first to Mary Magdalene, asking *her* to proclaim his resurrection.

Don't want to believe me? Look it up.

Of course, that only proves that Mary Magdalene was one of the most important supporters of Jesus. I also recognized her for reasons that were admittedly less solid, from a scholarly standpoint. One was the Gnostic Gospel of Mary Magdalene—it's a real work, but of arguable authority. Another clue came from myths, pure and simple. In one of her main legends, the Magdalene escapes first to Egypt, and later to France, arriving with two other Mary's—Mary Salome and Mary Jacobe—and a dark-skinned girl named Sarah. In some versions, the girl is the Magdalene's daughter by Jesus. In others, Sarah is simply an Egyptian servant.

I knew all that. My name is *Magdalene,* remember?

I suspect people named Jezebel or Sheba also do a little research.

Overwhelmed by possibilities, I tried some deep breathing, which moved me naturally into some badly needed Tai Chi, to draw my scattered energies back into balance. Stepping slowly, shifting my weight deliberately, I kept my arms and wrists curved and soft. I moved from basic forms of "ward-off" and "press" into the more complex "waving hands in clouds" and "fair lady weaves shuttle." Tai Chi is, above all else, a moving mediation.

It centered me.

By the time I'd stilled again, I had a better grasp on things. On the downside I had no more knowledge of exactly whom the Marians worshipped than I'd had before. On the upside—

I might have just gotten a glimpse into one of the biggest mysteries of the Western World!

None of that was as important as my immediate concerns about the mosaic, Simon Adriano and the safety of the children. So I grabbed the lantern and went out after the other women.

They were seated on the floor of the antechamber, in low conversation, but didn't look displeased to see me. It probably didn't hurt that, to judge by the echoes, the men had apparently finished scoping out the cave's security and were on their way, as well.

"We've come to a compromise." Eve patted the floor beside her for me to join them. "Since you're going to be gone for a few days anyway, looking for the Stuart tiles, Tru's going to use that time to make a duplicate mosaic."

My drop to a seated position was nowhere near as graceful as my Tai Chi forms had been. "You can *do* that? In *days?*"

The dowser's blond hair bounced as she shrugged. "I can try, if I have help with the firing and the glazing. But people, this is still a long shot. We need thousands of ingredients, *today*— well, tomorrow anyway. We're talking gold, sapphires, rubies, opals, all couriered same- or next-day service. Just because the kids are worth any price doesn't mean we actually *have*—"

Someone cleared his throat, and we looked up to see Lex, Griffin and Nick. Three guesses who had interrupted.

My husband met my gaze, and I nodded. "Lex has that kind of money."

Their widening eyes filled me with pride and something more like…embarrassment. I still wasn't used to the fact that, now that I'd married Lex, I, too, was richer than God. Not that I was complaining—I'm not an idiot. But it was a transition.

"Okey-dokey, then," said Tru, recovering. "Next question—is the duplicate meant for Simon, or are we sending him the original and keeping the duplicate?"

The idea of double-crossing Simon just plain scared me, not because he didn't deserve it, but because of the likely consequences. "Can he tell the difference?"

"Not if we make it full strength." Tru seemed to recognize just how brazen that sounded, because she added, "I mean, probably not. Assuming we stain them a little to age them. But do we want him to have a full-strength mosaic, either way?"

"Just because our mosaic can protect against a negative surge of energy," clarified Eve, "assuming it can really do that, doesn't mean it can protect against one that's been powered by inverted tiles."

"Inverted tiles are bad, right?" I asked.

Catrina nodded, an eyebrow arched.

By now the men had settled onto the floor with us, each by the appropriate woman. Nick rubbed Eve's shoulders. Griffin, his elbow on one knee, watched Tru's confidence with admiration.

Lex had settled neatly between me and Nadia, who'd been poignantly silent through all this. But it was my hand he found with his.

"We all want to save the children," Tru continued earnestly. "But there are millions of other children throughout Europe who could suffer and die if we arm Simon and disarm ourselves. Still, I think I understand the energies of the tiles well enough to make *near* duplicates. Almost identical to the originals but without as much power to filter or enhance the earth energies Simon's trying to manipulate."

"If Simon detects the ruse," Nadia noted quietly, "our children could pay the price."

Catrina said, "If we send him the real mosaic, they will not be alone in this."

"It's up to you guys," Tru insisted, looking around at the parents among us. "Catrina and I decided that we can't make the call for you."

I glanced at Lex, whose expression was annoyingly unreadable, then at Nadia. She looked as ill as I felt. If we made the wrong call, we could be condemning our daughters to the gas.

We must never abdicate our powers completely, I thought. The woman I suspected was Mary Magdalene had said that. *Even to the most competent defenders.*

And Simon Adriano was neither a defender nor competent.

"It's worth a try," I said. "There'll be time to change our minds when Lex and I get back from Scotland, if it looks like the duplicates won't fool him."

"Yeah," said Tru. "About Lex going to Scotland…"

I stiffened.

"Hey, maybe I've missed something. But if he's going to be paying for specific stones, shells, metals, petrified wood and gemstones from across the world, isn't he going to have to be the one buying them? Maybe it's too big a job. It took the Marian priestesses centuries."

"I can do it," insisted Lex, sounding more as if he were sitting on a throne than on a stone floor. "From Scotland, if I need to."

It was Nadia who, seeing where Tru was going, put her hand on Lex's arm. "Without the Adrianos suspecting that you're doing it?"

Crap.

Oh, Lex flew with me to Edinburgh, just as we'd planned. He'd brought my passport with him from the States, so we didn't have to worry about customs. But almost as soon as we'd checked into the Balmoral, after one last embrace and lingering kiss, he slipped away on foot for the nearby Waverly Station. He would head south into England by train, then catch a flight—or a train, if planes were still grounded—to Brussels. He was confident he could lose any Adriano agents who might be watching us. Belgium was close enough to France for one of the Marians—an antiquities thief named Aubrey de Lune—to smuggle his purchases back to the Marians, hopefully staying under Simon Adriano's radar.

Apparently, Simon thought she was dead.

So there I was, on my own to find Kestrel's tiles somewhere in Lex's ancestral country of Scotland. As soon as possible.

And I had no idea where to start.

Chapter 9

My decision was on par with closing my eyes and throwing a dart: I chose to check out Edinburgh Castle first.

At least it was a decision.

One of the several surprises waiting for me at the Balmoral, besides its six stories of palatial splendor, had been a collection of boxes from a store called Jenners, stacked in our suite's front room. Apparently our hotel reservations hadn't been the only arrangements Lex made.

He'd had a laptop computer delivered and a small selection of outfits in my size. Those included sturdy walking boots, gloves and a hooded cloak of dark blue, lined in a bright red plaid. A plaid scarf matched the lining.

I hadn't exactly been kidnapped with luggage. Now, considering how much colder the weather was up in Scotland than in Naples, I couldn't think of a more practical gift. I wanted to call him on his cell and thank him. I wanted to hear his voice, as if we hadn't just spent most of the morning, including our latest turbulent flight, hand in hand. I wished I hadn't lost the gift of knowing soul deep exactly where he was.

I wished we'd made time for a quickie before he'd gone.

But we both had desperately important jobs to do and, to judge by what the Marians had told us, reason to be paranoid. So I got a grip, wrapped up and headed out into the windy, sleety streets of Scotland's capital city, glad for the heavy clothes. Taking the car Lex had rented at the airport, I quickly reached the stone fortress that dominated Castle Rock, overlooking the city.

I'd only been there once before, about seven years ago. I hadn't remembered just how *brown* the city was—from castle to government buildings to historic tenements, everything was built from brownish-gray rock with slate-black roofs. Tall buildings, four- and five-stories high, dominated the narrow old streets. It gave the whole city a claustrophobic air. Even the sprawling castle, when I hurried through sleet across the ice-pebbled esplanade, seemed brooding and brown. This was no Cinderella's palace, despite its four-story military barracks and lofty great hall—neat, rectangular buildings, each with rows of small, glass-paned windows. Despite such seemingly modern symmetry, you could look in any direction and still see places where an intact boulder, ten feet high, completed the bottom of a curtain wall, or where raw rock cornered a building.

This place was as severe as the weather, and it was getting to me. Instead of thinking of the heroism of William Wallace and Robert the Bruce, whose bronze statues flanked the castle entrance before the drawbridge, I found myself remembering their tragic ends. It was the latter to whom Lex was distantly related. More important for my purposes that afternoon was Mary Queen of Scots. And like Robert the Bruce—and quite unlike my husband—she had *ruled* Scotland.

The Crown Jewels, aka the Honours of Scotland, were housed at the castle. It seemed as good a place to start as any.

I struggled my way up steeply inclined courtyards and icy steps, first far beneath the looming Half Moon Battery with its cannons overlooking the city, and eventually on cannon level myself. Normally one could see all the way across Edinburgh to the docks at the Firth of Forth. Gray sleet obscured almost all of it today. I squinted and kept my head down against the wind.

At least when I reached the palace itself, through the entrance in the base of its turreted clock tower, I was able to step in from the awful cold.

Trying not to give way to sniffles—this time, at least, caused only by weather and exercise—I paid the separate admission and found the dark-paneled room with its requisite glass cases displaying the Honours of Scotland. What was I looking for? Anything, absolutely anything, that could have incorporated alabaster tiles. Better yet, it would be nice to find a collection of the tiles all by themselves, though how I would then steal them was anybody's guess. Through glass cases I examined an ornate crown—one of those with an ermine band and red velvet under the golden frame, all done in pearls and diamonds. A delicate sword and silver scepter finished out the main treasures.

"The three Honours were first used together in the coronation of Queen Mary Stuart," offered a kilted man nearby, his voice thick with brogue. "She was nine months old at the time, so the crown had to be held over her head."

I nodded in vague politeness and searched the rest of the room. The only other significant piece was a huge slab of sandstone.

"'Tis the Stone of Destiny," said the Scot beside me, as if I couldn't read the plaque. "It served as Scotland's coronation chair until 'twas stolen centuries ago by the English. In 1950, three Scottish students stole it back and hid it. Only recently has it been on display."

Normally such examples of stolen history would have fascinated me, but not with my baby's safety at stake. There were no tiles. No extensive collection of jewels beyond the Honours.

"One of the students," added my guide, "was also a Stuart."

Now I looked directly at him, suspicious. The first mention of my married name had been innocuous enough—if Mary Queen of Scots hadn't been a Stuart, and very likely a Marian, I wouldn't be here. But this one?

The fortyish guide grinned, and his rugged, red-bearded face turned handsome.

"Is Stuart not your name then?" He looked me over, but not in a creepy way. "Are you wearing the tartan only to bring out your eyes?"

Of course. Tartans are the Scottish equivalent of coats of arms. Why wouldn't Lex have dressed me as a Stuart?

"It's my husband's name," I admitted, taking his offered hand. "I'm Maggi Stuart."

This didn't seem a time for hyphenates, either.

"Jamie MacDonald, at your service." He made a slight bow. I wondered if I should've known his surname from the green and red of his kilt. "Forgive me for noticing, but you're nae eyeing the Honours with quite the awe I've come to expect from visitors."

"And you see a lot of visitors?"

"Indeed I do. I'm a guide. But with the mucky weather we've had of late, it's a wonder any of us can get work. Since you seem to be looking for something in particular—and nae finding it—I thought I would be so bold as to offer my assistance."

I hesitated. On the one hand, this seemed suspiciously convenient. On the other…

Well, he wasn't the only man in a kilt who seemed to be twiddling his fingers over the scarcity of tourists. Other guides were watching us.

"I know what you're thinking," Jamie challenged, a smile in his thick brogue. "It's as plain as the nose on your lovely face. You're thinking to yourself—can I trust this handsome rogue? But me being a MacDonald— that's something a Stuart can trust. Now if I'd been a Campbell…."

He shook his head and clicked his tongue on his teeth, his opinion of the Campbells amusingly clear.

Hell, at some point I had to stop suspecting everybody. And even if this man were somehow involved with the Adrianos, what was he going to do—kidnap me again? The Adrianos wanted me to find the alabaster tiles as much as anybody.

My only immediate concern about the Adrianos was to keep up the illusion that Lex was also in Scotland. If asked, I'd say we'd split up to cover more ground.

"I thought there would be more personal items or jewels," I admitted. "Things Queen Mary brought back with her from France."

"Aye, in 1561," he supplied effortlessly. "The difficulty there, you see, is that from '68 to '87, the poor queen was a prisoner in England. Her son would have inherited anything she didna give to individual supporters, and he eventually became king of England himself. Many of her jewels are on display, but at the Tower of London."

Crap. I could try checking online once I got back to the

hotel, but the idea of having to pop down to London on what was already a wild-goose chase made me feel ill.

"Is it something in particular you're looking for?"

"Playing pieces," I lied, flat-out. "Little alabaster playing pieces, from a game she learned in France. They may be jeweled with pearls or opals, or so I thought… Well, I'm a professor at Clemens College, in Connecticut, and I'm researching this game for a paper."

Jamie MacDonald considered that. I suspected he recognized the lie, but he was kind enough to pretend not to. "You'll have a better chance at the gallery at Holyrood Palace, at the other end of the Royal Mile. 'Twas the queen's favorite residence in Edinburgh. But as long as you're here, we'd best see the room upstairs where the she gave birth to her only living child. If a woman ever had time to play a parlor game, it would be during the early hours of her confinement, aye?"

Lex and I had played cards during mine. And trivia games. We'd tried to watch a movie but couldn't concentrate. It suddenly seemed like yesterday. Goddess, we'd been excited.

"Yes," I said, letting him lead the way. I felt sorry for any woman who'd had to go through childbirth without modern medicine or technology. At least I'd been able to monitor Kestrel's heartbeat the entire time. At least I'd had some of the best neonatal care in the world just down the hospital hallway. "Her *only* child?"

"Poor wee bairn. Only eight months old when his father was murdered, and two months more when his mother fled to England. He would ne'er see her again."

He'd been one month younger than Kestrel, when she'd left. I didn't like that story at all.

Not surprisingly, the dark room where the Scottish queen had gone through her confinement offered no tiles—it's not as if nobody would've remembered to sweep up under the curtained bed over the last four hundred years.

"So if these pieces aren't at Holyrood Palace," I said, hurrying Jamie MacDonald toward the exit, "Where would I look next?"

"Stirling was the queen's favorite castle. 'Tis no terrible long drive, if the weather cooperates."

"And what if the weather doesn't cooperate?" I asked, and he grinned at the idea of such a challenge. So I said, "You're hired. Where's the closest public phone?"

The castle gift shop had a phone box. I gave Jamie a $50 bill U.S. and asked him to buy the best books on the Queen of Scots that the shop had. Then, with him busy, I telephoned Lex's private cell phone. All he said when he answered was, "Got it."

Then he hung up. A minute later the public phone rang. He'd captured the number off his cell phone and returned the call over a land line, for security's sake. The Adrianos couldn't bug everything.

"So far so good," he said—even without details, I felt comforted to know that much. "Have you found something already?"

"Not yet. Lex, are the MacDonalds and the Stuarts really allies?"

"Sure. You've heard how Flora MacDonald risked her life helping Bonnie Prince Charlie escape after the Jacobite uprising, right?"

It sounded familiar, but only vaguely. "Then I've got a guide," I told him. "A MacDonald guide."

"Good idea. I—" He'd clearly covered the mouthpiece, probably with his hand, but I thought I heard train-station sounds. He probably couldn't get a flight out. "I've got to go. Can I reach you here later?"

"No. I'll call back when I stop for supper. Thank you for the cloak. You have no idea the time and trouble it's saved."

"I wish I could save you from all of this. You and..." But he didn't have to say it, and I didn't have to respond. Kestrel was our number-one priority. "Maggi, if anybody can find what we need, it's you. You know that, right?"

But by then Jamie was returning with a Heritage of Scotland bag. Lex and I exchanged overly hasty love-you's so that he could catch his train, and I headed out with my guide.

Into more awful weather.

With Jamie MacDonald navigating, we made it to the sweeping, iron-fenced majesty of Holyrood Palace before the Queen's Gallery—built in a restored church on the grounds—closed for the afternoon. We were the only visitors, too. After shaking snow and ice off my cloak, I started examining the exhibit at a speed to break the hearts of whoever had designed this peaceful display, with its vaulted ceilings, blond wood and pale blue walls. It was a waste of time; most of the treasures had belonged to the Elizabeths, Victoria, Anne or the two Queen Marys who *weren't* Scottish.

After the last glance across everything from countless fans to decorative door hinges, I turned to my guide. "She spent time at Holyrood?"

The entryway into the palace proper—which was marginally more Cinderella-like than Edinburgh Castle, with turrets at all the corners—boasted Scotland's coat of arms, two unicorns rearing over a shield. The motto, *Nemo Me Impune Lacessit,* made me nervous. It basically means, "Nobody screws with me and gets away with it."

Lex had agreed to the Marians' plan, I reminded myself. He wasn't actively working to go to war with Simon. He would have told me if he was. Wouldn't he?

Then fate gave me *real* cause to worry.

"So sorry," said a guard, blocking the doorway. "Last admission was at three-thirty."

"But you're still open," I protested. "You're open until four-thirty."

"You'll need more than an hour to see everything. We open again at nine-thirty tomorrow."

"I can't wait until—"

"You're a MacIan, aye?" asked Jamie, interrupting me. "Can't you see she's a Stuart, man?"

And somehow I ended up inside the palace, my guide grinning broadly as he led me toward an upstairs room where Mary Stuart had seen her jealous second husband commit murder.

"Doesn't sound like she chose her husband very well," I said, to distract myself from just how overwhelmingly powerful the Stuart name seemed to be around here, even now.

Not that I was complaining. Really.

"Neither the second time nor the third," Jamie agreed. "Rarely did Stuarts marry well. An unhappy lot, that one."

"How's that?"

"Two different Stuart rulers were beheaded. Two of them were assassinated. Four were exiled. Seven of them were but wee bairns when crowned, having lost their fathers young. Five of them left no legitimate heirs."

Not a track record to cheer me. "We'll make more time if we split up," I said. "You take everything to the west, I'll take everything to the east, and we'll meet back at the entrance by closing time. You're looking for alabaster tiles."

The Palace at Holyrood boasted huge galleries with molded and medallioned ceilings, chandeliers, tapestries, portraits. As I moved from room to room, I couldn't fight off a sinking sense of futility. The incessant sound of sleet against the windows wasn't helping—would the sun never come out again? When I'd been after goddess grails, there'd been a sense of recognition, almost an instinct that helped draw me to them. But this was different. These were Kestrel's inheritance, not mine.

On top of all that, I hated not being prepared. I wouldn't be cracking a book about the Queen of Scots until every site I could possibly search was closed for the night.

Knowing that still didn't make it any easier when a tall old man, in one of the palace doorways, said, "I would have thought more of you, Mrs. Stuart."

I frowned at him, this slightly built man, gray-bearded, bright-eyed. He wore an expensive suit, expensive shoes. *Mrs.* Stuart, he'd called me. Despite that I had the cloak slung over my arm and wore a wedding ring, something about the way he said my name made me think he was more than guessing.

Then he confirmed it. "But you prefer Sanger-Stuart, do you not?"

"If you know anything that will help me help my daughter," I told him, cutting to the chase, "you tell me. *Now.*"

"I've been waiting here most of the afternoon in hopes of doing just that." He made a slight bow. "I feared you would start with the obvious, and the only thing more blatant than this would have been the crown jewels."

We were wasting time. "Give me something I can use," I warned, "or get the hell out of my way. You're with the Adrianos, right?"

"I prefer the name Myrddin, now." He seemed to make a decision and nodded. "But, yes. I was born Maximilian Adriano."

"Simon's father." I'd heard one of the Marians mention that connection, and the name *Max*.

"Sadly, yes. And you're looking in the wrong place."

"Oh? Then where *should* I look?"

"My dear lady, if I knew that, I could have found the tiles decades ago." Maybe he read in my expression just how dangerous I was feeling today. "God knows I have looked. We had access to a precious book once, before I lost it in the War. The Joan of Arc manuscript had family crests of the more significant Marian families drawn in the margins. We used it as a kind of reverse genealogy—in an attempt to find more tiles, mind you. We gave up trying to kill all Marian descendents some time ago. Such actions are hardly discreet. Only when we sensed a threat…" He shook his head, as if to clear it of unpleasant memories. "Well."

"Bully for you. What about the tiles?"

"I suspected Simon would send you or Ana Reisner on this quest and am here warn you against redundancy. I hired men to seek the Stuart tiles in my youth. I have sought them more recently, since I mended my ways. Rest assured, they could not possibly be on display in Edinburgh Castle, Holyrood Palace or Stirling Castle, or I should have found them. They are not to be found in Linlithgow Palace, where Mary Stuart was born, nor around the pile of masonry that remains of Fotheringhay Castle in England, where she was imprisoned and executed. It is obvious from her embroidery that she was aware of her Marian legacy. She would have kept and protected her family tiles. But if you are to do better than I, you must look beyond the obvious."

"*How?* I'm not a Marian myself. I'm not exactly a historian. And golly, Professor, I only got this homework assignment yesterday."

"Nevertheless, it is your only hope. And you do have one gift that none of the men I hired, nor I, had."

"And what—"

But we were interrupted by the arrival of Jamie Mac-Donald. "The palace is closing, Mrs. Stuart. I'm afraid we're done for the night."

I shouldn't have looked away from Myrddin—from Max—from whoever he was. Not even startled as I'd been. But I did, just for a moment, to face this sudden distraction.

When I looked back, the old man had vanished.

Chapter 10

"Where did he go?" Cliché or not, I asked it.

"Who?" Jamie looked at the dark-paneled, portrait-ridden room around us.

"The old man. He was right here, and he disappeared." I saw Jamie's expression and added, "Of course he didn't *poof* disappear! There must be another exit or secret passage!"

I began to search the paneling for a trigger.

"Indeed there is," agreed my guide, catching my hand back before I could push a portrait out of the way. "'Tis how the king would come to his queen's room, and how his conspirators murdered the queen's secretary. But such passages are nae open to the public."

I pulled loose and moved to a second wall. "I don't care."

"Holyrood is closing."

"Let them close."

"Stop!" Now he did take my arms and draw me back—or tried.

I slipped away from him, though not as easily as I should have, and glared. "I thought I hired you to help me!"

"Keeping you from jail *is* helping. Holyrood is a royal residence to this day, Maggi Stuart. They take their security quite seriously."

Two of the guards arrived to repeat Jamie's first announcement. "The palace is closed. Come along now."

Now I either had to fight three of them or let the whole thing go. Damn it.

I hated letting the old man get away. He may not have had more to tell me. But still. You want to tick off a college professor?

Call her "stupid."

The worst part was that Max-Myrrdin was probably right, no matter how little I trusted him. I *had* been seeking out the obvious, skimming the surface.

But if I needed expertise...

Halfway to the car, I stopped pulling against Jamie MacDonald's firm hold on my arm. There could be more value in slowing down. Even in standing still.

Even with your child's safety on the line? demanded the maternal protector side of me, the side that had been silently screaming for a fight since I'd left Kestrel behind.

But this time a deeper wisdom whispered, *Especially with your child's safety on the line.* What counted was success, not battle.

What I needed, even more than quick access to every Mary Stuart site in Scotland, was to understand the person more than her geography. No, not just the person. The *woman.*

The gift I had that other seekers—men—had not. I needed

to connect to what we had in common. It should have been the first thing a woman devoted to the Goddess—no matter which face She wore—had thought of.

"Let me buy you dinner," I said, in the silence of my rental car. I didn't even complain that Jamie had bundled me into the left-hand passenger seat. To his understanding, I was behaving pretty irrationally.

"I am flattered," he said, starting the car. He'd already cleared the windscreen of the worst of the ice; the wipers took care of the rest. "But are you nae married?"

"Not that kind of dinner. I need to understand everything there is to know about Mary Queen of Scots as quickly as possible."

"Ah. Then if that's all you need." He saw I wasn't joking. "I dinna ken everything about the queen myself, and I studied the Jacobites at university."

"But you know a lot more than I do. Please. I know I've been acting like a crazy lady, and someday I might explain why. But this is more important than you'll ever know."

He considered it, then nodded. "For a steak at the Witchery, I'll do my best to make you an expert of an evening. Mucky as the weather and tourism have been, we may even get a table."

"Oh," I heard myself saying, just as Lex might have done, "We'll get a table."

The Witchery lay back at the other end of the Royal Mile, just outside the walls of Edinburgh Castle. Entry took us down a mysteriously tight passageway, but the result was…opulent. The ceilings were lavishly painted in gilt. Antique paneling boasted intricate carvings and was hung with rich tapestries and mirrors. Cherub sconces held pillar candles aloft over chairs of red leather or white-clothed tables.

At my request, we were seated away from the windows. Large leather screens gave us the privacy I'd hoped for.

Jamie MacDonald started with butter-roasted quail with braised endive. I started with salad of Buckie crab and lobster with mango and tarragon dressing. And I began questioning my guide about the one thing that, in the end, matters most for the majority of women. Not politics. Not even power.

I asked about Mary Queen of Scots' relationships.

Her father had died when she was only six days old. She'd left her mother at age five, when the child queen was sent to France for safety but her mother stayed to help run Scotland. The French royalty had been like family to her after that. She'd married the Dauphin at fifteen, and "seemed to have loved him well enough," according to Jamie. They became King and Queen of France the following year, when her father-in-law was killed in a jousting accident. The year after that she lost first her mother and then her young husband to illness.

"As she'd borne no heir, she had no more place in the court o' France," Jamie explained. By now we were starting our main courses. We'd both chosen the Angus steak with smoked garlic broth. "So she came home to Scotland."

As if it had been her home anymore. *Brave girl.*

Jamie began to explain the politics of Mary's situation—who else wanted the crown and why—but I turned the conversation back to her personal ties. She'd had no legitimate siblings, and her illegitimate half brother became her enemy. She wanted to be friends with her cousin, Queen Elizabeth of England, but Elizabeth had seen her as a threat. Mary's second marriage, to the murderous jerk and father of her only son, had been a disaster. Many people still suspected that she'd had a hand in the plot that killed him. "But tha'," explained Jamie, "is only because she married the man who likely led it."

Apparently, scholars were also split on whether husband number three, the Earl of Bothwell, had abducted or eloped with her. Either way, it had ended badly. Mary miscarried twins. Bothwell fled to Europe, was captured and died some years later as a political prisoner. Mary was forced to abdicate to her infant son, fled to England and was shuffled from one castle to another until her eventual beheading.

So where in all of that, I thought, *would you have hidden your tiles, Mary Stuart?*

"Who were her best friends? She had them, didn't she?" Doesn't every woman?

"Aye," said Jamie MacDonald. "The Four Marys."

I stared over the edge of my dessert menu, suddenly alert. "The what?"

"Young noblewomen, all near her age, who'd accompanied her since she first left for France. Mary Seton, Mary Fleming, Mary Beaton and Mary…Livingstone, I presume. Folks've always called them the Four Marys, as they were so close to their queen. Seton even shared the queen's captivity with her."

First I'd run into the Two Marys who, along with Mary Magdalene of legend, made three. Now I'd run into Four Marys who, with their queen, made five. Three. Five. It didn't take a cryptographer to guess what came next in this numerical sequence. *Seven.* But that had to be coincidence, didn't it? It sure couldn't have been planned by human design. Could it?

In any case, the secret of the seventh key wasn't as immediate a concern to me as finding the Stuart tiles. "So what happened to Mary Seton, after the queen's execution?"

But that Jamie didn't know. Ask him what happened at the battle of Culloden, he was your man. But ask what happened to the Queen of Scots' best friend? Not so much.

It was only as we were finishing our dessert puddings that I remembered one more significant relationship in many women's lives. Beyond husbands and lovers, beyond children and parents, beyond siblings and friends.

God—or Goddess, depending on how you view the Deity.

"How religious was she?"

And that, *that* was the question which cracked the mystery.

"She was Catholic," I explained to Lex, on the phone in the back office at the Witchery. Less chance of the Adrianos intercepting us this way. It had been harder to convince Jamie MacDonald that I could drive myself to the Balmoral on my own—since his car was also parked outside the castle—than it was to persuade the manager to allow me to use his private phone. "When England and most of Scotland were devoutly Protestant, Mary Stuart was pretty much a French *Catholic*."

"I kind of knew that, Mag." Lex sounded glad to hear from me. He'd called right back when I gave him the number. But I could hear an edge of impatience in his voice, that drive that made him such a good businessman and leader. He was taking a break from whatever wheeling and dealing would get the ingredients for the Marians' faux mosaic. But it wasn't effortless. "I thought you did, too."

"Sure, I knew it with my head, but I didn't…" I was babbling. "Look at it this way. Assume she was a Marian, since none of the rest of this makes sense if she wasn't. It would have been easy to hide that in Catholic France, because anyone who saw the statues or embroideries of the Black Madonna would assume they were representations of the Virgin Mary. Heck, for all we know, even the Marians thought so by that point. A lot of scholars believe that the reason the

Virgin Cult flourished in the Middle Ages was the people's subconscious desire for a goddess figure, and that the—"

"I know that part, too, Mag. I'm not one of your students."

For a moment I blinked at the lush tapestry on the manager's office wall, since I couldn't blink at Lex. He must have recognized how snappish he'd sounded. "I'm sorry, goddess. I've been racing the clock since I got settled here, and end-of-business still hasn't hit in Asia and Australia. Most of the legitimate courier companies are grounded by the weather, so the more time I can give them…"

"You're right," I made myself say. As much as I wanted to linger with him, even over the phone, he had a job to do, too. "Here's the shorter version. It was safe to be Catholic in France. Not so much in Scotland. Imagine the kind of suspicion Mary would've drawn if she hadn't just been Catholic, but toted around relics from a Black Madonna figure? The Protestants were already accusing the Catholics of black magic, because of the candles and the incense and the ritual. If the queen's Marian beliefs got out and she was pegged as a goddess worshipper—whether or not it were true—she could've died for it. Jamie tells me that Scotland was a very, *very* bad place to be accused of witchcraft."

"'*Jamie*'?"

I laughed at the new note in Lex's voice. I had his attention now. "The MacDonald guide I've been with since we last talked. The one you approved, remember?" I made my voice breathy. "He wears a kilt."

"You were saying about witches?" Lex prompted, with an exaggerated patience that made me grin.

"Over four thousand people were burned as witches in Scotland. If the queen suspected this level of threat before leaving France…"

"Wait." The last edge of bored distraction faded from Lex's voice. "You're saying she never brought the tiles to Scotland at all?"

"She would have been an idiot to do it, and from what I can tell, she was no idiot. Except maybe when it came to marrying powerful men, and even that—" But I was digressing. "Lex, any woman of sense would have left some kind of map. And I think she did. *She left the embroidery.*"

"Christ," he whispered.

"There are legends about the secret codes in tapestries. Why should embroidery be different? Like nursery rhymes and fairy tales, it was women's stuff, so powerful men wouldn't have looked too closely. I need to have the embroidery sent ahead to Paris so that I can meet up with it there. Can you tell me who to call?"

"I'll do it."

"You're already—"

"The Cloisters knows me better." He wasn't lying there. He'd donated more medieval pieces to the New York museum than just the Queen of Scots tapestry. Our wedding took place at the Cloisters. "I'll have it sent to the George V."

He said the name the French way, as *Georges Cinq*. "What is it with you and super-ritzy hotels?"

"They're safer," said Lex. "They have tighter security and a higher staff-to-guest ratio. They're better able to handle emergencies. They're more discreet—yes," he insisted, when I snorted. To me, a ritzy hotel was still a place to see and be seen. "They're trained in discretion. Nobody's likely to slip up and admit that you're staying alone, not even to an Adriano."

I gave up. What kind of an idiot complains about five-star hotels? "Okay."

"And they can provide services that are beyond the—"

"*Okay,*" I interrupted more firmly. "If you feel that strongly, I'll stay at the George V."

Lex said, quietly, "And it's something I can actually do for you."

If I could just touch him, this awkward edge between us would evaporate. "You aren't solely responsible for my safety, Lex," I reminded him. "Or Kestrel's. You don't have to make up for anything."

"Maggi, no offense—"

"No. Never mind. I know." We often discussed this when we weren't feeling stressed, and argued about it when we were. *You're mine,* he would say, his hazel eyes pleading with me to understand exactly what he meant. *I know I don't own you. I know I don't control you. But you're my wife, and Kes is our daughter, and anyone who interferes with either of you interferes with me. In that way, you* are *mine.*

On the surface it could seem sweet and caring. I got that. I'd married him, hadn't I? But beneath it ran something more…unnerving. Heaven knows we were both too stressed just now to reopen that particular discussion.

After a long exhale, he repeated, "I'll have the tapestry sent to the George V. It won't be there until midday tomorrow at the earliest, so you might as well spend the night in Scotland and head out in the morning. I'm glad you're closer to figuring this out."

"Are you closer? Assuming I let you get back to Asia and Australia before close-of-business?"

"Yes. And I should do that. And I love you." That last came out muffled, as if he'd rubbed a hand down his face.

I considered insisting that none of this was his fault. But I knew what he'd say—that it was still his responsibility. And we'd wasted enough time already. "I love you, too, Your Highness. Have you eaten?"

"I'll have something sent up to the room."

"Lex, you've got to—"

"I'll catch you at the Cinq, Mag." And he disconnected, damn it. I unclenched my jaw, reminding myself that if I had the right to run around Scotland on my own without him complaining, he had the right to choose when to eat. But at that moment, I kind of understood Lex's point of view. He was mine, too.

After thanking the manager—and tipping heavily for his hospitality—I wrapped up in my heavy cloak and my Stuart scarf and headed out into the sleet, back toward my rental car.

The ice had recently been scraped from the windshield.

Spinning around, I scanned my surroundings. The car park. The Royal Mile, stretching off across the dark-brown breadth of Edinburgh, streetlights dimmed by the winter storm. The great, floodlit hulk of a castle climbing the rock above me. Then back to the car park. Someone flashed his parking lights, just enough to catch my attention, not enough to blind me, and I squinted through the wind and wet.

Jamie MacDonald raised his hand in salute, from the driver's seat of a Ford Mondeo. For a moment it felt as if he was a courtier, watching out for the safety of his liege lord's lady. But of course, he didn't even know Lex. Lex's family hadn't been liege lords in Scotland for centuries. I'd spent too much time immersed in history today, was all.

I waved back, glad to know there were decent people like that in the world, and drove myself back to the Balmoral. But I was followed.

Only when I reached the hotel did Jamie MacDonald flash his lights at me from behind and drive away.

* * *

The next morning, when my prepaid cell phone rang, I wasn't confused by the strange ring tone. Confused about where I was, for a moment—what was it with all the heather green, the leather furniture and the paneled walls? But not by the fact that Simon Adriano would probably send me a wake-up call every freaking morning until I finished what he'd asked me to do.

"Good morning, Duke," I muttered, after thumbing the green button.

The last thing I'd expected was a little voice saying, "I want my mommy."

Chapter 11

For a moment—a stupid, desperate moment—I could almost imagine it was Kestrel. But Kes could barely do words, much less sentences.

"Lexie?" I realized, with that automatic, forced cheer we mothers adopt to try to fool the children. "This is Aunt Maggi."

"Mommy gone." I could hear the pout in her two-year-old voice, and it wrenched my heart.

"No, sweetheart, your mommy isn't gone. She'll come get you very soon. She and your daddy—and Daddy Lex—just as soon as they can. Nanny Olga's there with you, right?" Surely they hadn't dragged Lexie away to a telephone without Olga, had they? If only I could talk to Olga, learn how the hostages were doing. Yeah. Right. *The hostages.*

I needed to know about Kestrel. Almost more than I needed air.

Lexie breathed hard into the phone. Then she said, "My ice cream fell down!"

We'd gotten close, during the previous weeks. I knew that just because she could talk didn't mean she always made sense. But I couldn't keep myself from asking, "Lexie, how's Kestrel?"

"It's dirty," she whined. Probably about some part of her the ice cream had hit when it fell down. Lexie didn't much like being dirty. When she noticed it, that is.

"That's okay, sweetie. We can clean it. How's the baby, Lexie? Have you seen the baby?"

"Little baby and big baby. I'm a big girl."

I'd forgotten about Mara. "There sure are two babies. How's the big baby? How's Kes?"

But with a shuffling noise and a squeak of protest the phone was apparently taken from her. "Take her back to the others," I heard Simon Adriano say, before he deigned speak directly to me.

"Good morning, Mrs. Stuart."

"Duke Adriano." I got that he preferred the social niceties, and that I needed to keep him happy. More or less. But wishing him a good-morning would be reaching. The best I could do was to pretend speaking to Lexie hadn't shaken me to the core. "I met your father yesterday, at Holyrood Palace."

"Indeed? Is he as mad as ever?"

"From your perspective? Probably. He said that the Adrianos have already searched Scotland for the Stuart tiles."

"Then you will simply have to search it again," he warned.

"Lex and I have been doing some research," I assured him, as if Lex were there with me. The last thing we wanted was for him to realize that Lex was off buying the ingredients for a counterfeit mosaic. "We'll find them."

"Make sure that you do, Mrs. Stuart. I shall see you in four days." And he disconnected.

He'd given no indication that he'd guessed Lex's true activities, or my upcoming departure. That was a good sign. So why, sitting up in my heavy wooden bed in the Balmoral, did I have to rest my head against my knees, just to stop shaking?

I want my mommy....

The bastard.

I should have noticed before then just how badly the weather was battering Europe—not just blowing pedestrians around and icing cars, but undermining commerce, transportation, infrastructure. I'd already known that commercial flights had been grounded from Naples to France two days before—and, remembering our roller-coaster ride with Geno, and again on Lex's private jet to Edinburgh the previous morning, I understood why.

"This," my husband had murmured to me at the time, "is why I don't fly my own planes." Though Lex had his license, he considered himself a recreational pilot. The men he hired for the day-to-day work were ex-military.

But now, despite that Lex had left the Hawker for me in Edinburgh, even the grizzled Captain Harris refused to take off into the storm. "There are occasional lulls, Mrs. Stuart," he admitted over the echoing clamor of hail on the roof of the hangar where we stood together. "I've got her fueled and ready to take advantage of it, the minute one hits. But I've been watching the satellite photos, and we aren't getting a lull anytime before nightfall."

"But this is important," I insisted, still shaken by the earlier phone call. "I'm willing to take my chances."

"No offense, ma'am, but I'm not. Not with my life, and especially not with yours."

Take me to Paris, or you're fired. Heaven help me, I almost said that. As soon as I swallowed back the words, I took an actual step backward from the older man, as if I were afraid of hitting him next. Who was I becoming, to be so casually throwing around first money and now threats?

Almost throwing around threats.

Fighting the ugliness that the power of wealth was stirring in me this morning, I made myself give in. My protective-mother side screamed at me to force this man to fly us to Paris at gunpoint, if necessary. Luckily I didn't have a gun.

My voice almost sounded steady. "When you get that lull then, Captain, please take her back to Lezignan-Corbieres in southern France. I've got to get to Paris today, so…" There were always alternatives. "I'll take a train."

"Yes, ma'am," he said. "Good luck with that."

The train I took south from Edinburgh's Waverly Station was crowded to capacity—people stood in the aisles or swapped out seats for the entire, almost-five-hour journey. Me, I found a nice corner seat tucked against a window and did Internet research on my latest laptop. I was only drawn out by the occasional "ahh's" and "look there's" of the other passengers, when lightning struck particularly close—which happened a lot—or when we crossed trestles and saw rivers running high beneath us, far closer than rivers should get to train tracks. Only once did I give myself a break from the Queen of Scots to skim the weather.

Europe and the U.K. were shut down by massive storm cells. *Stranded Travelers Enter Day Three. Hotels Overflowing. Car Rentals Reach Record Highs. Markets Claim Shortages on Imports.*

But it was one thing to read the headlines. It was another to step off the train at London Kings Cross station into chaos.

The platforms were pandemonium. People pushed and yelled and were jostled apart in the crowds. Far above us the curved ceiling, like a long checkerboard of corrugated skylights, only echoed the unending rain that was at fault.

Except that the Adrianos were at fault, for screwing with the weather, I thought. Them, and the time of epic transition Simon kept predicting for next Monday.

Slinging my satchel more securely over my shoulder, I dove into the melee. The usually easygoing Brits were behaving as if this were one huge soccer game—and they were losing. With the Underground closed due to flooding I had to find an overcrowded bus to Waterloo Station. I wasn't the only person hoping to take the EuroStar to Paris.

At one point the bus began to drift as it plowed through water. But it regained traction. We passengers cheered as we drove on.

The long bank of turnstiles into Waterloo International made me feel like a cow being herded unknowingly to my doom. Once in the main terminal, itself a high-ceilinged cacophony of echoes, I found the Eurostar desks and stood in queue for over an hour. Even before I reached the desk, word was being passed back and bandied about.

"They're saying no tickets are available until the day after tomorrow."

"Paris or Brussels?" someone asked. The trains through the tunnel could go to either destination.

"Paris. Brussels is first thing tomorrow night."

"How about first-class?" I called. Because I could.

"Leisure Select *or* Business Premier. Standard class, no tickets until Thursday night."

This was Tuesday. Some people gave up in disgust and

stalked away, to the relief to the rest of us in line, who got to move forward. I reviewed my options and wasn't encouraged. The car rental agencies were empty and the storms had shut down the airports. Damn it! What good was it to marry someone richer than God if I couldn't even manage a two-and-a-half-hour train ride from the British Isles back to France?

Then I realized—Lex *was* richer than God, or close to it. Yes, there weren't any flights going out. Yes, the trains were overbooked. Yes, the car rental agencies were empty.

But I had an emergency credit card, matte-black, with no credit limit.

Shouts from across the terminal caught our attention—several panes in the high skylight roof, above an elaborate architecture of girders, had broken under the pressure of the storm. Water gushed downward onto stranded passengers. With a crash, another one caved in. I realized it wasn't just glass coming down onto the neon-lined kiosks and plastic chairs—it was hail.

People ran. People screamed. A lot of people rushed in to help others—stunned into paralysis—take shelter toward the edges of the terminal. And Goddess help me—like most of the people in line, I didn't budge. There would be a karmic price to pay for not helping, I knew it.

But I would waste every bit of karma to help Kestrel.

And at least I wasn't a medical or rescue professional myself. And when some of the people in line began to surge forward, trapping a couple up against the EuroStar desks, I did join in to drag the worst offenders back and keep anyone from being trampled or crushed. One of the clerks stood on her chair and shouted at us, as loudly as possible in a no-nonsense East Ender drawl, that they could only help people one at a time, no matter how many tried to come over the desk.

"Do that again, and we're shutting down," she warned. "Then nobody gets on any of the trains."

I would have honestly worried for her life, had she tried it, but her threat worked. The queue subsided to muttering discontent.

It helped that only one more skylight fell in.

"What about the shuttle cars for drivers—I mean, motorists?" I called, both because I needed to know, and to reestablish that all-in-this-together air we'd had going a while back. Sure enough, a handful of helpful Brits passed the question ahead.

The answer came back that there were still slots for cars on trains leaving tonight, but not from London. "And good luck getting to Kent!"

I was half-afraid that with each minute that passed in line, even that would change before my turn. But it didn't. England and Europe don't have quite the car-happy culture as the USA. They actually count on their public transit.

"What kind of automobile will it be?" At last the clerk typed in the appropriate information off my passport.

"I don't know," I admitted—and, with the sound of another crash from across the terminal, I felt increasingly less embarrassed to be rich. "I haven't bought it yet."

But once I did, I came back and picked up three other stranded passengers before we headed East.

You don't just drive under the English Channel like you would through the Lincoln Tunnel—the whole thing is built for rail traffic. Instead, after the two-hour drive from London, you exit into check-in booths near Folkestone, in Kent, and then drive through the "frontier controls," aka Customs. This was the trickiest part for me, testing whether or not the salesman had really managed to set me up with all the proper documentation for my new silver Audi. But we got the all-clear to drive up into one of the automobile "carriages." That part was pretty similar to driving into the bay of a ferry, except that it had temperature controls and better lighting, and that drivers were expected to stay with their cars, though we could get out and stretch our legs.

Thirty-five minutes after the train left England, it arrived just outside Calais, France. I wouldn't say the trip was stress-free, especially not the last five-hour drive from Calais to Paris. And not just because Greg, the medical student, snored or because poor Elise, stranded in an attempt to go check on her mother's health, hadn't bathed in two days. Normally the drive only took half that time, but the storms had caused a disturbing number of accidents, and in several places traffic slowed to a crawl. I don't love driving at night, much less in foreign countries, and it was well past dark by the time I dropped my passengers off at the appropriate train stations and pulled up in front of the George V.

But those Audis? Darned comfortable cars.

And speaking of darned comfort…

Maybe the Cinq, like the other hotels across Europe, was also full up with stranded travelers. If so, these were the crème de la crème of stranded travelers—and Lex had still gotten us in. Even as I let the valet take my car, a bellman shouldered my one bag with a polite, "Good evening, Mrs. Stuart." Entering the grand lobby—"Good evening, Mrs. Stuart," the doorman greeted—felt like entering a museum. The floor was gleaming marble. The architecture was Empire. Crystal chandeliers, Greek statues and more lush, fresh flowers than I'd ever seen outside a botanical garden all fit perfectly. Far better than I did!

"Good evening, Mrs. Stuart," repeated the concierge, coming

out from around the front desk. "Your husband has made all the necessary arrangements. May I show you to your room?"

Everyone spoke English, despite that I speak fluent French. That, and the fact that they seemed to recognize me on sight, indicated that they'd done enough homework to know my nationality—and possibly had downloaded a picture of me. Lex may even have provided one with the reservations, for security reasons.

"It's Sanger-Stuart," I heard myself correct the concierge, gently but firmly, and felt like a major ingrate. Except…that *was* my name. It wasn't meant as a slight to Lex, or a complaint about marriage… As I've said before, what kind of idiot would complain about all this? And yet…

It was my name. If I stopped insisting on my individuality just because of the expensive hotel, incredible service and new car, wasn't that the *definition* of selling out?

The concierge didn't bat an eye. "But of course, Mrs. Sanger-Stuart. My apologies for the mistake."

An older woman, who'd seemed to be waiting for somebody in one of the silk-upholstered chairs in the lobby, overheard. She more than batted an eye. She stood and adjusted her fur stole.

"*Si,*" she applauded, with the grand gesture of a society wife who has imbibed too much sherry. "Do not let any man own you, Mrs. Sanger-Stuart. Once we let the husbands own us, it is over. Over!"

Another staff member hurried to her side—probably to avoid a scene. I smiled to reassure all involved that I hadn't taken offense. "Thank you for the advice," I told the Italian lady, as the concierge led me to the elevators.

"*Prego,*" she dismissed. Her hand flashed with diamonds. Her clothes were classy and expensive. And she looked miserable.

Goddess, I hoped I never turned into that. But I had Lex. Of course I wouldn't.

I waited until the elevator doors had closed to turn to the concierge and the still-silent bellman. "My husband is having a package delivered here."

"It is in the safe in your room, Mrs. Sanger-Stuart," I was assured. Excellent.

The Black Madonna embroidery, done by the hand of Mary Queen of Scots herself, was the best chance I had of figuring out where Kestrel's great-great-great-whatever grandmother had hidden the alabaster tiles of the mosaic.

Now if I could just figure it out before the world ended.

Chapter 12

"Good morning, Mrs. Stuart," greeted Duke Simon Adriano. "May I speak to your husband?"

"No," I said, still groggily trying to place my newest palatial surroundings. My chic suite made a strange contrast against the sound of rain rain rain on the seventh-story terrace outside the French doors. "No, you may not."

"Pardon?"

I couldn't let Simon realize Lex was somewhere else, working to help the Marians dupe the duke. But the only way I could convince him was to convince myself. So I imagined that the other half of the huge canopy bed was equally rumpled. I imagined that the sound of the rain outside was the sound of running water from the vast marble bathroom. It wasn't a half-bad fantasy.

"He's in the shower," I hissed into the phone, as if trying to hide my voice from said husband. "There is only one reason I would interrupt him, and it has nothing to do with saying the man who abducted our daughter is on the phone."

Maybe it was the deliberate distraction of shower sex. Or maybe he'd just been teasing me? But he let the subject go.

"Three days, Mrs. Stuart." And Simon disconnected.

Or maybe he meant to *test* me. Immediately I rolled across the bed—it was huge, and took two rolls. I snatched up the phone, dialed out as quickly as possible, even if I could only remember his cell phone. *Answer. Answer. Please don't be on the other line yet....*

"Good morning, gorgeous," answered Lex, his voice thick with sleep. I'd checked in with him the night before, to let him know the embroidery and I had arrived. He recognized my number. "I'll call you right—"

"Simon may call. Don't answer."

That cleared the sleep from his voice fast enough. "Excuse me?"

"I told him you were in the shower. If that was true, and your cell phone started ringing—"

I heard the faintest blip on his end of the line.

"Someone's beeping in," announced Lex darkly. "That son of a bitch. He *called* you?"

"—normally I would ignore it…except that of course knowing it's him I would probably answer and tell him to fuck off, but since we aren't actually sharing a hotel room, let's pretend your phone is in the bathroom with you. Actually…" I probably should have mentioned this before. "He's been calling every morning."

"That motherfu—" Lex bit off his own curse. He hardly ever swears like that. *Click.* Then, worse, "He hasn't said how she is, has he?"

As much as I hated being forced to play nice with Simon,

I hated hearing Lex do it even more. I was all about compromise. He wasn't. "No. He put Lexie on yesterday morning. She sounded fine. She had ice cream. But he won't say a word about Kes."

Click. "It's not enough that he takes her, and sends you running errands like you're his damned servant—" His temper was building.

"Lex! Just don't answer."

"The hell I won't!"

"He can't know that we aren't together! Remember? Big picture?" To my relief, the clicking of Simon's call ended.

Lex's breath came out as more of a snarl, but I thought I could hear a marginal release of tension. "He'll probably call back, you know. Even if I was too busy showering to answer the first time. And then he'll ask to talk to you on *my* line."

"Just tell him we've split up for the day. If you answer at all."

"Are we in Paris, then?"

My half laugh was sheer tension, nothing more, but it had the effect of soothing Lex's voice into reluctant humor when he said, "You know what I mean, Mag."

"I haven't mentioned it. I'm afraid that if he catches us in even a little lie…" But I didn't have to voice what scared me. "Call me back on the land line, just in case."

"Yes."

It hurt, to put the handset back into its cradle. It actually *hurt* to disconnect from him. Picking up again, after the first ring, was nowhere near enough to soothe the ache of being separated. Especially since, for a moment, we had nothing else to say.

"How close are you to being finished?" I heard myself asking at last—like a 1950s wife asking her husband when he'd be home from work. But it wasn't like that. Really.

"By tonight, if I'm lucky. Have you made progress with the embroidery?"

"Not much. I should probably call an expert from the Cluny, damn it." The Cluny was Paris's museum of medieval antiquities, the Continental version of the Cloisters.

"I thought you loved the Cluny," said Lex.

"Yeah, the problem is that their best expert on tapestry and embroidery is on sabbatical in the south of France. In Lys, to be exact."

Now Lex laughed—a rare and wonderful enough occurrence that even my disgust at having to ask Catrina Dauvergne for help eased. "Wow. You sure can hold a grudge."

"So you've said." We probably wouldn't have been "off-again" quite so often in our dating lives if I'd had more of a forgive-and-forget personality. "I know she gave us this embroidery to make up for that business with the Melusine Chalice. I've got to respect all that. I just…don't like her."

"Because she's sleeping with your friend Rhys?" Now Lex didn't sound so amused. But only someone who knew him as well as I did would hear the subtle jealousy. He was trying, anyway.

"Don't worry—I disliked her long before that." Then, to distract myself almost as much as him, I said, "So…what are you wearing?"

"Mmm." Lex's voice thickened, and I heard him sitting back in bed. "What do you want me to be wearing?"

It was still very, very early, after all. Neither of us would even be awake had Simon Adriano not called. Surely a half hour's distraction—voices, touch, more remembrance than fantasy—wouldn't hurt our individual efforts to help our baby daughter.

Goddess knew, it helped *my* mood. And I needed it. Especially when afterward, once we'd disconnected, I stopped on my way to the bathroom to look out the glass doors with their view of so much of the city beyond the terrace. I watched lightning striking the Eiffel Tower—again and again and again. For a moment it seemed as if it would never stop. I felt scared then—really scared. Would *any* of us get out?

When I first called for Catrina, Eve answered the phone. Catrina was off at the caves, where phone signals didn't reach. Eve would ask her to call me as soon as she got back.

In the meantime, deciding I'd better have some pictures of the embroidery—and some rain gear that wasn't for weather as cold as Scotland's—I showered, dressed and headed out. I asked at the concierge about the best place in the area to buy a digital camera.

He protested. "There is no need for you to go out into the rain. We can purchase a camera for you! Do you have any special photography needs? A camera that also has video capability? Waterproof, perhaps?"

I stared at him, then asked, "Did my husband instruct you to keep me inside?"

I think his surprise was honest. "No, madame. We at the George V offer this sort of service to all of our guests."

Well…didn't I feel silly. "My apologies, uh…Hugh." I'd read his name tag. "Thank you for your offer, but I also need to buy a raincoat, so I think I'll do my own shopping."

"Will you at least let us drive you? This, indeed, your husband encouraged when he made the reservations. Many of the streets are flooded, madame."

Remembering the lightning striking the Eiffel Tower, I consented to a driver. I sat in one of the silk-upholstered lobby chairs to wait while Hugh leaped to fetch him.

Someone sat next to me—the older woman from the previous night. Today she wore sapphires on her ears and around her slim throat. She looked to be well into her sixties, despite the quality of her dye job.

"Do you just sit out here and listen in on people's conversations?" I asked.

"I only eavesdrop on the interesting people," she assured me. "It is a skill I learned in my own house, where I am a shadow, unnecessary to my husband and—" her eyes clouded "—and my children. It is a useful skill, to listen."

She'd complained about her husband the night before, too. While I felt sorry for her, I didn't want to encourage that kind of conversation just now. "So why would you find me interesting? I'm just another stranded traveler."

"You have an air about you, Mrs. Sanger-Stuart." She cocked her head, as if seeing me even more closely. "I see who I would like to have been in you. I was never so strong as to demand my own name. I would have allowed the concierge to fetch for me, and stayed obediently in my golden cage."

A gesture at the marble and chandeliers, the flowers and crystal and soaring columns, encompassed the George V as just such a cage.

I considered saying, *It's not that hard.* But who was I to tell a woman from another generation and another culture—not just the culture of Italy, but of wealth—what was and wasn't hard? Instead I said, "I'm afraid I never caught your name."

"You may call me Signora di Spedalotto. *Hugh!*"

The concierge looked immediately concerned by her shout.

"I am now Signora di Spedalotto!"

"Si, Signora," he agreed.

"It is my maiden name," she explained, quite pleased with herself. "You are an inspiration, Mrs. Sanger-Stuart."

I was just as glad that my driver arrived—a solid man in

his midthirties, with the brown hair and blue eyes of the classic French.

There had been times when the energy of the Goddess was so thick in me, I could inspire women with a handshake or a hug. But I hadn't been hunting goddess grails for a while, and in any case, I hadn't touched the woman.

Signora di Spedalotto seemed a bit unsettling...and more than a little desperate. Or maybe that was me. I even became suspicious of Alain, my driver. Something seemed...off, about him. Not threatening-off. More... overly friendly–off. I'd grown accustomed to how professional drivers behave—or, more specifically, how skilled they are at being invisible. Alain was not invisible, not to me. He escorted me into and out of stores. He offered that he had grown up in Paris and knew a great deal about it, in case I wanted to explore.

I told myself that if over-attentiveness was the biggest problem I had with the man, I was fine. And I let him show me the drenched city, bridges closed due to flooding, troops sandbagging Notre Dame and the Louvre.

And this was probably happening all across Europe.

Crap.

Back in my suite, I changed into dry clothes and took pictures of the sixteenth-century Black Madonna embroidery from every angle. It really was a gorgeous work, one I was starting to know very well. The Madonna herself, child in arms, dominated the piece. But behind her, as with many medieval and Renaissance tapestries, the negative space had been filled with scores of flowers and animals...and, unfortunately, not a single hint at location. If only the queen had bothered to embroider a particular church or abbey into the scene!

By the time I'd installed the digital camera's software on

my laptop, uploaded the pictures from the camera and sent the best of them to Catrina, she finally called me back.

"Magdalene," she greeted coolly, when I answered.

"Catrina. Hi. I…" *Aye-yi-yi.* Bad enough to ask favors. Worse to ask them of someone I didn't like, who I knew didn't like me. But I'd gotten out a wallet shot of me, Lex and Kestrel for motivation. "I have a favor to ask. Would you be so good as to look at some pictures I just e-mailed to you?"

She said nothing, perhaps waiting for a reason why.

"I think—hope—that Mary Stuart may have left some kind of code in her embroidery, telling us where she hid her tiles before she left France."

"You believe she left the tiles in France." She did not make it a question—and she spoke in French. Fine. I answered in the same language.

"Yes. But I have no idea where. I don't know very much about the hidden language of tapestry."

"It is not a tapestry."

I stuck out my tongue, for my own satisfaction. "*Or embroidery.* Could you just, please—"

"I am already looking at them."

Oh. So I sat silently and distracted myself turning the pictures in my wallet. My parents. Kestrel, newborn. A picture of me and Lex on our first date, in the eighth grade—that one always made me grin. Kestrel, three months old. Lex's and my wedding picture. Kestrel and the dog.

I didn't have a picture of my friend Rhys with me, but he was in Lex's and my wedding album. He hadn't been dating Catrina back then. He hadn't been dating anybody. I really shouldn't be surprised that he'd eventually changed that.

"Hmm," said Catrina, which, after the building tension of her long silence, seemed unfairly ambiguous.

"What, 'hmm'? Do you see anything or not?"

"Ah, I forget. Unlike the rest of us, you are trying to stop an apocalypse." Her cool French was made for sarcasm. Luckily she continued. "The Madonna herself? Rhys has already studied her iconography. This version, though crude, shows no significant differences. Thus it is likely that any message lies in the design that surrounds her. Embroidery— and tapestry, especially after the development of the *mille fleurs* background—often used a language of flowers. Have you noted the ivy?"

"Is that the green border, to her left? By the two deer?" One deer had been stitched in black threads, the other in white.

"Ivy symbolizes eternal fidelity. This mixes with forget-me-not." Okay, so that second one was pretty self-explanatory. "Yet the yellow roses to her left—by the snake—mean infidelity."

"Really? I'm not disagreeing, it just seems that yellow roses wouldn't sell that well today, if people knew."

"Since Roman times, yellow roses meant infidelity. The flowers mixed with them may be oleander, which signifies danger, and tansy, for war. But the Madonna is turned away from those, turned slightly toward the positive flowers."

"And lilies, right?" I could at least recognize a fleur-de-lis when I saw one. "With the ivy and forget-me-nots, those are lilies."

"Symbol of the French nobility. Perhaps for Marie's husband Francois II? Yet behind her is the crescent moon."

"A goddess symbol," I reminded her. "The snake, too."

"Perhaps. But…the deer with the crescent moon make me think of something else."

"Diana's bow," I murmured, in English.

"Excusez-moi?"

"I have a friend who's a Wiccan. She said that the new

moon, curved that way, is sometimes called Diana's bow. After the huntress of Roman mythology. So along with deer…"

"But of course! The Duchesse de Valentinois."

Now I was the one who asked, *"Excusez-moi?"*

"Marie Stuart was raised in the court of France. At that time the French queen—her mother-in-law—was Catherine de' Medici. But the king's true love was his mistress, Diane de Poitiers, the Duchesse de Valentinois. The crescent moon, it was her symbol, because of the goddess Diana. And her colors were black and white."

"Like the black and white deer in the ivy," I murmured, starting to see what she saw.

"The snake, to the other side, was the symbol of Catherine de' Medici, Marie's mother-in-law. In the battle between the two powerful women—"

"Mary's siding with her father-in-law's mistress over his wife?"

"But of course. If Mary wishes us to think of Diane de Poitiers, she means one of two sites. Anet, the *duchesse's* late husband's estate, is where she is buried. But her royal lover gave her the Château Chenonceau, on the River Cher."

"So which one would Mary—?"

"You had best hope that it is Chenonceau," said Catrina dourly. "Much of Anet was destroyed after the Revolution."

"That isn't much to go on," I muttered, but got only silence. I suspected she'd probably raised an eyebrow, or shrugged or something. And annoying though that might be… "But thank you, Cat. I mean it. Thanks."

She did not say *de rien,* that it was nothing. She said, "You are welcome. Good luck, Maggi."

It was a start.

I was packed—including putting the embroidery safely

back into its packaging and into the safe—in a matter of minutes. At the desk, after asking to have my Audi brought around, I had the concierge provide a current road map and directions to Chenonceau. The château lay about a hundred and fifty miles south-southeast, in the Loire Valley.

"Please, Mrs. Stuart," said Alain, surprising me with his presence as I turned away from the concierge desk. "Allow me to drive you. There may be a great deal of flooding in the valley, and it would help if you had a companion."

Remember what I said about that driver? My radar was going off again. "No," I said. "Thank you."

"But I could be of help. I'm really quite familiar with the area, and the history."

"The history of what, exactly?" I challenged.

"The sixteenth century. Henri II. François II. Marie Stuart."

He was just another driver at the Cinq huh?

"Okay," I challenged, folding my arms. "Who hired you?"

"Pardon?"

"If it was Simon Adriano, tell him I don't need the help." Even if I did need the help, I sure didn't need the supervision.

Alain took a step back. "Mrs. Stuart, you've misread my intentions. I only mean to assist you—"

"*Un,*" I ticked off on my finger. "You're calling me Mrs. Stuart. The concierge would have told you to call me Mrs. Sanger-Stuart. Hence, you're not merely connected to the Cinq. *Deux,* you just happen to know a great deal about the time period I'm researching. *Trois,* you're way too helpful for it to be coincidence. *Quatre,* you are *not* a professional driver. You have too much of an air of importance around you. And…"

And *cinq.* The last piece, clicking into place, shook me.

He'd approached me exactly the way Jamie MacDonald had, in Edinburgh. As if the same person had arranged their presence.

I felt sick at the obvious explanation. Luckily, my Audi slid up to the entrance of the hotel and the valet climbed out.

"Stay the hell away from me," I warned Alain. "I do not need a babysitter. And if you talk to my husband before I do, tell him—" What? That Lex was busted wasn't the half of it. That I was pissed didn't even come close. That he'd promised to give me my space, when we married, and this did not count as space? That was too personal.

"Never mind," I muttered. "I'll tell him myself."

At length.

And I left the hotel, got into my new car and headed south.

Chapter 13

A hundred and fifty miles. A three-hours drive, right?

Not with verge-of-apocalypse weather. The traffic was terrible. In one place a bridge had been washed out, requiring back-road detours. In another place, emergency crews responding to tornado damage had closed the road. And the whole time? Sheeting rain. Twilight-colored skies in the mid-afternoon. Blurry views even the windshield wipers couldn't completely combat. Poor traction.

Lex only called once while I was driving. "Where are you?"

"Ask your friend Alain," I suggested.

After a moment of silence, he said, "Oh."

So much for the chance that I was wrong.

I hung up. The problem wasn't that he'd found people able to help me in my search. That was actually a good thing—I knew that with my head, even if the rest of me was still pissed. The problem was that he hadn't bothered to tell me. He hadn't just hired guides, he'd hired babysitters. And I'd thought we were so very past that. Knowing that we weren't…

It didn't lift my spirits, any more than the continuous rain.

With the full realization that any visiting hours at the château were long gone, and with a slow awareness of not having eaten since I'd left Paris, I finally had to stop at Blois, almost thirty miles from Chenonceau, and get a room. Luckily, Blois wasn't a large enough city to have a major airport, and thus wasn't having the no-vacancy issues of big cities.

Once there, I called Lex back. Angry or not, I needed to let him know where I specifically was.

That, and I'd just suffered another disappointment.

"It's closed," I admitted, after giving Lex my number at the inn to call back. "Chenonceau. They told me at the café here. The château is built on a bridge over a river, and it's been closed to tourists because of the flooding."

"So your plan of attack is…?" Lex prompted.

"Break in," I said. "I'll figure out the details tomorrow. So good—"

"Maggi, about Alain—"

"And Jamie."

Another guilty silence. "You made Jamie, too."

"I shouldn't have had to *make* either of them, Lex! You're my husband, not my hall monitor!"

"They were there to help you, not—"

"This isn't a conversation for the telephone. Good night."

"I love—" Actually, I hadn't meant to hang up in the middle of that. The receiver was already on its way to the cradle when I heard his distant voice start the endearment, and I couldn't stop in time. Then I just lay there, in yet another strange bed, in yet another foreign town, and felt miserable and mean and confused…and lonely. Lonely for my baby girl.

Lonely for the man I'd thought I'd married. Lonely for a dose of goddess energy.

I listened to the damned unending rain.

"Good morning, Mrs. Stu—"

"There's someone at the door," I interrupted, before Simon Adriano's ritual greeting could go farther. The pounding noise was hard to ignore. "Just a moment, please."

"I will not be put on hold, Mrs. Stuart." But I didn't have to put Simon on hold. He was on the prepaid cell he'd given me. I took it with me to the door, looked through the peephole—

And gasped.

"Mrs. Stuart? What is it?" But now, phone caught between my shoulder and my ear, I was too busy unlocking the door…there's some kind of law about French doors having a minimum of three locks. A new note tightened Simon's voice as he said, *"Magdalene?"*

And then I had the door open, and Lex was there. He looked tired and rumpled and gorgeous. A paper bag and two cardboard cups sat on the suitcase beside him, but he was holding flowers. "Maggi, I'm—"

"Sorry, Simon," I said quickly, just in case Lex was about to say *I'm done* instead of *I'm sorry.* "I mean…Duke Simon. Lex locked himself out when he went for breakfast."

I heard my voice begin to smile with the wonderful normalcy of that last statement. Problems or not, Lex was here.

"It's Adriano, is it?" asked Lex coolly, as if he hadn't known from yesterday exactly when our daughter's abductor would be calling. "Let me talk to him."

"I don't think that's—"

"By all means," insisted Simon. "Put him on."

Behave, I mouthed at Lex as I traded the phone for the

flowers. Part of me was still mad about his high-handedness in setting me up with Jamie and Alain. Part of me was terrified that he would antagonize Simon, who…

Had Simon just called me Magdalene?

But most of me was so damned happy to have Lex there—his voice and his presence, his wet scent and his warmth—that I wanted to hug him. But he was kind of busy…and, suddenly, not at his most huggable.

"Lex Stuart," he said, upon getting the phone, and listened a moment, his jaw tight while I left the flowers on the bureau. "My wife said that much. But if any harm comes to that baby, it won't matter."

Another pause—I took the coffee and pastry bag inside—and Lex's eyes narrowed in quiet fury. His voice was even calmer. "No, that would be Maggi. Me, I don't give a rat's ass who gets hurt as long as my girls are safe. Don't confuse me with one of the good guys, Adriano, or you'll make mistakes neither of us want."

A grab at the suitcase, and I was able to close the door for privacy. I didn't like this. The contrast between Lex's expression and his voice was getting eerie. I said, "Let me have the phone back."

"That's probably as close to an understanding as we'll get, then," Lex said to Simon. Then, so toneless he sounded dangerous, "Looking forward to it."

And he hit the red disconnect button. "Adriano says he'll see you in two days. *Damn* it!"

"Give me the phone, Lex."

"We have to get her away from that bastard. Kes and Lexie both."

"The phone." I managed to ease it out of his hand and put it beside the flowers. "Come here."

"God *damn* it."

I had to take his face between my hands to ease his gaze back to me. In doing so, I pressed myself against his solid body, his rainy wet seeping through the cotton of my sleep shirt. "We will get them away from him. We *will*. And then you can hire an assassin or have the president authorize a nuclear strike against his compound or whatever it takes to wipe his sorry ass off the face of the earth, okay? *Just be patient.*"

He stared at me, his golden eyes almost brown with fury…and something else. I could feel the something else in the warmth between our wet clothes, too. "Maggi…"

Then he kissed me so hard I had trouble remembering why he shouldn't. Instead, I wound my arms over his wet, solid shoulders and kissed him back, opening to him, welcoming him back to me. In a smooth sweep, the hand he'd slid under my butt caught up my weight and he deposited me on the bed. He followed me down, continuing to kiss me as if I were some kind of sustenance without which he couldn't survive much longer.

It was a heady sensation. So were his talented hands, one sliding up my leg, one weaving into my morning-tangled hair. So was the wet weight of him, and the press of him, and the depth of his moan. "Oh, Mag…"

Something niggled at the back of my mind, even as I ran my hands over the plane of his shirt-covered chest and kissed along the smoothness of his clean-shaven jaw. Lex would have shaved at a truck stop before he would show up stubbly. There was some reason we shouldn't be doing this. Why…?

Then—in a lull as he stopped to push his raincoat off and lift his half-unbuttoned shirt over his head—I remembered. "I'm still angry at you," I warned him, even as I writhed beneath his weight, even as my hands itched to latch on to his belt and speed up the undressing. "I'm pretty sure I've got good reason, too."

The shirt was gone now, and his bare chest presented a powerful distraction. When he took off his watch and tossed it onto the clothes, I knew we were golden. "Be angry over breakfast," Lex suggested breathlessly, ducking back to resume his attentions along my neck, my collarbone…and, with one hand, under my sleep shirt. "Just don't push me away. Please, Maggi. I've needed you—"

I shut him up with a kiss, just as demanding as his. His sigh of relief, across my ear, shook with a kind of exhaustion that went way beyond the fact that he'd just made the same rainy, detour-ridden drive I had yesterday—but he'd done so during the dark of night. He *did* need me. No matter how wealthy, no matter how influential, he'd rarely tried to hide that.

I found an incredible kind of feminine power in my ability to give him just what he so desperately needed. So I did.

It didn't hurt that I needed him so badly, myself.

Of course I wasn't angry over breakfast. Breakfast was too cozy with afterglow, the two of us curled together against the headboard, eating the pastries he'd brought, drinking the lukewarm coffee. Sometimes we kissed crumbs off each other's bare skin. Mostly he caught me up on his progress.

"Aubrey de Lune took the last package of gemstones late yesterday," Lex finished. "She said the ladies at Lys are running the kiln twenty-four/seven, helping Tru fire and glaze the false tiles she's been making since Monday. It's going to be close."

I looked at the clock—still not very late in the morning, between Simon's early wake-up calls and Lex's arrival—and nodded. "We'd better get to Chenonceau, then. Or as close as we can, with it closed to visitors."

"Yes. About that…"

I rolled more solidly onto my shoulder to better face my

husband. He moved his hand with me, so he could go on petting some of my wild hair between his fingers and thumb, as if the very feel of it was soothing. "*What* about that, Lex?"

He held my gaze with his own, as if silently asking me to be okay with this. "I placed some calls, made some promises…"

The keys and security codes for the château were waiting for us at the Chenonceau gatehouse, just outside the half-flooded car park. As soon as Lex signed for them, the guard who'd delivered them closed the gate behind us and drove away, leaving the entire castle to us.

"You are amazing," I muttered, as we slogged our way across the grounds toward the château.

"In a good way or a bad way?" asked Lex warily, wading beside me. He'd let me drive the Audi from the inn, so that he could catch a quick nap in the passenger seat. He'd been up most of the night—and exerted himself pretty well that morning—but you couldn't see his exhaustion now.

"I'm glad we've got the keys," I said honestly, avoiding the real question. The slide of his gaze told me he noticed that, but he didn't challenge me. The water was almost knee high, at its deepest along the path, and we had to concentrate on that.

I recognized Chenonceau from its photographs. If you've ever bought a calendar of castles, chances are you've seen it. White-walled with slate-blue roofs, it's not just built *beside* the River Cher. Most of it is built *on* the River Cher. With the exception of the old tower, on land, the main keep rises gracefully up out of the water toward one side of the river. The rest of it is built atop a stone bridge, which crosses the river in five beautiful arches. The entire place is surrounded by wide, incredible gardens to rival those of Versailles, and all that is surrounded by the verdant forests of the Loire Valley.

Well, that's the usual Chenonceau.

The Cher must have overflowed its banks upriver. Much of the gorgeous, manicured gardens were now soup, new spring flowers drowned, dirt pathways a spill of mud, flotsam and jetsem catching against carefully shaped bushes. All I could see of the famous arches were tiny crescents of space over the top of the brown river, which had risen to a height mere feet under the ground-floor windows.

If this didn't stop soon…

But I couldn't distract myself with those concerns. And whether it's a feminist thought or not, I found it easier to be hopeful now that Lex and I were slogging through this together. He was the one who'd suggested we bring a change of clothes in with us, because of the likelihood of getting soaked before we'd made it inside. He was the one who'd shouldered the satchel.

When I stepped on something that moved beneath the muddy water and stumbled, Lex firmly caught my elbow. Even that casual strength, the easy assistance he would give any falling woman, felt charged with innate power.

I watched his face as he helped me regain my balance, glancing back as he spotted me a few steps. The sense of security shook me. I'd known I could help him. But…if I'd hurt my ankle, he could have carried me. If I were half-drowned, or bitten by a water snake, he could get me to the best hospital faster than anybody. We were a team. He was…

Mine?

Sort of. Just because I couldn't put it into words didn't mean I couldn't glimpse the edge of understanding about what us belonging to each other really meant. But even so, despite knowing him more than half my life, there was so much about him I would never see. Stuff I couldn't even imagine. Like this.

This wasn't like getting the keys to some small town's Pioneer Village Park. Historical significance-wise, Chenonceau was more along the lines of…well, a step under the Smithsonian, but several steps above Monticello.

"Why do you keep looking at me like that?" my husband asked. And no matter what I didn't know about him, I knew enough to sense the wariness again. For someone so in control of the rest of his world, he could still get awfully nervous about me.

I grinned at him, half reassurance, half woman-of-mystery, seriously glad that he was here. "Let's break into the gift shop first, Your Highness. We're going to need a floorplan."

The gift shop was in the narrow Tour des Marques—the oldest part of the château, the part on land. After I selected a book and a map and Lex left money, we reset the alarms and headed through more rain, then through one of the green double doors into the main structure. We changed out of our clothes beside what would normally be the ticket desk, muddy from the knees down and wet everywhere else, and into the dry outfits we'd packed for this purpose. We left our shoes drying, and just made do wearing dry socks.

Then we began exploring.

The first floor hall had rib-vaulted ceilings and dark, red-tiled floors that must have once been beautifully painted—near the walls, you could still see ghosts of the design that had been worn away by foot traffic toward the middle. Tapestries draped the guard room, and we peeked behind each. The chapel was glorious—more rib vaulting, two stories high, stained-glass windows. Since Mary Stuart had been religious, and we *were* after Madonna tiles, Lex and I examined every bit of wall and altar space, especially a marble virgin-and-child frieze. We looked under rugs and pressed everything that might have led to a secret compartment. When we found nothing, we kept going.

The decor turned increasingly richer with the Louis XIV living room—all in rich reds—and François I's bedroom. They got even more promising with Diane de Poitiers' bedroom—more tapestry, a canopied bed of the deepest blue velvet, and a huge white fireplace carved with nymphs and lions and an interlaced HD monogram that made me remember what Catrina had said about her being King Henri's mistress "and true love."

"We might come back to this one," I said, after our initial look-through. "Apparently she and Mary Stuart were friends."

Then Lex and I reached the gallery, the first floor of the bridge part of Chenonceau. I caught my breath at its grandeur, briefly forgetting why we were even here. According to the literature it had served as an above-water ballroom. The most striking elements were the vast black-and-white checkerboard floors, the exposed-joist ceiling above it, and all the high, double windows that looked out over the Cher, something like nine windows on each side. Small, manicured, potted trees sat in niches between the windows.

"Wow," breathed Lex, as distracted as I.

"Isn't this the life you were born into?" I teased.

"No, it's the life my great-great-great etc. grandparents were born into." But he drew me into a few waltzing dance steps across the slate-and-chalk squares of the floor in our stocking feet, in this echoing gallery where only we existed. People in high society still know how to waltz, and Lex had taught me long ago. For a moment it was so easy to imagine him as one of his Stuart ancestors, and the gallery filled with courtiers…

And me as what?

He ended our brief dance with a long dip and a kiss, then said, "C'mon. Let's check out the next floor."

I was momentarily distracted by the sight of the river out the windows, so close beneath us—all that water pushing against the bridge supports. According to our stolen brochures, the château had survived for over five hundred years. Surely it had weathered its share of floods. But this was an end-of-an-era, every-other-millennia flood.

Worrying about it wouldn't fix anything.

I raced my husband upstairs.

More vast bedchambers. More tapestry-covered walls. More canopied beds, all in rich, heavy fabrics that were the antithesis of the frilly pink some people equate with canopied beds. I noticed that Queen Catherine de Medici's bedroom lay directly above that of her husband's mistress, and wondered what we'd find if we looked under *her* rugs…she must have been at least tempted to spy on the lovers, right? But here on the second floor—what the French called the first—our best hope lay in the Five Queens' Bedroom, glorious with its tapestries and red drapes and dark, medallioned ceiling.

One of the five queens who had supposedly lived in these rooms had been Mary Stuart, Queen of Scots.

"We should stop for lunch soon, if we want to stay at the top of our game," Lex suggested as we reached that one. "I've got some bread and cheese with our things downstairs."

"After this one." As I had with each room, just to be on the thorough side, I looked under the bed. "Do you suppose all kings took mistresses?"

"I wouldn't," said Lex.

Still kneeling, I looked over to where he was studying the fireplace. "Well, that was a non sequitur."

"No, it wasn't."

I sighed, impressed at how well he knew me. "No, it wasn't. But I'm not worried about you cheating on me."

"Good. Because I wouldn't. Haven't. Don't want to. Never will."

I knew that most people think that—especially in their first year or so of marriage. And I knew that things often changed between people. But as much as any living human could make that promise—or prediction—Lex had one of the better chances of keeping it. He had a remarkably old-fashioned sense of honor. The chivalric, knightly kind.

"I believe you," I said. And I did.

"So what's the problem?"

"There isn't a problem. I was just thinking about the people who lived here, and how many of them had mistresses, and I wondered about it."

"Uh-huh." Lex left the fireplace and moved on to a writing desk by the window.

I stood and started looking behind tapestries, musing to myself. *Come on, Mary Stuart. Where did you hide the damned things? If you don't want to show me, show your great-great etc. grandson over there. Your great-great-great etc. granddaughter needs us to find these. She's a redhead, you know. Like you.*

"Maggi," said Lex, his voice muffled by the woven cloth draped across me.

"Yeah?"

"Mag!"

I came out from behind the tapestry and he waved me over to the writing desk. It was a lovely little piece in walnut, with intricately carved slim legs and an inlaid surface…and a mosaiclike design edging it, just beneath the lip.

In white.

I kneeled beside it, looking closer. "Some of these are pearls. But these…these uneven ones look like alabaster to me. Do they look like alabaster to you?"

"Yes," said Lex simply, as I ran my fingertips along the tiles. The same sense of power I'd felt back in the Black Madonna's temple, kind of a bounce-back of energy, was in these bits. "They look like alabaster to me."

"Thank you, Mary Stuart," I whispered—almost prayed. It's not that I thought the woman herself was a goddess—not equal to Isis or Melusine or Demeter or Persephone. I knew Mary Stuart had been a flesh-and-blood woman, just as I was, just as my husband was a flesh-and-blood man. But I'd almost forgotten one of the first lessons of grailkeeping.

Women and goddesses are a lot more similar than they are different.

Lex pried the alabaster pieces off the desk—yes, it was theft, and at this point we didn't care; we would find a way to make it up to Chenonceau. There were fourteen of them. I put them in my pocket, for lack of a bag until we could get back to our things. Then he slowly stood.

Done.

He scooped me up and spun me around and kissed me.

The most uncertain part of our quest was over.

Except for how Lex stopped—so suddenly that my feet kept going—and the sound of a gun being cocked, by the chamber door.

Chapter 14

I expected Adrianos.

What I got was Signora di Spedalotto. The fur stole she wore was absolutely soaked, as was the hem of her skirt. Her leather boots were caked in mud. But her eyes shone, and she looked marginally tougher with a pistol in her hand. "Ah, good," she murmured, almost to herself. "At last I have somebody's attention."

Lex's grip on me loosened so that I was standing on my own feet again. He seemed to be leaning against me, while I braced against him, and I realized that we were each trying to edge the other one out of the main line of fire.

"Stop it," I hissed, before greeting more loudly, *"Signora."*

"You stop it," murmured Lex. "You know her?"

"From the Cinq." I couldn't keep myself from putting a little extra emphasis on the hotel name, but at least I didn't say, *the hotel that you insisted would be the safest possible place, Your Highness.*

"Tsk-tsk," chided the signora, coming closer. Considering the breadth of the Five Queens' Bedroom, *closer* was a relative term. She wasn't exactly in jumping distance. Though shooting distance, yes. "Has nobody told you that it is rude to whisper? I require that you give me what you just found."

What we just found? "You don't know what it is?"

"I am certain that when I search your lifeless body, I shall learn. But this way, it is so much neater."

Lex tensed—easy to feel since we still stood shoulder to shoulder, though we'd stopped trying to crowd each other out of the way. "Don't," I warned him, not bothering to whisper. "I have a feeling she'd be even happier to shoot a man."

Signora di Spedalotto laughed. "You are clever, Magdalene Sanger-Stuart. *The treasure,* please. And you, the husband I presume? Step back that way. Toward the bed."

"No," growled Lex, even as I risked taking my eyes off the gunwoman to tell him *yes.*

In a flash the signora shot out a diamond-paned window, just behind us. I cringed at the crash. She laughed with delight. I didn't get the idea that she used guns much...but inexperience made her more dangerous, not less.

The novelty of having the château to ourselves was wearing off. Nobody would hear the gunshot.

"I am done," she said, her voice shaking, "with men who think themselves in charge because of their wealth, because they are men. You, Signor Stuart, I will you shoot gladly, if only to save your wife what my life has become. Her, I will only shoot if necessary. Do you wish to make it necessary?"

Lex murmured, "You *touched* her, didn't you!" He knew that the more I dealt with goddesses, the more my touch strengthened other women as well. I hadn't mentioned my fears that my goddess gifts were fading.

"She was like this when I met her. Please, Lex. *Go stand by the bed.*"

"So that she can take—"

"We can't get them back if you're dead." Well, *I* could, but… *"Go."*

His golden eyes narrow and his jaw tight, my husband strode to the bed. He'd never looked more regal than he did in this setting…and rarely more dangerous.

"Grazie." The signora risked coming closer to me yet. "Now, you show me."

"We need them," I said, trying to meet her on the level of woman to woman. "Our baby daughter's life could depend on them."

"Show me!"

So I reached into my pocket and, with a quick prayer to any goddess close enough to hear, I pulled out three of the alabaster pieces and placed them on the writing desk. "There."

Again with the *tsk-tsk.* "You are lying to me, Signora Sanger-Stuart. I heard far more pieces being retrieved. Your pocket is still heavy with them. The rest, please. And turn your pocket out to show me that is all."

Crap. I did as instructed. The best I could manage was to hide the final tile between the fingers I used to turn my pocket inside out.

"Very good. I believe…" Her eyes flicking between me, Lex, and the tiles, she withdrew a black velvet square from her shoulder bag. "Yes," she murmured, tossing it onto the inlaid surface of the writing desk with a faint thud. "Put them in here."

I tipped the velvet, silk-lined bag, and an antique silver

mirror slid out. I'd known women to carry mirrors like this. Rich women. Expensive mirrors.

My gaze met Lex's where he stood, ready to pounce, near the scarlet-draped bed. *See,* I tried to tell him with my gaze. *She's not here to kill us.*

Not that we could let her keep Kestrel's tiles. But I'd take any silver linings I could get.

I must have taken too long. With a bang and a crash, she shot out another window. *"Now."*

"Please don't do that." I hurried to put the tiles—all of them except the one I'd kept for my pocket—into the black velvet bag. "This castle is a piece of history. The rain's going to get in, and…"

"It is the home of a famous whore, and does not deserve such veneration. Now give it to me."

I handed her the velvet bag.

She told me, *"Grazie,"* and began to back away, moving the gun from me to Lex and back.

I pocketed the silver mirror in case we needed fingerprints. "Signora, my baby daughter—"

"Enough about your daughter! You can have more children. I cannot."

Now *my* eyes narrowed.

I didn't try to stop Lex when, the moment the signora reached the doorway and turned her back, he went after her, silent on his stocking feet. Actually, I raced him for it. But he had a head start. I reached the broad hallway in time to see him tackle her. Her smaller body vanished under his. With a cry, she hit the floor. The gun skittered across red tile, under one of the neat wooden benches that alternated with flower arrangements along the chalk-white walls.

I dove after it, turned around with it heavy in my hand…

In time to see Lex drag Signora di Spedalotto up by the fur collar of her stole and slam her, hard, against one of the hallway's tapestries. In a moment, he had her turned against the tapestry, her arms twisted behind her back. She had to turn her head, her jaw and cheek against the wall so that she could breathe.

Her mouth opened, and an awful wailing sound struggled from her throat.

"Get the tiles, Maggi," spat Lex, barely panting.

I don't like guns. I put on the safety of this one, slid it carefully into the back of Lex's waistband, then patted down the wailing, weeping figure who had just robbed us. In a moment I had our tiles back, safe in the black velvet bag, which I stuffed securely into my back pocket. "There. I've got them. You don't have to hurt her."

"He is!" cried the Italian woman, tears running down her cheeks. "He *is* hurting me! My arm, I think he broke it!"

"No, he didn't." I knew my husband that well. If her arm was broken, it was from the fall, not from his holding her.

A brief nod from Lex, his glance warm with gratitude, agreed with me. But then he leaned over Signora di Spedalotto's shoulder and whispered something in her ear that made her close her eyes. Her wails turned to whimpers, riding her ragged breath.

All he said to me was, "Get something to tie her. We'll drop her off with the local gendarmerie. We can't just leave her to follow us again."

I used the ties from the lush draperies to bind the signora's uninjured hands in front of her, for easier movement. Lex was the one who wrangled her down the walled, curved stone stairs, although she'd stopped struggling by then.

"What did you say to her?" I demanded.

"I plead the fifth," he muttered. But something about the

way she kept her eyes closed, something about her whimpers and rocking, made me think that the signora had gone someplace else entirely from fear of...*Lex?* Why she wanted the tiles—or wanted whatever we'd found, which just happened to be alabaster tiles—was still a mystery. In my opinion, nobody who waved a gun around deserved much sympathy—*I could have more children?* But it was hard not to worry, with that moaning.

We reached the hallway below, our traumatized prisoner hanging from Lex's grip. The exit from the château was only a room's length away. I said, "I'm not accusing you of anything, I just—"

Then both of the green double-doors pushed open, and four men in black came in with the rain, rifles at the ready. Fear lurched through me. Not just because I recognized them as Adriano men, but because of the memories they brought with them. The gallery in New York. My dead bodyguard. Lexie and Olga. Kestrel.

We backed away from them, deeper into the château. Lex muttered, "Take her and run."

Suddenly I had the semiconscious form of Signora di Spedalotto in my arms, and Lex had drawn the gun and stepped between us and the bad guys. Crap.

Trust him not to use even a villainous woman as a shield, but...*crap!*

"The duke, he sends us," announced the head black-coat, spreading his hands as if to show that he was unarmed. The gesture was contradicted by the rifles the other three men held. "He requests that you give us the tiles now, *si?*"

More Italian. An ugly suspicion about the signora struggled through the chaos. *You may* call me *Signora di Spedalotto.* Could her name actually be...?

No. It would be too big a coincidence. There were a lot of Italians in France. And I couldn't imagine Simon Adriano easily sending women to do his work…or the signora doing anything willingly for the men in her life.

"We will give you the tiles, *no,*" countered Lex. We continued to back down the hallway, me and the Italian woman first, Lex and her pistol second. Even as he spoke I realized a new dilemma.

"They're *the duke's* tiles," I added quickly.

"You need not wait," insisted the head black-coat. "We will take them to the duke for you, and then you may travel back to Lys unencumbered. Better for everyone."

Inspiration hit. "But how do I know you really work for him? I have to put them in *his* hand, not yours."

"I am afraid you will have to take our word, signora."

Speaking of signoras, I'd gotten no help from di Spedalotto. She was barely walking. I was taking almost her full weight. I'm in decent shape, but there's a limit. We somehow made it to the doorway at the end of the hall that, if it hadn't been open, would have looked like more white stone wall.

"I'm clear," I told Lex, dragging the *signora* through and holding my breath.

The moment Lex backed safely through the door I pulled it shut behind him and exhaled. Now, between the two of us, we could make more time.

I was turning toward the other end of the long, ballroom-like gallery when the shot sounded. That's how I saw the six new gunmen—with enough black coats between them to scream *Adriano*—who'd entered behind us.

They weren't all carrying the rifles I associated with tranquilizer darts, either.

Lex shot back once, twice—then grunted. I dropped

Signora di Spedalotto onto the checkerboard floor to fend for herself. I grabbed my wounded husband and, as he continued to fire, dragged him back. I pinned him against the wall behind the marginal safety of a window niche.

He'd dropped two of them.

"It's okay, Mag," he gasped. "I, uh, think it's okay."

His upper sleeve blossomed red. I tore the material. From the stripe of blood, it seemed the bullet had grazed him, nothing more. This time.

But something else…something niggled at me.

Still, Lex wasn't dead, and he wasn't down. That put us in the positive column for a few more minutes, anyway. "Yes," I assured him, with a quick kiss to his jaw. "It's okay."

"Shouldn't we…?" He nodded toward the older woman.

"No." I watched her crawl to another niche opposite of us, unable to forget my suspicions. "She's only slowing us down."

"Yes, but she's—"

"*No.* I don't think they'll hurt her…and I doubt she can go where we're going."

"Which is?" I could hear our pursuers approaching from both ends of the gallery, speaking quietly to each other in Italian, readying for whatever trouble we might give. We'd be stupid to stay and cause more trouble. What we had to do was get the hell *away* from these men, us and our tiles both.

I unlatched one of the tall windows overlooking the swollen River Cher. "Your arm won't keep you from swimming, will it?"

"You're joking."

I shook my head.

"Maggi, the river's at full flood." When I didn't answer, he added, *"And we're upstream."*

"Yeah," I agreed. "I wouldn't have planned it that way." If

we jumped out the window on this side, we wouldn't have just the maddened current to deal with. We also had to make it all the way under what was left of the archways, beneath this very gallery. *Under the castle.* Underwater.

"Simon still needs you, right?" Lex asked. "He needs you to deliver—well, he wants you to decipher the seven—"

But he was figuring out what I already had. Once Simon Adriano had the Stuart tiles, he could get someone else to perform either of those two tasks. Oh, sure, I'd be convenient. But I was nowhere near necessary. What Lex *hadn't* figured out, however—

The men came closer yet. I heard a brush of wet material. Someone breathing through his teeth.

"They're going to kill you," I whispered.

"Me and not you?" Lex actually looked relieved. Bastard.

"I'm not sure about me. But I'm pretty sure about you. You're both too damned macho."

"Excuse me?"

"You can't put two stallions in the same paddock or two roosters in the same cage or—"

"I get it. The evils of testosterone. But you think—"

"He called me Magdalene, this morning." When that made no sense to Lex—hell, it barely made sense to me—I used the one argument that I thought he would believe. "Call it an instinct. My throat hurts."

That's how I used to sense danger, before I'd let my goddess-championing duties lapse. It was also true. Adriano's men were even more dangerous than a torrential river.

"Okay." And Lex straddled the windowsill. He trusted my instincts. I adored him for it. Water, hitting one of the piers between the arches, splashed high enough to dampen my socked foot as I joined him. "You know I love you, right?"

I looked sharply up, into his noble, strong-jawed face. "We're not going to die."

"I won't risk not saying it, though. You're everything to me. You and Kestrel. I need you to always know that."

So I held his solemn, golden gaze. "You're everything to me, too, Lex Stuart. So *don't die.*"

I reached for my back pocket, to secure the tiles before we dove into the river—and went cold.

Three things happened simultaneously then.

The Adriano men came around the niche, weapons drawn.

Lex said, "Now!" and pulled me out the window with him, into the flooded river.

And just as I went over, just before the muddy waters of the Cher sucked me down and the stone archway of the castle swallowed me, I caught a glimpse of Signora di Spedalotto smiling—and, with her bound hands, dangling the black velvet bag she must have grabbed out of my pocket as I'd helped her evade the gunmen.

Chapter 15

Hard, cold water swallowed us. I struggled not to gasp, not to give in to the single instinct that probably drowns more flood victims than any other. I longed to hold on to Lex, but we needed our hands and our strength for swimming…at least, that was my excuse when the river wrenched us apart, as if Lex's and my death grips were no more than a casual pinky-hook.

Lex…

But I couldn't distract myself, not even with him. The crushing need to breathe took over. I knew only the anger of the once-placid Cher rolling over me, forcing me down beneath the château, dragging me under the curved stone of its arched bridge. The rush of current deafened me. There was only darkness and fear and floundering—and absolute helplessness against Nature's fury.

Except that I don't do helpless. Not even for Mother Nature.

As black became gray, when the river finally spat me out on the other side of the château, I struggled upward—what I *hoped* was upward—with my last remaining strength. I broke the surface of the churning, rushing current and gasped blessed breath, life. I flopped onto my back, the only way not to inhale water in this kind of flooding.

Then I saw riflemen at the fairy castle's beautiful gallery windows, and I dove again after all.

Even a tranquilizer dart would be fatal in these rapids. Something hot touched my hand, and I rolled underwater to see not darts but bullets disintegrating above me—who would've guessed only a few feet submersion really would stop bullets!

The current dragged at me, didn't want to let me break surface again. I did anyway and gasped another breath, farther downstream. Again I dove, again I dodged shots.

The third time I surfaced, the castle was only a memory. That's how fast the current rushed past the sodden green woods of the Loire Valley. Swimming on my back again, choking at the water surging into my face, I looked for Lex's head over the roar of water and nearly went down. One emergency at a time. Backstroking as hard as I could, struggling not to be pulled under for good, I edged toward the left bank at a slow diagonal. The river fought me, tried to push me back, push me down, with every stroke. I felt myself faltering, weaker, colder, losing my coordination—

Then I glimpsed trees ahead, combing the current like fingers. One chance…

Reaching outward, I caught myself against a branch and, with my last strength, heaved myself up and out of the Cher. I barely had the strength to climb up onto a higher branch. I did it anyway, in case the water rose further. Then I lay there, gasping, panting…praying. My heartbeat deafened me. And my need…

Lex.

Melusine, you were once goddess of the springs and rivers, not so far south of here. Protect him.

Isis, you once helped me find him as you found Osirus in the Nile—be with him.

Lady Mother…

But I didn't know which Lady Mother the Black Madonna symbolized. Any of them? All of them? And the goddess I'd found just before my wedding, Sovereignty, was more about taking charge of yourself than asking for help. As soon as I'd caught my breath, I climbed from this tree—a chestnut—to the next, then another, until I'd made it away from the flood-waters and could climb down without immediate fear of being swept away.

My legs almost buckled when I hit the ground. Goddess, I was wiped. But after scanning what I could see of the banks upriver, I took a chance and began to walk downriver.

Looking. Hoping. Praying. And feeling increasingly ill, the farther I stumbled—and not just because of all the water I'd swallowed.

I'd convinced him to jump into a flooding river, to be swept under a castle, based only on instinct? It was one thing for me to make those calls for myself, but him? *What if I'd been wrong?* What if Simon's men would only have taken us both captive? But now, because he'd trusted my instinct, the only man I'd ever loved may have drowned. He may have been shot—again. And since I'd lost my ability to sense his location when I'd given birth to Kestrel, I couldn't even know…

Then I saw it, an uprooted tree intercepting the current and something human-size trapped in its watery branches, half-hidden under the wash of diverted water.

Something dead.

Something I desperately didn't want to see—and had to.

Dangerous or not, I balanced my way out onto the wet tree trunk, off the river bank and back over the rushing water. I barely had any strength left. If the tree's roots gave way, I would be back in the river. Even without branches to entangle me, I might easily drown. So I stepped carefully. I clung to branches when I could. But I had to see…

It was a deer. An eight-point stag, drowned and snared. Relief warred with a strong sense of foreboding. The stag is often a symbol of the sacrificed king.

In everything I'd understood about Lex's own mythology, my husband embraced the figure of the sacrificed king. Arthur. Osiris. Christ.

But not now. Not this time.

Somehow I made it back to shore, made it off the downed tree just as its trunk suddenly rolled beneath my feet as I jumped. I backed away from its muddy roots as, with a great groan, the force of the river wrenched it sideways and dragged it away down the flooding river to catch and drown other frantically swimming creatures with its churning branches.

Rain beat the ground around me.

I felt empty.

And then—

The whistle sliced through the sound of rainfall, through the low rumble of thunder, through the closer roar of the flood. My head came up, and there he stood on the opposite bank.

I spotted him just as, hand to teeth, he whistled again.

Lex.

It took everything I had not to just sink down onto my butt, in the mud, and weep. But I couldn't. Not only did I have a reputation to maintain—with myself even more than my husband. He would want to comfort me, and we had a river the width of a four-lane highway rushing between us.

He looked soggy and muddy and fit—his clinging clothes and proud posture emphasized just how fit, as if he weren't exhausted at all. Jogging to catch up to the section of bank across from where I stood, Lex gestured at the river between us and spread his hands, as if to ask, *What's up with this?*

I could see his grin, even from this distance. He'd clearly been as scared for me as I'd been for him. This pleased me so much that I pointed at him, then gestured at my side. *You were supposed to go left.*

He shook his head and gestured at his side. *No, right.*

I laughed. Goddess, I loved this man. And speaking of which…

Thank you, Melusine. Thank you, Isis. Thank you, Holy Mother, whichever one You are. I won't forget your cause, I promise.

With an exaggerated shake of his head, as if we were hopeless, Lex beckoned me to keep walking downstream. I was glad to parallel him on my side of the flooded Cher. But I kept sneaking peeks at him.

Was he trying to use his cell phone? Either way, he then pocketed it. At one point, he spread his hand deliberately over his chest, then crossed his arms on his chest like a hug, then spread his hand toward me. *I love you.*

I repeated the message, holding out both hands toward him. *I love you bigger.*

He repeated it, spreading his arms very wide. *I love you biggest.*

Then I caught a glimpse of the bridge we were heading toward, obstructed by several downed trees, farther downstream, and I doubted that was possible. *Good plan, my love.*

Lex broke into a jog in that direction, and I heard another noise, beyond the sound of wind, rain and rapids. A far more worrisome noise.

The steady beat of a helicopter.

Adrianos?

I wouldn't have thought I had it in me, but I broke into a run myself. If they were coming after us again I wouldn't be caught on the other side of the river from my husband. Lex beat me to the bridge, which wouldn't likely survive against this flood much longer...between the current pushing against it and the trees slamming into it, even stone would eventually give way. Rather than put us both in danger, I hung back while Lex waded through the water running over its surface.

We were both aware that at any moment he could be swept off with the overflow. At any moment the whole thing might collapse. *Hurry!* But could he also hear the helicopter, getting closer?

The last bit of danger came when he reached my end of the bridge—the water was flowing around it, not just under and over it. But Lex waded almost effortlessly through the treacherous current, and then he was there, with me. He buried me in his embrace, covered my mouth with his own. His cold lips warmed against mine—but I pulled back. I tried to drag him into the tree line.

"Helicopter," I managed to gasp against his lips, shivering. To judge by the noise, it would be past the trees, over us, at any moment. *We needed to take cover!*

Again, Lex grinned. "Ours," he shouted into my ear.

That surprised me so much that it took me a moment to notice him kissing me again—well, a millisecond or two. Before the rightness of his kisses became everything. Then I sank against him and his strength, let his arms hold me up, let his body shelter me from the blowing water—which just blew worse as the helicopter sank into view over the river. A man, leaning dangerously out of it, gestured something that Lex seemed to understand. Lex gestured back—the symbol for okay—and the chopper ascended.

"There's a clearing down this road," he explained against my ear. Then, since he was there anyway, he kissed the ear. And the sensitive stretch of my neck just beneath it. Mmm. "They can pick us up there."

"You called for help? What kind of a waterproof cell phone do you have?"

"One I put into a sealed baggie." He kissed me again, unimpressed by his own preparedness.

"But how'd you get a *helicopter?*" The cacophony lessened and my wits returned from the wonder of my husband's skilled mouth, and my sheer joy at our survival, to lingering concerns about other matters.

"I do have connections, Mag," he reminded me. But that same uncertainty about his sheer power—the same thing that had eaten at me on our way into Chenonceau—was a lesser concern.

No way to say it but to say it. "I lost the tiles."

Lex's grin faded into sudden, absolute composure. But I knew his composure for the mask it was.

"Kestrel's tiles, Lex. They're gone, all but one of them."

"In the river?"

I shook my head. "That bitch Signora di Spedalotto took them while I was dragging her to safety. I only realized it as we went out the window."

His clenched jaw added subtle annoyance to his composure. "I should have tied her hands behind her."

"I should have put the tiles where she couldn't get them."

"It's not your—"

"—fault," I said at the same time to him. Now I felt even sicker.

"Come on. We don't know how long the weather will hold." And, taking my hand, he set a rapid pace up the country road toward the promised clearing. Not that the weather was particularly clear, but I guess the helicopter pilots had deemed it clear enough. "Maybe Adriano's goons have them now."

We both knew that Simon Adriano wasn't the kind of guy to not hold my losses against me—or worse, against Kestrel. So neither of us even suggested that.

Lex, because he really did understand powerful men. Too well.

Me, because I didn't want to introduce Simon back into the conversation until both my husband and I had warmed up and gotten into some dry clothes.

And maybe not until well after that.

To Lex's credit, he didn't bring it up until we were back on the road, late that afternoon. He drove the Audi. The gendarmes had recovered it from Chenonceau's car park when they went in to investigate the shootings and to secure the château against further damage. Although Lex wouldn't see a doctor about his arm, one of the guys on the helicopter was a medic, who applied a competent field dressing. We'd both taken a hot shower at the inn—together—which led to other delicious activities, which led to the necessity of a short nap…although really, surviving a river in full flood may have required the nap anyway. It didn't feel as though we'd wasted *too* much time. Then we were on our way back to Lys. What might have been a five-hour drive promised to last well into the night.

Only then did Lex ask, oh, so casually, "He called you Magdalene?"

I'd pretty much figured that one would come back to haunt me. My husband has a brilliant memory.

"This morning, when I saw it was you, I gasped. Simon asked me what was wrong, and he called me Magdalene."

"And that's unusual?"

Nope. Not at all. But that would be disingenuous. I'd used Simon's increased intimacy to justify a death-defying dive into the flooded Cher. "Normally he calls me Mrs. Stuart."

"Oh." We drove a few more kilometers before Lex said, "You think he's falling for you?"

"I'm not sure what I think. But when his thugs started shooting at us—at you—with real bullets, it seemed significant."

"So not only does the bastard steal my daughter, he's hot for my wife."

"Hot would be overstating things."

"I doubt it." Lex always believes other men find me as attractive as he does. Sure, I clean up okay. But I'm no top model.

"He's seen me for barely ten minutes," I reminded him. The flashing numbers on Simon Adriano's computer screen wouldn't fade from my memory anytime soon.

"And any amount of time he may have been watching you from his ceiling-cam," Lex reminded me tightly. "And calling you every morning."

"You can't be jealous. He's calling to taunt me."

"Which I bet he just loves."

When I didn't say anything, Lex cut his gaze from the road to me and back. "You think he does, too."

It wasn't a question.

"I think that any routine can become seductive." Well, *that* was the wrong word. Now his eyes flared at me. "It's the power of anticipation, Lex. Of waiting. You know that."

He didn't even have to ask if I was anticipating the morning calls, too. It wasn't a pleasant given…but it was kind of a given, all the same. My mistake was being embarrassed enough to try to explain it. "Lex, he's my only connection to Kestrel."

Open mouth. Insert foot.

Just as well his gaze stayed mainly on the road, because he was stony.

"Other than you," I added. That could not possibly have sounded more lame.

"Don't sweat it," he bit out, his knuckles white on the steering wheel.

But we'd both had a hard day. A hard week.

And considering that I now had to go back to Simon Adriano without Kestrel's Mary Stuart tiles, with the counterfeit makings of a fake mosaic and without any idea why the seventh Marian was key?

Things were about to get harder.

Chapter 16

We arrived in Lys sometime just before dawn—or when dawn would have been, if it would ever stop raining. I didn't expect to find anyone awake yet, much less welcoming us. But as I climbed out into the rain and Lex reclaimed our bags from the back seat, the front door of the farmhouse wrenched open. A beautiful, honey-haired woman stood there in the light of the entryway, barefoot, in an oversize T-shirt.

Only after my initial blink of surprise—and as disappointment soured her expression to something more familiar—did I recognize the slim build and feline eyes of Catrina Dauvergne.

"Ah," she said dully. "It is only you."

And she went back in, leaving the door ajar for us.

Well that had been strange. I had to be more tired than I'd thought. Lex and I went in, shutting out the rain behind us—and we got to face the others.

Bad leg or not, Nick Petter must have vaulted down the

stairs to get there, with his rifle, so soon after Catrina. Eve was still descending the steps, also in an oversize T-shirt, socks on her feet, her black curls pulled back in a scrunchy. Her shirt read, *Epidemiologists do it Feverishly.* A glance toward Catrina, where she'd flopped into a large chair with a quilt—apparently she'd been sleeping there—showed me that her shirt sported no friendly messages. No surprise there.

Tru and Griffin descended together—both in men's underwear, though Tru wore a tank top—and a new woman, small and dark and marginally older than the rest of us, seemed to simply appear around the doorway from the kitchen. She wore pajama bottoms, similar to those worn to practice yoga, and a black tank top with small, Gothic red print on it that I couldn't read without getting closer. Something about the way she stood, both relaxed and ready, kept me from getting closer. That, and the way she seemed to take up a post at Catrina's side.

The dark-haired woman rolled her fingers at Lex. I realized she was the one who'd been secreting the ingredients back to the Marians, even as he said, "Maggi, this is Aubrey de Lune. Aubrey, this is my wife, Maggi."

"You got here safely," I said, realizing even as the words came out how foolish they sounded. It was one step above, *Great smuggling, you.* But I felt so damned uncomfortable. I'd felt that way since Lex's and my nonargument.

Aubrey raised her eyebrows in noncommittal acknowledgment.

"Sorry," I said, feeling their need to hear of our progress like a physical pull. "I'm sorry for waking everybody, and—and I lost them." It seemed kinder than revealing that part *after* the story of how we'd finally found what we'd sought. "The tiles."

"*We* lost them," corrected Lex firmly, guiding me to the sofa, beside Eve, and sitting on the arm above and beside me.

"Yeah," I muttered. "*We* got my pocket picked by a woman I think is involved with the Adriano family. Doesn't Simon have a wife?"

"Not so you would notice," said Aubrey, when the others looked to her. Apparently she was our resident Adriano expert, in the absence of—where was Nadia? "I've only seen her once. She has her own wing of the compound. She provided Simon with his heir, his spare and his contribution to the church. That was the original family plan, in any case. Simon provides her with expensive clothes, trips to Paris and enough designer drugs to keep her comfortably numb."

"Let's go back to the part where you found the tiles," suggested Tru. So I recounted the basics of my last four days. If anybody noticed that Lex and I weren't sitting as close to each other as Tru and Griffin, or holding hands like Eve and Nick, they didn't comment. The one person who might have...

"Where's Nadia?" I asked.

"She went back to Naples," explained Eve. "To be closer to Joshua."

And to Lexie. But nobody needed to add that part. Suddenly I felt jealous of Nadia and not, this time, because of Lex.

"So we're still missing the alabaster tiles," I finished, passing the one piece I'd managed to keep to Tru. "All except this one. I'm sorry. I know how important they were. But if Signora di Spedalotto really was working for Simon—"

"Unlikely," said Aubrey firmly.

"—but *if* she was, or if the men who ambushed us searched her, at least the tiles are with him."

Tru's eyebrows shot up even higher than Catrina's. "That's the *bright* side?"

But Eve understood. "If Simon has the tiles, he's less likely to take Maggi's presumed failure out on the children."

That was a hell of a lot to leave resting on an *if.*

Lex said, "He won't be able to take anything out on the children if we rescue them first."

"I've been thinking about your idea," agreed Nick Petter. Even without the cargo pants, boots and sweater—and without the rifle—he would just ooze Special Forces. "And if we had a better description of the room where the hostages are being held—"

"No!" Now I *definitely* wasn't sitting close to Lex. I was standing, facing him as I backed toward the others. *His* idea? "No rescue attempts."

He stood too. "Maggi."

"I told you about the gas. I told you about the code."

"We're almost out of time." He ventured a step toward me, then apparently changed his mind. Smart guy.

"He'll kill them." I believed that with every instinct I had. I'd seen the man's cold eyes. I'd heard his fervor.

"And what do you think he'll do when he figures out we gave him a fake mosaic?"

So we give him the real mosaic. But I couldn't say that. It was one of those protests that your despair wants to make, wants to believe—like *I'll do better,* or *we can change*—but even as it tears out of your throat, you know you're lying. If the Black Madonna mosaic had the ability to either intensify or neutralize the powers that had been plaguing Europe for a year now, then giving it to Simon Adriano would be like handing him a nuclear bomb, one he'd already vowed to use this coming Monday.

It was currently very, very early Friday morning.

But *not* to give it to him, when he had such precious hostages. Or worse, to risk all of them in a rescue attempt, after all Simon's warnings about spies everywhere... If

Kestrel died because we made the wrong call, I wouldn't want to live.

Well…not longer than it would take to crush Adriano.

"Even if we give him everything he wants," Lex continued, more quietly now. "Even if we help him destroy Europe with tornadoes, earthquakes, tsunamis and plague, he won't leave her alive, Maggi. He won't leave any of you alive once he's done."

Wait. "This isn't about you being jealous of Simon Adriano, is it?"

"Is it about you thinking you can sweet-talk him out of being the murderous, power-hungry sociopath we know and hate? Because you can't."

"I can be pretty damned persuasive if I need to be." When I have a goddess or two on my side.

Lex's eyes narrowed at the idea of me *persuading* Simon. "No."

That sounded a lot like him trying to tell me what to do. But we'd had an agreement. Before I would marry him, we'd made a pact about never trying to order each other around. And he'd promised—squeezing my hands, laughing with relief, kissing me all over my face, *he'd promised*. And now…*no?*

"She's my baby," I warned him now, "and I'll do what I need to do."

Words barely escaped Lex's throat, he was so angry, struggling so hard to keep his composure in front of all these people. "Why do you keep forgetting that she's my baby, too?"

And what's worse? What twisted in my gut? *He was right.*

I had no idea what I would have said to that, if Catrina hadn't interrupted. "Yours is not the only child there."

"Thank you," said Eve, quietly.

"How's this for a plan?" intercepted Nick, beside her. "We give this matter the thought it deserves. Mrs. Stuart doesn't have to be in Naples with the tiles until tomorrow. That gives us a little time. So, everybody who needs more sleep, get it— especially you two," he added, indicating Lex and me, still in our stand-off positions. "Tru has a few last tiles to fire or age or…something…to finish the fake mosaic, right?"

"Especially now," the sun-bleached dowser agreed, examining the single piece of alabaster in her hand. "Then we have to finish laying them out beside the real one, to make sure they're a match."

"So we meet in the temple after lunch. Stuart, Sinclair and I will come up with our best rescue proposal. Just for consideration," he added quickly, toward me.

At a disgusted sound, I turned and saw Aubrey de Lune's exasperation. For a small woman, she had attitude. I could also read the Gothic print on her tank top. *No More Miss Nice Guy.*

"And Aubrey," Nick conceded with a grin. "The rest of you finish the mosaic and come up with an alternative plan. Midafternoon, we compare our options and come to a decision. Agreed?"

We didn't find out. Alarms sounded again.

"Car," said Griffin Sinclair, going to the window.

Tru tapped in an alarm code to shut off the klaxons and then, when Catrina wrenched the door open, Tru tapped it in again. Catrina, the farmhouse's purported owner, was too busy racing into the rain. As a tall figure unfolded from the driver's seat of a familiar Citroën Saxo, she hurled herself up into his arms. Her bare legs wrapped his jeaned hips and her arms went around his neck, his own long arms pulling her even closer. In just that position, Catrina Dauvergne and my old friend Rhys Pritchard kissed in the blowing, sheeting rain. Another man, grinning tiredly, pulled two duffel bags from the car's hatchback.

In a few minutes the new arrivals were safely inside.

Catrina's hair was wet and her feet muddy as Rhys lowered her to stand on the floor, not that they were separating much farther than that just yet. She looked radiant as she studied his profile and felt his shoulder, as if making sure he was real. *She does love him,* I thought, somehow surprised. I'd expected the tenderness on the face of my tall, black-haired friend as he looked down at her—Rhys wouldn't be involved with someone halfway. But the blond Frenchwoman…

Until this moment, I guess I'd thought she was toying with him.

Maybe I was wrong.

Oh, Rhys had his own smile and hug for me, when he recovered enough from Catrina's ambush to notice who else was in the farmhouse. Rhys and Lex traded manly handshakes. The man with the leather jacket and dark-brown ponytail greeted Aubrey with real friendship. Rhys introduced the man as Robert Fraser, Analise's husband and baby Mara's dad. But even as I started telling Robert everything I'd seen of his family, during my first day as a hostage, Rhys sank into the big chair, Catrina on his lap, and he didn't even look embarrassed by it. And not just because seating was getting scarce. They kept exchanging little whispers to catch up.

Tru and Griffin got coffee for everyone. Despite that she'd heard the story before, Eve was hungry to revisit the details of her niece and nephew—her *children.* Although he was keeping guard, I could tell that her husband Nick was listening, too.

After Robert and Rhys—and Aubrey—were caught up on that part of the story, our new arrivals related their attempts to solicit help against the Adrianos from the Vatican.

"Nothing," admitted Robert, as much to Aubrey as anybody. "We got pretty high up—Ana and I made some interesting contacts at St. Peter's, last summer—and apparently the pope himself had calls made on our behalf. Simon Adriano isn't taking them."

It was Aubrey who asked, "Not from the *pope?*" Then she explained. "The Adrianos have been close with the church for centuries. Half the atrocities blamed on the Catholics started as Adriano power plays."

"Apparently," said Rhys, while Catrina watched his face with concern, "Simon has decided to change their game. He's ignoring the pontiff."

"It's out of character," insisted Aubrey.

"Unless that's not where he sees the power anymore," offered Lex, from where he leaned against a dark beam, across the room from me. As I've said before, Lex would know from powerful men. "The Adrianos aligned with the Catholics in order to ride the coattails of their power. Didn't the church once rule Europe?"

"Its influence only began to truly wane in the seventeenth century," said Catrina.

"Maybe Simon thinks some other person or force is about to become more powerful, after this time of transition everyone keeps talking about."

We all exchanged uncomfortable looks.

"Him?" I guessed.

"That," admitted Aubrey, "is more in character."

My daily wake-up call from Simon came while Lex and I were stripping down for bed, in the same simple room we'd shared a few nights earlier. I was just beginning to say, "I'm sorry."

The "sorry" part got drowned out by ring tone.

Lex's golden gaze cut to me, seriously unhappy, but he just went on undressing. I particularly loved watching him take off his watch. There was something so symbolic about that, not just that he didn't want it to catch in my hair, but that he was divesting himself of the need to control his schedule, at least until we woke again.

Another ring, and I picked up. "Good morning, Duke Adriano."

"Good morning, Mrs. Stuart. Am I to understand that you had some excitement at Chenonceau?"

A muscle in Lex's jaw twitched as he shrugged off his shirt. The bandage made a large white patch near his shoulder—damn right, we'd had excitement. But my husband showed no more pain than that.

Why was it so easy for me to forget how well Lex hid pain?

"Nothing we couldn't handle," I assured Simon, not giving him more information than necessary.

"Obviously." Simon's annoyance came through as sarcasm. "I look forward to seeing you tomorrow. At noon. Be at the airfield from whence you and my son's bitch left Naples."

So he knew how Nadia and I had gotten to Lys last Sunday? I wondered if our original pilot, Geno, worked for him.

If not, I wondered if Geno was still alive. "The timing may be a little tricky," I said, watching Lex drop his slacks. He had great legs, too. He could easily wear a kilt. "The roads are awful, and planes have been grounded for days."

When Lex left his clothes folded on the bureau and turned toward the bed, dressed only in his briefs, I stopped him with a hand to his chest. His warm, solid chest. His gaze, as it slid to me, held suspicion. Then, as I stepped up against him, it warmed into an understanding words couldn't have given him.

Not Simon, you idiot. Never Simon. You.

His arms slid hard around me as I turned in them, leaning

back against the solid support of my husband to finish the call, while Simon said, "The skies should clear."

That surprised me. Not enough for me to push away the distraction of Lex's silent lips down the side of my neck, as his hands slid helpfully to the waist of my slacks. But still. "Not even you can't know that!"

Simon said nothing.

Lex slid my slacks off my hips, down my thighs.

"I mean, I knew the storms are connected to whatever you've been doing with the ley lines, but weather control can't be *that* exact a science."

"I will expect you," warned Simon, "at noon tomorrow. Your plane is to land and to leave, without hesitation. You are to disembark alone with everything I requested."

Just as well that he disconnected then. As Lex slid a warm hand down my belly and into my panties, I'm not sure I could have answered coherently. I barely managed to fumble the phone onto the bureau before I lost all dexterity, and could only brace my own hands on his corded forearms. Oh… Goddess…yes.

"Don't say his name," warned Lex, into the nape of my neck.

"No," I agreed, then gasped satisfaction at my reward. I still had plenty of reason for mixed feelings about my husband. His hiring of babysitters, his unnerving power, his stubborn plan—a plan the other men knew about!—to rescue Kes by force. But let's be honest. I knew what kind of man he was when I married him. And he was trying to use his powers for good. He'd put himself between me and gunmen today. He would gladly die for me or Kestrel. I knew that, too.

Still, he was a guy. He didn't want words.

And I wanted what he wanted.

Only afterward—my world still spinning, my skin damp,

my breath tearing from my lungs—did I watch his profile in the gray light of rain-muffled dawn and know that even mind-blowing sex hadn't been enough.

Lex was usually so damned sure of everything. Everything except me, maybe. But not now. Not lately.

"Of course she's your daughter," I whispered.

Lex's breath stuttered into what I recognized as a breathless laugh. We both clearly remembered the night Kes had been conceived.

"I mean," I tried, and he kissed me.

"I know," he whispered. "You never implied otherwise."

"None of this is your fault."

His eyes searched mine in the shadows. "Yes," he said, finally. "It is."

"Lex—"

"I've been too complacent, since you and Kes. I haven't moved hard enough, aggressively enough, to strengthen my own position. If I had, even someone as desperate as Adriano would have left us alone." He looked back up at the sloping ceiling. "Anyway, if I can't stop it this time, how can I ever stop it happening again?"

This wasn't an argument I would win. Besides, we were beyond exhausted, and needed to be awake in a few hours.

"I won't let you trade yourself for her," Lex warned at the ceiling, then. Because of course that was an option, if a lousy one. Kestrel for me. As long as Kestrel was safe…

"You may not be able to stop me," I said.

"I can damn well try."

So that was that. Lines in the sand. The one thing that could turn us back into enemies was the one thing we both loved more than life.

But we slept in each other's arms, all the same. His essence still felt wet between my legs, because neither of us had thought of a condom.

We weren't enemies yet.

Chapter 17

Simon was right. By the time the late-night travelers woke and had sandwiches, us included, the rain had stopped.

It should have been a relief.

Instead, it felt…malevolent. Not only the rain but the wind had vanished. I wondered if even the ley lines beneath us had washed to a stagnant stop. The sky had taken on an ugly, greenish cast. Nothing stirred—not birds, not rabbits, no hint of insect life.

"As if anything with half a brain is hiding," I muttered, as the five of us hiked across the muddy-but-drying foothills toward the Temple Caves.

"And yet here we are," teased Catrina. Injury or not, she seemed in a remarkably good mood, walking carefully beside Rhys. I suspected I knew why. The fact that Rhys had only met my gaze once over sandwiches, and blushed deeply when he did, made for a pretty good hint.

None of us said much until we reached the privacy of the

caves. A downside of the sudden lull in the weather was that anyone with binoculars and a shotgun microphone could capture everything we said and did.

Not every sniper positioned in these hills would be working for Nick or Lex.

But damn, this change in the weather felt ominous. As if the last few days had been the eye-wall, and now all of Europe lay in a false calm before even worse would descend upon us.

As if, at any moment, the world itself would stop turning.

Once we reached the safety of the caves, deep enough to foil eavesdroppers, that's when the conversations began.

"How close are your forces?" asked Nick Petter, who'd met us at the entrance to unlock the barred gate.

"Switzerland." Lex intercepted a glare from me. "Adriano said not to bring anyone into Italy."

"So the other women are in the temple, right?" I asked, having to get away before I lost my temper again.

Any attempts to rescue you or your daughter will result in dire consequences....

But Simon wasn't here as a target for my frustration.

Catrina and Rhys kissed again, before parting. This time, as he met my gaze, Rhys's expression was more one of amusement, probably because he was staying with the plan-a-military-coup faction. Rhys had once been a priest and, as far as I knew, was still a pacifist. But he was also a guy.

Catrina and I didn't say a word on our walk deeper into the caverns. But it wasn't an uncomfortable silence. Once we reached the others in the temple itself, with its nearly complete Black Madonna mosaic laid into the natural pillar in its center, we distracted ourselves helping the others piece together the faux-mosaic, laid out at the feet of the first. Both images were gorgeous, glorious. And yet the energy that all but hummed from the original somehow added to Her luster.

Who are you? I wanted to ask. *Thank you for helping Lex, but…* who are you?

Gaia, the Earth Mother? Isis, the Black Mother Goddess? Mary, Mother of Jesus? The Magdalene, Beloved Apostle? *Was* she a goddess, or simply a priestess or a saint? On all my previous adventures, I'd known who I was dealing with.

But this isn't just your adventure, I reminded myself.

A deeper wisdom said, *It is now.*

"We should drink from the chalice," I suggested, after the five of us had stood and gazed at our handiwork. "It's how the ancient Marians would worship her. I don't know about the rest of you, but I could use some inspiration about now."

And some guidance. And some comfort.

We sat in a semicircle, more than half surrounding the pillar with the Black Madonna, and passed the carved marble chalice from woman to woman. Catrina first. Then Aubrey, as she joined us. Then Tru and Eve. Each time, my lips moved in a voiceless plea beneath the temple cave's beating heart. *Show her something….*

Although each woman seemed to take strength from the ritual, nobody announced visions or insights.

Then it was my turn. "We are one," I whispered, raising the marble to my lips—

"We must start now. Of course all men shall not turn bad. But their values…without balance, we and our daughters, and their daughters, shall suffer unspeakable atrocities. We must create some kind of sanctuary, before it is too late."

The younger of the original two priestesses, dark-skinned and delicately boned, pleads with a cluster of

*women in this very temple room. Rather…what this
temple room would have looked like before the stalactites and stalagmites had been carved into glorious
adornment, before the mosaic. I do not see the older
woman, the one I believe is Mary Magdalene.*

Another priestess asks, "What does Mother wish?"

*Sarah says, "Mother says that she is old, and that
this is a challenge for the future. She says that we are
the future."*

*"My Lady would not allow such dark times to come
upon us," protests a lady of Norse paleness. A freckled
woman with a hint of red hair escaping her veil—Celtic,
I think—nods. "Nor mine."*

*"Foolish superstition," protests another, her blue eyes
luminous in the torchlight. "The Lady helps those who
help themselves. Why else would She have sent such a
warning to Sarah, but for us to act on it?"*

*"We know that this is Her heart." Sarah gestures at the
cavern around them. "To protect it will take lifetimes. But
it is our only hope of preserving Her, and Her children,
until the water bearer replaces the fish."*

*The Norse woman remains stubborn. "Mother must
have some opinion."*

*"Mother's opinion," states the older priestess then,
appearing in the doorway, "is that, faced with threat,
it is better to do something than nothing. We all die. The
test is how."*

*I can see the conflict on Sarah's face—her relief that
the others are beginning to nod, beginning to consider
her proposal for the great mosaic versus her frustration
that she needs the older woman to intercede.*

My eyes opened.

"Well?" prompted Catrina, a touch sarcastic. "Did the Black Madonna reveal her hidden secrets to you alone?"

"I didn't get a vision of the Black Madonna. Only Her priestesses." Briefly, I filled them in on my suspicions about the older mother-priestess being Mary Magdalene, as well as the legends regarding the Magdalene and dark-skinned Saint Sarah.

"Could an apostle of Jesus be a goddess worshipper?" asked Tru, more curiosity than challenge.

"Rhys has told me," said Catrina, "that Judaism sees God as beyond gender—and Jesus was, after all, a rabbi. Hebrew words for god can be masculine, feminine, singular and plural. They only default to 'he' because the language has no genderless pronouns, and most of the speakers were, themselves, masculine."

Just as a powerful woman might default to a feminine pronoun? By this theory, God was a parent—mother or father, equally.

"But what we really want to know," teased Eve, "is how close this particular apostle really got." We'd all heard the most recent debates. "And is this where the Marians began?"

"The priestesses are calling themselves Marians by this time," I admitted. "They aren't worshipping her."

But maybe the feminine face of God…

With no more insight than that from the chalice, we had to explore alternatives to the guys' rescue plan on our own mortal level. The harder we tried, the more painful the truth became.

Anything we offered would be about as dangerous as a rescue attempt, and with even less hope. As for the *when,* part…

Better to do it before the apocalypse than after. And as Eve and Tru agreed, the earth Herself seemed to be bracing for disaster.

When the men arrived to compare plans, the Marians and

I had no choice but to listen and to hope that their overall suggestion was better than ours.

In the end it wasn't. Not by much. But it was more…immediate. *Better to do something than nothing.* Maybe the priestess had been onto something, there.

"We do it *before* Maggi goes back," Lex insisted, after the initial overview of secreting their hired soldiers in from Switzerland. Nick Petter knew some routes. "At the same time Adriano is expecting her at the airport tomorrow, we move in on the complex. It gives us more element of surprise."

"No," I argued back—I knew he was trying to protect me, but he had to knock it off. "I've got to go back first, or the others won't know what to expect."

Aubrey shook her head over a whole different point. "No matter how many commandoes you can bring in, no way will a frontal assault on the compound succeed. You'll have to use the back way in, the tunnels. I'll lead you."

"But you can't be sure they haven't blocked that route since you and Max escaped last year. The element of surprise is everything, or else the gas…" That was Robert's contribution. His infant daughter Mara was the one who'd suffered worst from the previous release of gasses.

"The gas that killed the gerbil isn't explosive, in case you have to blow your way in," Eve assured us. "But without masks, the children couldn't last very long breathing it."

Finally I dragged everyone's ideas into a summary. "Let's say Aubrey *can* get the commandoes close enough to blast into the bunker where the hostages are kept." I felt like I was betraying Kes with each word. But I had nothing else. "It's always possible Joshua and Nadia have found a way in over the last week, as well. If we go with that, then tomorrow night's probably the best timing."

"No," said Lex. "You aren't going back."

But of course I was, and even he had to face it. "We don't know how much time will pass between me delivering the tiles to Simon and me getting back into the bunker, so we'd better plan for evening. I need to tell Ana and Olga what will happen before it does. And Eric, if possible," I added for Aubrey, who was apparently close to the bodyguard. "Them knowing what to expect could make the difference between panic and an organized escape. Especially with all the children involved. And as Nick said, we'd need to get everyone away from the wall you're coming through."

Nick rubbed his leg in thought. "I wish we knew which wall we'd be using. We'll have to devise a warning system. A knock of some sort."

"Which the guards may hear," said Tru.

"If we know what's coming, we can get the kids across the room in under thirty seconds." I tried to remember the size of the bunker and hoped I'd gotten it right. "That may be enough time to survive any gas released, as long as you bring in gas masks. And that's assuming Simon's quick enough on the uptake to respond immediately. If I could distract him—"

"No," said Lex, firmly.

Catrina's brows arched as she looked between us.

"Lex, I wasn't suggesting—" But neither was I crossing that possibility off the list, and Lex damn well knew it.

Even I didn't have the ability to face down his glare this time.

"You need to be with Kes when this goes down," my husband reminded me. Goddess knows, I'd be pissed if Lex was suggesting he seduce someone as a distraction.

"If I showed up at the front door," said Aubrey, "that would certainly distract Simon. He thinks I'm dead."

"Except that we need you to show us the tunnels," Nick insisted.

"But—"

"That's enough!" To everyone's surprise, that was Rhys. He hadn't said a word since we'd reunited in the temple room. He'd only sat against the cave wall and put his arms around Catrina, when she'd leaned back to listen. And really, what would a quiet-natured pacifist have to contribute to this?

Just as surprising, we all fell silent.

"Nobody sacrifices themselves," Rhys decreed. "There's a good chance that this will work, if you move quickly and stay together. But for every person who suggests going off to distract Simon—" he aimed a blue glare from Aubrey to me "—or to find the alabaster tiles that were stolen, there's someone else who will rush off to rescue *them,* with even more disorganization, more delays and more risk to everyone, including the children. Either you plan this for everyone to get out, or don't bother planning it at all."

For a moment we said nothing. You forget what kind of authority a priest—or even a former priest—can wield.

"Padre speaks the truth," said Griffin, who had some military training himself. He only winked at Rhys's glare over the nickname. "Let's keep it simple, folks. Thirty seconds warning should be adequate."

We really needed more information but we just didn't have it. So by the time we headed back to the farmhouse, we'd cobbled together something that only vaguely resembled a plan. A frightening, brutal, uncertain plan.

Or we had until the arrival of Max Adriano.

Chapter 18

"I can help you," was all the old man said, there on Rhys and Catrina's front stoop, using his neatly pressed handkerchief as a white flag. "Let me help you."

We couldn't let him say more out in the open. Not that Max Adriano—the man who preferred to be called "Myrddin"—looked like a physical threat. He was tall, thin, graying, pushing eighty.

But even a child can be a threat, with the right armaments. Boys and their toys. So Nick patted him down before bringing him inside. Greetings ran the gamut from Eve's affectionate hello to Tru's glare.

And Aubrey—

Aubrey had faded into another room, so as not to be seen still alive by an Adriano. Any Adriano. That made for as good a vote against pure trust as anything.

"What do you mean, help us?" demanded Griffin, once Nick indicated that it was safe to talk.

"You don't plan to go meekly like sheep to the slaughter, do you?" The old man seemed to realize that he wouldn't immediately be offered a chair. Our rudeness seemed to amuse him. "If so, I've woefully underestimated the ladies."

"If it's that obvious to you, then it must be that obvious to Simon," I challenged him. Honestly? I still hadn't gotten over how stupid he'd made me feel in Edinburgh. "Why would we do anything he's expecting?"

"Except that my son still thinks as I once did, that he can actually control people by threats. Even women. Even angry mothers. He hasn't the insight I was granted. My guess is you will need to get into the compound by stealth. And nobody knows that compound better than—"

"Nick and Robert," interrupted Catrina, from the doorway to the kitchen. "Keep watch on him, *s'il vous plaît*. The rest of us must speak alone."

"If I could bother you for some drafting paper," suggested Max, nonplussed, "I'll begin sketching the tunnel layout."

Rhys laid some paper and pencils out at the trestle table while the rest of us made our exodus. He then closed the heavy doors between the two rooms behind him as he joined us.

"No way do we trust the son of a bitch," hissed Aubrey, who was lurking near the back entrance. "He had my entire family killed, and Nadia's as well."

Griffin leaned back against the whitewashed wall. "I thought you rescued him from Simon's compound. Isn't that how you know the tunnel route back in?"

"He never told me who he was!" Aubrey didn't strike me as the forgive-and-forget type.

"Perhaps he was ashamed of who he'd been." Eve, like

Rhys and Tru, had sat at the smaller kitchen table. "Everything he told me proved to be correct. And, Catrina, didn't he help you in Paris as well?"

Catrina looked from Eve to Aubrey—but she was standing nearer Aubrey. "At least he did not slaughter my family."

Tru laughed, then looked embarrassed.

Eve said, "Myrddin—"

"*Max*," interrupted Aubrey. "His name is Maximilian Adriano. He was a member of the Hitler Youth. He and his father may be personally responsible for the Catholic Church not speaking out against the Holocaust—"

"The Church *did* speak out against the Holocaust," interrupted Rhys gently.

"Not as strongly as it could have, and it helped Nazi war criminals escape afterward, except that was Max, too. Max Adriano didn't just kill a few people. His commands murdered hundreds, probably thousands, and he turned his son into the monster who *stole your children*."

"And he's trying to make up for it, right now. If we let him. People can change," Eve insisted, looking to Rhys. If anybody would be into the turn-the-other-cheek, all-souls-can-be-saved angle, it would be him, right?

"People can change," my friend agreed slowly. "But not so easily as we might hope. We'd be fools to wholly trust the man without a better understanding into his conversion. But if we do accept that conversion…" Now he looked apologetically toward Aubrey. "His assistance could make all the difference."

"That's what he wants." Eve looked from one of us to the next. "To make a difference. To make up for—"

"He's done things he can never make up for," warned Aubrey.

"But we can let him *try*."

In the end, we headed back to the living area to judge the

old man's supposed conversion for ourselves. But none of us—not even a wearied Eve—had argued Aubrey's insistence that we had to search him much more closely for communication devices and to keep guard on him the whole way.

Lex and I exchanged a silent glance as we settled onto one of the old, comfortable sofas, vaguely relieved that for once, we weren't the ones providing the drama.

"Why I have changed," murmured Max, after Rhys—by group decision—presented our challenge to him. "I don't suppose any of you are willing to merely take my word?"

He smiled but didn't see much responding sympathy. At least Aubrey had stayed out of sight, in the kitchen, to listen in on this particular revelation without revealing herself.

"You can understand our reluctance," said Rhys, nonjudgmental but firm.

"I suppose I can, at that." With a sigh, Simon Adriano's father, the former Duke Maximilian, proceeded to explain. "Many of you have heard reports that I collapsed at an art exhibit in Portugal, several years back."

"But you did not collapse," challenged Catrina. "Joshua said you were shot."

"Both I and my dearest grandson speak the truth, Mademoiselle Dauvergne. I *did* collapse. The only misrepresentation given to the press was that I did so from age and weakness, and not because an assassin's bullet destroyed my chest. Only the uninformed would believe the lies. My family is renowned for dying only of violent deaths. Some call it a curse, like those of the Kennedy or Onassis families."

Again Lex and I exchanged silent looks. We'd discussed curses and powerful families ourselves, more than once.

"What fewer people know," continued Max, "is that the assassin did succeed, if only briefly. While doctors struggled to repair the bullet's damage, I died on the operating table. The experience is surprisingly similar to what one hears."

I felt Lex's whole body tensing beside me on the sofa, and didn't know why. Plenty of people are skeptics about near-death experiences, but I hadn't thought my husband was one of them. Was he sure Max was lying?

"I floated above my body," Max explained, "watching the doctors shock my injured heart in an attempt to restart it. I became aware of a tunnel, a bright light and lost friends and family waiting to greet me. Friends, family…and victims."

He hesitated—shaken, or putting on a nicely understated show of it—and Eve thought to pour him a glass of water. With a deep breath and a murmured "thank you," Max took a sip and continued.

"I apologize. I do not mean to be coy, but the experience defies earthly description. I find myself unable to name names, relay conversation…or even confirm that there was conversation. What I do remember is a slow, horrid clarity, a true understanding of my earthly evil."

"You had not noticed until then?" inquired Catrina dryly.

I think Rhys kicked her under the table. She scowled. Robert, standing over the table, continued to watch Max.

Max laughed, looking somehow relieved to do so. "I had certainly been aware that some people, through what I deemed ignorance or subjectivity, might label my actions as evil. But I honestly did believe that I was sacrificing the few for the good of the many, teaching people lessons they needed to learn. I believed that the majority of people would prefer to be told what to do, that my family had been granted special status, not just the ability but the *responsibility* to quietly run whatever we could."

The tension in Lex, beside me, had grown so palpable that

I took his hand in mine. He didn't seem to notice. I asked, "And your family's campaign against the Marians?"

"As a whole? The Adrianos have always believed the Marians to be fanatics—dangerous women proclaiming the existence of false deity, when the security of Europe depended on one God, on one holy, Catholic and apostolic Church. The Cathar Inquisitions, the Holy Wars of the Protestant Reformation, the bloody excesses of atheism within the French Revolution—all of those could have been avoided by simple conformity. We saw those devastations as a precedent for what would occur should the Age of Aquarius shift Europe's power base to a more fragmented, uncertain future, and we took it upon ourselves to interfere.

"As for me personally, and the individual Marians, I justified myself by targeting only those individuals whom I believed had wronged me or my family. Mistakenly, I know now," he insisted, holding up a hand when several of us started to protest at once. "Some women, like poor Aubrey de Lune's family, refused to hand over property to which I believed we had the better claim. Others, like Nadia Bishop's grandmother…well. When one is raised to believe that one deserves anything, that sense of entitlement stains many aspects of one's life."

"And what, exactly, do you believe now?" Rhys challenged.

"It is difficult, after so many years of rationalization, to confess one's sins." Max seemed to take some refuge in Rhys's gaze. "To face that one has been walking on the side of darkness, has taken pride from a family lineage that made an empire of doing the same. I was tempted to simply go into the light, to leave my messes for someone else to clean up. Instead, given a clear choice, I chose to return and attempt the task—I know it is impossible—of somehow atoning for my sins and, if possible, stopping my bloodline from perpetrating more and worse evils."

It was Tru who asked, "So why didn't you just kill Simon? Wouldn't that have stopped everything?"

"Murder my own son?" Max shook his head, staring at his hands. "So tempting, to believe the villains capable of anything. Bad enough that I held the gun that killed Caleb, despite that I did not pull the trigger—I shall mourn that boy to my dying breath. No, Miss Palmer, I was allowed back to *atone* for my evil, not to perpetuate it. You found no weapons on me because I will not risk taking another life, certainly not in defense of my own, for which I was given only temporary reprieve.

"I don't think you understand, ladies. I was not allowed back to save the world. That was never my destiny. It has ever, always, been the destiny of you, the Marians. I am only here to surrender my services to you, to do my small part in assisting you in your destiny without insinuating myself into it. I apologize if my struggle with that balance has, at times, made me less than forthcoming."

The rest of us exchanged silent, weighted gazes.

"I believe him," said Eve, at last. She looked relieved when her husband, Nick, said, "As do I. I think we can trust him."

Griffin said, "I don't *not* trust him, but…"

Tru made a face, and Rhys stepped in to clarify. "But we're not the ones risking our own children."

"I am." Robert Fraser never had sat—he stood over Max's shoulder. And he didn't address us. "My baby daughter's life is at stake, and my wife's. I'll trust you, old man. But if you betray me in this, I'll make you suffer into eternity. There won't be a corner in Hell where you can hide from me."

The old man nodded.

From the next room I thought I heard a door open. I knew

I should say something. But I was distracted by Lex's strained energy, beside me. *What was wrong?*

Catrina's cat walked in, as if returning from a day of mousing, and Cat picked it up. Perhaps thinking of Aubrey in the next room, she said, "I am less confused by his current beliefs than by how he could have believed otherwise, in his youth. How could he have been blind to his evil for so long?"

Max made a sound vaguely similar to a laugh, but not the least bit happy. "You would not understand the seduction of it, being told from birth that one's family is better by blood and ability than all others, until one must either believe it, or doubt the fabric of one's reality. To think oneself—to think *myself*—evil would be to admit that my father was a monster and my mother a victim, that my own blood stinks with such iniquity that nothing could ever cleanse it. Which life would you choose? No, you cannot understand."

"Some of us can," said Lex. "I believe him."

And he headed out the back.

Aware of everyone's gaze on me, the last parent not to weigh in, I said, "If Lex says we can believe him, we can."

My husband knows from powerful men.

But then I followed him through the empty kitchen and into the frighteningly still evening. Springtime in southern France should have been soft, gentle, heaven on earth. Instead it just felt…ominous.

Part of that might have been Aubrey, standing just outside. Her wet eyes reflected the starlight, but her jaw was set as she fondled a dagger. "Universal balance," she whispered under her breath, or something like that. "Balance is justice."

If the seven people inside couldn't protect Max from her, then so be it. I only nodded acknowledgment of her and kept walking. I found Lex by one of the outbuildings, in the direction of the orchard, standing with his back against the brick wall—and I don't think just literally.

Not unlike Aubrey, he was staring at nothingness.

Chapter 19

I couldn't have kept myself from going to him, from touching him, if I'd tried. I didn't try. At first he moved as if to shake me off, but I wouldn't let him. I rubbed his tight shoulders, buried my hands in his thick, gingery hair until he finally gave in. He leaned his forehead against mine, wrapped his arms around me.

"I love you," I said. It seemed important that I say it first this time. He relaxed even more against me.

"I love you, too."

Okay, so I knew that. But it never gets old.

The night seemed unnaturally silent. No crickets. No frogs. Mother Nature herself, waiting for the other shoe to drop.

"I never told you something," confessed Lex, finally.

My stomach sank. Crap. It was a too-tired habit to look over my shoulder, to make sure that Aubrey de Lune wasn't in hearing distance. Secrets and Lex were not my favorite combination. I tried not to tense too much in his arms. I don't think I wholly succeeded.

"There are a lot of things you never told me," I reminded him. About his business, his family, his life as a powermonger. "I knew that when I married you."

"The reason I believe old Myrddin, back there." And, no, it didn't escape me that Max had become Myrddin to my husband now. "Mag, it happened to me, too."

Okay. For this? I had to see his face. But I framed it with my hands as I leaned marginally back. I didn't want him to feel abandoned. "A near-death experience?" At his nod, I said, "After that knife attack, in New York?"

He shook his head. He looked…haunted.

"That time your cousin poisoned you?" The number of times Lex had nearly died might've seemed amusing except…it wasn't.

"No. Long before that. It happened during my bone-marrow transplant, Mag. When I had leukemia. I died on the table, just for a few seconds, and I saw things—things a lot like Myrddin did. I saw the misdirection my family had taken, and I saw the hope of what I could become, how I could fix things, if I could shoulder the responsibility."

"You were just thirteen."

He shrugged off his youth. "I always told myself it was a dream. That's why I never mentioned it to you. But part of me suspected it was more, and after hearing Myrddin in there… I think he's really going to help us get Kes back, Maggi. God knows, if I were him…"

Click. Now I understood the rest of his upset. *Being told from birth that one's family is better by blood and ability than all others.* "You aren't him."

"But I could have been."

"Okay, first of all? Your family and the…society they keep?" No need to start naming names, out in the open. "Sure, they're patriarchal, elitist and corrupt—which I realize is why you need to fix them. They consider themselves above the law, I know that, too. You say misdirected. I say evil. But you can't compare even their evils to the wholesale massacre the Adrianos have perpetrated over the centuries. And second? You never participated in that evil."

I deliberately did *not* make that a question.

"But I would have. Like my cousin. Like my dad. If I hadn't been shown differently, before I had the chance—"

"Then there's a reason you *were* shown differently. You also didn't have to accept the responsibility of trying to change them."

"Yes. I did."

"No. A lesser person wouldn't. But you did, and I adore you for it."

"Mag, I may have screwed up."

It's surprising, how much that startled me. My Lex, admitting fallibility. "How?"

"This past week, ever since they took you and Kestrel. Keeping it out of the press. Leaving work behind. Bringing in the mercenaries. Even I couldn't do all this on my own."

I don't consider myself psychic, not beyond a few half-lost goddess gifts and the standard woman's intuition, but I could tell I wasn't going to like this. "So no more talk about a vacation home on the beach, huh?"

His gaze slid dryly to me, as if to judge if I was kidding. I was. Even without coming from his kind of money, I could guess that one's own individual army, much less managing to move it invisibly into and out of countries, cost far more than even the best beach houses.

Not that money was everything. He had a job. I had a job.

If he lost every asset, we would survive. What worried me was that he was talking more than money. That's why I hesitated before asking, "So how deep are you?"

Because I feared the very answer he gave me. "I can't tell you."

That meant he'd gone to powerful men, the same group of men whose secrecy, not unlike that of the Adrianos, had almost destroyed our relationship. Lex was a leader in many ways—it's a long story—but not the kind of leader who demands things without agreeing to pay them back. And with a few of them...

"Your dad, huh?" I asked. "Your cousin?"

Just what kind of deal *had* he made?

Apparently even that would be saying too much. If Lex told someone he would protect names, he would do so. Period.

Finally I understood my discomfort about the expensive hotels, about being able to just buy a car when the rental lots were empty, about our free run of Chenonceau. It hadn't been so much that I didn't trust Lex to provide those things; it had been because, on some level, I realized there'd been strings attached when *he* got them. Much of his money came from family and associates neither of us fully trusted. He'd been making deals with the devil, and I'd been helping.

And yet, what was done was done. So I said the only thing I could. "I trust you to handle it." I pretty much had to, right? At this point, the only thing that mattered was Kes. Anything else could make for its own damned adventure, in its own damned time. When Lex still said nothing, I tried, "Apparently we each dislike whom the other might get into bed with to save our daughter, huh?"

His jaw tightened.

"Joke," I whispered.

"I love you and Kestrel beyond reason. I won't apologize for that."

"I'm not asking you to. Just…be as careful as you can. Okay?"

"Will you promise the same?"

"For you?" I drew a hand down his cheek, willing him to relax a little. "Absolutely."

"I hate this."

"Mmm. I couldn't tell." The stillness out here was starting to creep me out, even in the safety of Lex's arms. I trusted him to keep me safe. But with so ambiguous an enemy as a pissed-off Nature herself, I wasn't as confident about my ability to protect him. "So shall we go back inside to help with your overly ambitious rescue plan?"

"You still don't agree with it, do you?"

His gaze asked me to agree, but he needed my honesty even more. "Guns. Soldiers. Explosives. Doing exactly what we were warned not to…" I couldn't help it. I smiled a little. "Okay, so normally, I'd be up for that last part, but I'm too scared to flaunt rules just now, even his stupid, evil rules. It's not my kind of plan, Lex. But I don't have a plan, so…maybe that's why I need you."

His arms pulled me hard against him, his face in my hair, for a long moment. Then his hold eased, as if he was ready, and I turned for the door.

Except that he still hesitated.

"Is there something else you wanted to mention?" I asked, hating it when he did that.

"Nothing imperative."

"Oh. That makes me feel tons better." But actually, when Lex looped an arm over my shoulder and kissed my cheek, *that* did the job his words hadn't.

I did feel better.

Especially considering that in under twelve hours we would be leaving for Naples and sure separation, and only a *possible* reunion with Kestrel…and goddess knew what else.

Simon didn't call me the next morning…either because he knew he'd see me in a few hours or, more likely, to play with my head.

Lex and I took the corporate jet flown by Captain Harris. True to his promise, the grizzled old vet had brought the Hawker 800XP to southern France as soon as the weather cleared.

The captain honestly didn't seem to notice anything wrong with the deathly still weather. "It's not raining, ma'am," he pointed out from the cockpit way up front—needlessly. "In my book, that's all to the good."

Lex and I, holding hands across the narrow aisle between our luxurious leather seats, exchanged looks, but otherwise said nothing about it. While Harris knew a great deal of what was going on—that Kestrel had been kidnapped, that we were paying some kind of secret ransom—he didn't know about the whole time-of-transition, possible-apocalypse angle.

Lower-case a on the apocalypse. I hoped. Considering that our hopes for stopping said apocalypse rested on a mosaic of a Black Madonna figure that even I, champion of goddesses, couldn't figure out? Silence seemed best on that front. Even if we tried to warn people, what would we suggest? Where would the worst of it strike?

Halfway through the flight, Lex's grip on my hand tightened to the point that I unfastened my seat belt and joined him in his seat, on his side of the aisle. He restrapped both of us in—safety first—and wrapped his arms around me, and I laid my head on his shoulder and tried to relax. A large leather satchel sat at our feet, heavy with all the aged, faux tiles Tru Palmer had spent the week creating from ingredients Lex had acquired. She'd deliberately made some of the tiles more powerful than others, and packed those into the top and the bottom of the bag. That way, she'd explained, if Simon had Pauline feel the energy off of them by reaching in, or by spilling them all out and touching those from the bottom, she would hopefully sense that they were real.

Fingers crossed.

"I hate that you're doing this alone," murmured Lex as we started our descent toward the private airport outside Naples. Not surprisingly, his body was so tense it felt like rock against mine. "I wish I could go with you."

"And I'm so glad that you can't, I can barely see straight," I murmured. "I'm pretty sure Simon wants you dead."

"You think he won't kill you, too?"

"Eventually, sure." I tipped my head on his shoulder to better see him. "But neither of us will let it get that far."

Lex kissed me then, right through the landing that pressed me hard against him. It was the only way he could try to own me, even a little, even enough to keep me safe for a few minutes more.

As we taxied toward a stop, Captain Harris said, "Here comes company."

Per yesterday's instructions, he didn't cut the engines.

Lex unfastened our shared seat belt, and I gave him one more kiss on the cheek before he could open the door. *See you tonight,* I mouthed, holding his gaze.

He nodded, unfastened the door and lowered the steps. I had to use both hands to heft the weight of the overstuffed satchel as I made my way, with short hitching steps, to the tarmac. Sure enough, there sat a black town car, flanked by four black-suited Adriano henchmen.

One of whom lifted a rifle.

Crap! I suddenly knew that this wasn't just a defensive tactic—knew it as a familiar pain in my throat—even before it happened. I spun. *"Go!"*

The crack of the gunshot sounded a millisecond later, hitting the edge of the open doorway into the jet.

"Maggi!" yelled Lex, at the same time. At any moment the damned hero would leap out of the jet, and Simon would murder him, and I couldn't—

Yes, I could.

I dropped the satchel, wrenched it open, and pulled out a heaping pile of tiles, as many as my two spread hands could hold. They glittered in the eerily green sunlight, shone with flecks of ruby and copper, as I held them up.

"Put down the guns," I warned at a shout. "Let them leave, or I'm starting to throw these. Everywhere."

The gunman simply aimed the rifle at me.

"Maggi," I heard Lex warn, loudly, from inside the Hawker.

"And if these aren't all of them," I continued, "you won't even know it until you've spent hours collecting them and looking for the rest. If you've killed me, you won't have any idea where I hid the others. Do you really want to tell your boss that, with so little time left to the big moment, you may have permanently lost what he's been after for his entire life?"

They exchanged glances—but I had them. Of course, I *hadn't* hidden any of the tiles. This was all of them. But they couldn't know that.

The man who'd shot at Lex lowered the rifle.

Biting back a curse I couldn't quite make out, Lex drew

up the steps and closed the door behind me. The whine of the Hawker's engines grew louder as Captain Harris taxied away.

They wouldn't be going that far, I reminded myself, to battle a sudden surge of loneliness now that I'd gotten what I'd fought Lex for—him leaving me behind. But not that far. The mercenaries would already be waiting in northern Italy.

When the Adriano men came forward—with satisfying caution—to take the satchel, I let them approach. As the plane turned and started down the runway, gaining speed for takeoff, I even dribbled the tile pieces from my full hands slowly back into the bag. My palms tingled from the energy off them, right up into my wrists. Tru had done her job well.

"Is this all?" asked the man I recognized from my previous visit as Sergio. The one who'd almost shot young Laurel Fouquet.

"I don't have to answer to you." I watched the Hawker take off as if I were really that confident of my own safety. "I'll tell Duke Simon if that's all of them."

That knowledge, after all, might be the only thing keeping me alive.

But only me.

Again my throat tightened, with a sensation I recognized as my own, goddess-given internal warning system. *It really was back!* I screamed pure rage, pure horror—

And saw the pilot's window of the airborne plane explode under the single gunshot from behind me.

Captain Harris slumped.

The plane dropped.

Lex!

Chapter 20

Goddess help them.

With a burst of jet power, the Hawker righted itself in midair—and its nose went up. But...

There was blood, and maybe worse, on the smashed window. Captain Harris was still down.

Lex had to be flying it, from the copilot's chair.

I figured all this out in the space of a blink. In the next blink I spun and kicked the satchel from a distracted Sergio's hands, spilling tiles across the tarmac—gold and silver, opal and lapis lazuli...

And my booted foot came down over the center of them.

Only my long practice with Tai Chi enabled me to hold my balance like that, without any actual weight on that foot. "Stop the sniper or I'm grinding them to dust."

"The duke still has your daughter," warned Sergio.

"And *I still have his answers*. The secret of the seventh key.

The location of the missing tiles. Don't forget how badly he wants those, wants them for something I'd normally die to stop. My daughter is his last hold on me." I made myself breathe. Breath is strength, life. "If he wants me to believe I'm buying her more than a few hours, then you'll have your sniper *stand down!*"

We glared at each other—but no more shots were fired. Yet.

I bent deliberately forward at the waist, as if to throw all of my weight onto the crushing of these tiles.

Sergio raised a single fist high in the air, a signal to *stop*. I'd won this round.

So I stood down, too, and arched a hand wide toward the sky in a slow wave. With the edge of my vision, I saw Lex's plane give me a slight waggle of the wings. Nothing flashy. Not Lex. Just a tiny acknowledgment that we were okay.

For him to fly away showed more trust in my abilities than I could ever have expected.

But I still noticed when Sergio swung at me. I wasn't so distracted that I couldn't spin, on the one foot that held my weight, smoothly out of his way.

Did anyone think I hadn't been practicing my Tai Chi in hotel rooms, farmhouses and temple caves over the last week? I'd needed it for stress relief if nothing else!

Having braced himself to connect with me, Sergio stumbled against nothingness. That's the beauty of Tai Chi. You don't so much hit back as you just let your opponent's attacks slide past you, as if through water. You let him do all the work. You stay insubstantial, play his weakness.

Speaking of which…

"Ah-ah-ah," I chided, pointing at his feet. "Mind Duke Simon's tiles."

Sergio was standing on them. He blanched. It was a testament to Tru's craft that none of them seemed to crack. Still, I backed deliberately away from the men, each step careful and soft. *Move with tranquility,* my sifu would say.

Showing his teeth, Sergio followed. As if trailing after me put him somehow in charge.

The plane, I noticed peripherally, was barely a speck in the sky. Lex had gotten away safely.

"Now that that's done," I began—

Throaty instinct warned me of the man circling behind me—instinct and maybe the heat of his body, the sound of his breath. Again I pivoted, sank away just enough that he connected with nothingness.

I'd forgotten something important about men, bad men especially.

They really hate losing.

"Um, guys?" Now three of them surrounded me—and all three came at once. I had to move quickly to stay insubstantial, dropping low between two of them, rolling through tiles as I did. The tesserae bit hard into my palms as I swept my legs around, tripping a suddenly vulnerable Sergio to the tarmac by hitting the right balance points behind his knees.

He fell hard. I finished the roll on my feet—and with two handfuls of tiles. "Don't we have business with the—"

Crap.

They came at me again, and I couldn't get that insubstantial. I threw the tiles into their faces and used that distraction to bolt for the town car. If it was like Lex's, I might be able to lock myself inside so that even the driver would have to break a window to get in.

I reached the car's sleek, black side, yanked the handle.

Unfortunately, also like Lex's town car, it hadn't been left unlocked.

I turned, trapped between four pissed-off henchmen and a luxury automobile, my stomach sinking. But, hey, I'd been through childbirth. That hadn't exactly wimpified me.

In fact, it pretty much convinced me that I was stronger than any guy here.

When Sergio grabbed first, I turned easily out of his grip, nudged his overly extended wrist into a painful bend, and launched myself up and over the hood of the car. I'd rolled off the other side well before Adriano's men could circle the vehicle, and quickly scanned the airport around me for some kind of temporary sanctuary. It's not like I wanted to escape. What I wanted was to see Kestrel, to see Ana and Olga and the other children. That meant getting these guys to take me, without detours or get-even breaks, back to—

The crack of a rifle shot ended that idea. A sharp pain in my shoulder startled me. So did the poof of orange plastic fringe suddenly protruding from me. Well *crap*…

As I had behind the antique store, barely a week before, I dropped to my knees on purpose, then to my butt, in a race with the tranquilizer. I didn't like the gleam in these men's eyes.

"The duke won't want sloppy seconds," I warned them, my words starting to slur toward the end, the world starting to stretch.

But then I was out. Out—and completely helpless.

I woke to a sharp slap on my cheek, then another one, and finally winced away with a thick, "Nooo."

Nightmare? Dreams? Memories?

Another slap established reality, and I glared blearily—at Duke Simon himself.

"Ah, Mrs. Stuart. I see that you have returned to us." His eyes narrowed in warning as he straightened. "Stay that way."

A surge of adrenaline helped clear more of the lingering, swooping drug from my system. I half lay, half sat slumped in one of the chairs in the duke's book-lined office, still fully clothed. My elbow hurt, and one cheek, probably from where I'd hit the tarmac. I didn't think I'd been gang-raped by Simon's henchmen, but I wasn't going to start squirming to find out.

I did have a vague memory, maybe only a dream, of Simon backhanding someone into a wall. *Idiot! We are on a tight enough schedule as it is.*

It took concentration to form my mouth around words as Simon paced to the bar. "Did you hit Sergio?"

"You caused far too much trouble this afternoon. If any of the tiles you scattered about have been damaged…"

"He's the one who stepped in them."

The slice of Simon's gaze, over his shoulder, told me how unlikely he was to put up with that kind of conversation. The fact that I had to struggle to even stay awake dampened my concern levels, though. *Breathe in. Breathe out. Blink.*

When Simon asked, "Would you care for a drink, Mrs. Stuart?" I answered, "Something with caffeine, please."

Normally I'm a bottled-water and fruit-juice gal. But I really did need to stay awake. The duke obligingly opened a small cola bottle and poured its fizzy contents over ice. Hopefully, with his *tight-enough schedule,* he wouldn't roofie it.

"Where's Kes?" But I figured that out on my own, even as Simon paced. The office was as I'd remembered it, with the dominant desk, the glass doors looking onto a now-sunny patio, and another chair. Again the waifish Pauline Adriano sat with big-eyed silence, barely fingering her necklace, as if not wanting Simon to notice she was actually there. Since he hadn't offered her a drink, I half wondered if it was working, but he was probably just being mean. The big, flat-panel monitor sat on the small computer desk to the side. On that monitor I could see, though a fish-eye lens, the stretched figures of Lexie Bishop playing beside Benny Adriano and Phillipe Fouquet—dark and light. Of Olga and Ana with their heads bent over baby Mara.

And of Laurel Fouquet carrying my daughter Kestrel on her ten-year-old hip.

Kes. *My baby.*

According to the ever-present, inch-high countdown, we had almost two hours before the code would need to be input to stop another release of gas. But was I watching a recording, or was she really there?

Goddess, it had been almost a week!

Simon shoved the cola glass none too gently into my hand. This was no time to get distracted. He'd clearly worked himself into a temper even before smacking me awake. "We have wasted enough time. You told my men you had answers I would want. Did you hide some of the tiles, against my explicit instructions?"

"No."

He stilled, clearly surprised.

"I told them that because they were trying to kill my husband." I took a sip of the cola, and it did help clear my head. "Was *that* against your explicit instructions?"

"My people are reconstructing the mosaic as we speak," he warned me, without answering. "It had best be complete."

"Of course it's not complete, but that's not my fault. The alabaster pieces to make the jug are missing. Your men were there when Signora di Spedalotto took them from me, back at Chenonceau."

Pauline gasped.

Simon blinked. He still wasn't handsome, not exactly.

His nose had too much of a hook to it, and his eyes were a shade too narrow. But there was something disturbingly sexy about him. Power, I guess. Power can do it for a woman, almost every time—unless she knows what to watch out for.

"Signora *di Spedalotto*," he repeated slowly, and their reactions encouraged me to pursue my own theory.

"Your wife," I challenged. "Right?"

With an angry jab, Simon said something in rapid Italian into an intercom, then turned back to me. "And what of the seventh key? Why must I bother to keep seven Marians alive in order to use this mosaic?"

That part, I wasn't so ready for. But I needed him to keep the Marians—especially the children—alive. So I spitballed.

"Here's the best I've figured out. Originally there must have been one figure, the deity who became the Black Madonna whom this group of Marians worshipped, with the key and the sword. I still haven't figured out exactly who she represents. What I do know," I added quickly, at Simon's obvious impatience, "is that according to legend, Mary Magdalene came to France accompanied by Mary Salome and Mary Jacobe. The worship of the one Black Madonna had been around before that, but it seems to have grown significantly on their arrival. Three Marys. You with me?"

The arch of Simon's brow warned me not to condescend again.

"The sixteenth century seems to also have been important, probably because of Europe's religious wars. That's when Mary Queen of Scots came into the picture, but she didn't travel alone. She had four ladies in waiting, coincidentally also named Mary. They were called the Four Marys. With the queen, that made five."

"This doesn't make sense," whined Pauline, but Simon raised a slow hand.

He might be evil, but he wasn't at all stupid. "One," he repeated, warming to the theory. "Then three. Then five."

"I doubt you need seven actual Marys," I clarified, for all of us. "The name may be figurative, for seven Marians."

"And if my great-great-grandchildren must use the power again, they will need nine."

"That's the theory." Actually, it wasn't half-bad, for something I'd pulled out of thin air. "I don't know why, other than the magical qualities attributed to odd numbers through the millennia."

Simon extended both hands to me. Still not clear-minded enough to risk rebelling, I put down my nearly empty glass to place my hands in his. He drew me to my unsteady feet— and smiled. "You are a pleasant surprise, Mrs. Stuart."

It felt like a punch in the gut, his smile was that powerful.

"Well done," he purred.

And he kissed me.

Pauline mewed a kind of protest—jealous?

The honest truth? He wasn't half-bad. He didn't have a lot of technique—probably never needed it—but he made up for that in confidence, which really can be sexy. But that said...

Lex Stuart had more confidence, and more technique, in his pinky finger. And since Lex was my husband, I should know from sexy. I smiled in actual relief—and Simon must have seen something of my true thoughts in that smile, because some of his own smugness faded to annoyance. He dropped my hands and retreated behind his desk. "However, you failed at your primary task, which was to retrieve the Mary Stuart tiles—"

My throat hurt. "I told you, Signora di Spedalotto—"

"Do not lie to me, and do not use that ridiculous name! That woman is no more capable of—"

But then the door to Simon's office opened, and we all got to see firsthand exactly what Signora di Spedalotto was capable of. Because the exquisitely dressed woman stood right there. She shut and locked the door neatly behind her, in the faces of several unusually pale guards, and turned to us.

Simon began to swear—I assume—in Italian, but stopped so abruptly that I knew *something* was wrong. I looked closer—and saw that the signora had something in her hand.

It seemed to be a grenade.

From the way everyone was acting, I assumed she'd already pulled the pin. I'm into mythology, not armaments. But even I knew what that meant.

As long as she held the grenade, we were all safe. But if her hand opened…

The term, at least for lawn mowers and Jet Skis, is "dead man's switch." If an operator is suddenly incapacitated, the machine stops operating. Now I knew where this phrase came from.

If Signora di Spedalotto was suddenly incapacitated, the grenade would go off.

And we would *all* stop operating.

Chapter 21

I looked toward the flat-panel monitor, where I'd avoided sneaking too many peeks at Kestrel lest I be unable to function otherwise—and I thanked everything holy, for the first time since I'd regained consciousness, that she wasn't here with me.

"If you wish to kill yourself," warned Simon, ironically polite enough to still speak English, "do it somewhere else."

The signora laughed harshly. "Kill myself?" she echoed, then launched into angry, shouting Italian.

I turned to Pauline, beside me. "Translate."

She widened her doe eyes at me. But when I glared, she made an attempt. "She often has wished to kill herself. Since their first year of marriage, since Simon allowed his father to teach her a lesson."

Simon glared at us both, and Pauline lapsed back into silence.

Seeing this, the signora reverted to English, as if she relished having as large an audience as possible. "To teach me a lesson about the role of women in your family—while you watched! In this office. *Over that desk!*"

She gestured, her free hand shaking as she did, and moved her accusations to Pauline. "Do you think you are the first Adriano wife to be taken by your father-in-law?"

My stomach twisted to realize that she was talking about genial old Myrddin—no, *Max*. Aubrey had been right. The man had committed more crimes than seemed forgivable.

"No—you are only the first to want it!" the signora continued to her husband's lover. "I never did. Never! But that did not matter. Nothing I wanted ever mattered."

Now she turned to me, maybe for understanding. "But I had vowed before God, good times and bad. And then the children came. Children are God's blessing. I had to live for them. But he—" a gesture at Simon "—he took them from me!"

"You exaggerate." Simon reached for the intercom button.

Signora di Spedalotto—Signora *Adriano*—lifted the grenade in threat.

With exaggerated patience, Simon let his hand fall. His narrow eyes warned that his wife had best succeed at blowing him up or she would regret the consequences.

His wife was beyond caring.

"We all lived here, *the same house,* but how long did I go without seeing them, once their voices deepened? Weeks? Months?"

"You were too often in Paris," Simon reminded her. "Or St. Tropez. Or Lake Como."

"More often I was not. And then—" her dark, wild eyes glittered with tears "—then they started dying. *Push yourself,* you kept telling Aaron, until he pushed himself into the grave! And Caleb—despite your twisting, he had a chance at love, at healing. You turned it to suspicion. You turned it into a madness, a murder he could never forgive himself, until he took his own life—"

"His was not the only hand on the gun. You cannot know—"

"He was my son! Dead like his brother. And now Joshua. You would kill him before you would see him choose love over your precious destruction. But I will not allow it. You have kept me invisible, kept me powerless, for our full life together. But I am neither now!"

I was tempted to say, *You go, girl!* Except…she was holding a live grenade. That was a pretty desperate measure, and I didn't know her well enough to trust her with it. Especially with phrases that tend to inspire high fives.

Especially when she said, "You have dreamed of your great moment for as long as I have known you. I wish to watch as your plans become nothing."

And she extended the grenade in a trembling hand.

"Wait," I interrupted. "Signora, shouldn't we get the children out first?"

Once she turned her husband into a faux finish for his den, all bets would be off. Angry guards could massacre the hostages. The gas could be released—the countdown on the screen gave us an hour and a half—and nobody could stop it. Not to mention, the grenade was as close to me and Pauline as to Simon.

That's when the older woman turned her maddened eyes to me and said, "You think I mean to let *you* live?"

What? "What have I done to you?"

"You hurt me! You let your husband push me into a wall—hard! You tied my hands!"

"Because you came at us with a gun! You stole the tiles I needed for my baby's safety!"

"You have all hurt me," she insisted, with a gesture that

somehow grouped me with Simon and Pauline Adriano. "You must all die with me."

"And with your grandchildren? Joshua's children are down there. Benny and Lexie. If Simon's dead, they might die, too!"

She said, "Better that the Adriano seed die here and now."

Crap. I'd forgotten how dangerous it is to sympathize with a victim, at least so completely that you forget how very cruel victims' pain can turn them. Abusers were usually once abused themselves—that's how they learned it. The dogs people kick are the ones most likely to bite. And this woman—

This woman was no longer a frightened bride, broken by her vicious husband and father-in-law. Nor was she simply a deserted mother, mourning the various losses of her children. I did not discount her tragedies—I ached with every reminder of them.

But the signora was now threatening *my* child, trying to make *me* a victim.

I had no intention of waiting decades to deal with that.

"This is not the only power left to you, signora," I said as gently as possible, praying that a goddess might guide my words. "The power to dominate over others is seductive, but it's nothing compared to our personal power, our ability to survive, our ability to choose for ourselves. If you only think for a moment, really think about those innocent children trapped beneath your home, and your ability to help them—"

"Silence!" She had no intention of thinking about the children at all.

So I had to. But I needed a distraction.

As Simon's wife launched into more excited Italian, I nudged Pauline's slim ankle with my booted foot. She widened her already large eyes at me, unaware of what I needed, completely useless. So I had to meet the gaze of the one man with whom I'd never meant to ally myself.

Simon had the nerve to look amused. But he also had the intelligence to know what I needed. With a last, disgusted look at his wife, he yanked open a drawer in his desk, winning her full attention. She spun, gasped—and in that moment of startled recognition, before she could consciously react, I grabbed her hand. My own fingers closed hard over her slackening ones, before they could fully open and drop the grenade.

She cried out at the betrayal, a victim to the end.

The bark of a gun splattered me with warm blood—and worse—finishing the ordeal. Signora Adriano's body sank heavily to the tiled floor. I bent with it, not releasing the deadly prize in her hand. My horrified gaze found Simon's cool one.

With a satisfied nod, he put the pistol back into his desk.

"Be silent," he commanded Pauline, who was screaming. "And unlock that door before—"

Too late. He swore in Italian as his guards kicked it in. The door hit the signora's body. Somehow I kept my hold on the beringed hand covering the grenade.

The signora's dead hand was all that stood between me and some goddesses of death.

One of the guards eased the explosive from me, his hand sliding into place as it forced mine away. Suddenly freed of that responsibility, that horrible power, I fell back on my butt, shaking. *Crap, crap, crap.* What had I just helped do?

I'd had to. I would do it again. But still…

"You didn't have to kill her," I accused, when I recognized the hands helping me to my feet as Simon Adriano's.

"I believe I did. You may clean up in there." And he gave me a slight shove toward a private bathroom off his study. "I have sent a man for one of my wife's blouses, so that you may change clothes."

Just what I wanted—to wear the dead wife's clothing. "Why do you care?"

His expression hardened. "I am unaccustomed to showing gratitude, Mrs. Stuart—take what I offer you with grace."

Since it got me away from him, I shut myself into the bathroom, away from Pauline's wails, away from the removal of the body, away from Simon's sharp demands for explanations from his guards. I stared in the mirror at my blood-freckled face, and my trembling ratcheted up a few degrees.

Shock, insisted the logical part of my mind. *Caffeine. Stress. Those damned tranquilizers.*

My logical side had me stripping out of the shirt I'd put on that morning, using clean patches to swipe across my face and hair before I dropped it. I turned the sink handles and stuck my head under a warm rush of water from the goose-neck faucet. I scrubbed my hair and face and neck with scented hand soap. Only when I turned off the water and wrapped myself in a couple of large, luxurious towels did I realize that some of the warmest water came from me.

I was crying.

Signora Adriano had forced me to help her commit suicide—suicide by husband. Duke Simon had goaded her, over decades, to that level of desperation. And the life she'd led...

A powerful man's wife. Despite the clear contrasts between Lex the hero and Simon the villain, I couldn't help feeling shaken by the equally clear parallels. Lex's mother had also killed herself. My mother had worried that, by marrying Lex, I might get equally lost. I'd been sure I could handle it, of course, or I wouldn't have married him.

But in the year and a half since our marriage, what had I

done with my own life? I hadn't gone after any goddess grails. I'd cut back significantly on my teaching hours.

Feeling stronger, I began to scrub my hair dry. None of that had been against my will. And to be honest, none of it had been for Lex. All of it had been for Kestrel. Kestrel, who apparently could survive, at least for short amounts of time, without me, and thank heavens. *Kes*.

She was somewhere *right below me*.

I was almost surprised when one of Simon's men returned, as promised, with a silk blouse of the type a fashionable woman in her sixties might wear. I was even more surprised when, as soon as I'd dressed, I was led to exactly where I wanted to be.

Down the stairs…

Through the hidden gallery of antiquities…

Past the alabaster jar that called to me from its lit display case—I did feel its draw, but a stronger draw demanded my full attention.

Into the bunker.

"Maggi!" exclaimed Olga, as the guards ushered me in. I heard the door being shut and locked behind me, but I didn't bother to look. I was too busy striding to Lexie's nanny—who was holding Kestrel—and taking my baby into my arms for the first time in a week. *My baby*. Mine.

A homecoming. A completeness.

Kestrel.

"Mamamama," she babbled happily up at me, as if she knew what the word meant. I buried my face in her sweetness.

"Yes, baby. Mama's here. Mama got here as fast as she could."

Kes continued to tell me about her week, I assumed. I continued to drink in her scent and her weight and her presence like ambrosia, like nectar from a goddess grail. It took everything I had not to hug her too tightly.

My baby.

Kes…

Too soon, I had to talk to the others, as well—they deserved to know where I'd been, what I'd been doing, how I'd gotten back. It was easy to convey messages from parents to anxious children, from Robert to a tired-looking Ana. I openly told both of the adults as much of my adventures as I assumed Simon knew.

"You gave him the mosaic tiles?" demanded Ana, horrified.

"All the Marians voted." I willed her to be patient until I could fill her in on the secret details. "We weren't willing to sacrifice our loved ones."

To which Ana had no comment at all. She was probably as conflicted as I'd felt, before Tru's brilliant idea for the faux mosaic. She would not want to endanger her child, any more than I wanted to endanger mine. But the cost…

More difficult, of course, was the task of privately informing Ana and Olga about tonight's rescue plan. I got Ana alone over the changing table, whispering only the basics. Olga I managed when Kestrel—fighting the restraints of my arms until I put her down—crawled with superbaby speed to the woman who'd been caring for her during my absence.

"Thank you for watching over her," I said, heartfelt despite an ugly kernel of envy, and gave the older woman a hug. Only then did I whisper, "We have to teach the children to run to the left wall on our signal. The guys are blasting through the right wall tonight."

She quickly schooled her expression. "You're welcome," she assured me, as if I'd said nothing more than thanks.

If either Ana or Olga disagreed with the rescue plan, they had no chance to say so. Everything else, I reminded myself, could be explained after our escape.

Assuming we did escape.

But we had to.

Olga's the one who thought of a running game, from one wall to the next, kind of like "red light, green light." The children took to it pretty quickly, even little Lexie, who seemed to have latched on to Benny as her closest friend. Despite his continued sense of distance from the other children, he cared enough to take her hand and help her with the game.

It was something.

The afternoon carried a strange sense of dualism. On the one hand, I felt more contented than I had all week because I was with Kestrel again—feeding her, changing her, talking to her, holding her arms so that she could walk. No wonder ancient women worshipped their god in the form of a mother. I'm not sure any force could really surpass this power.

On the other hand? Kestrel and I were being held hostage in an underground bunker, by a powermonger determined to use us to destroy much of Europe. According to Max Adriano—who claimed to have gotten the specifics off a Mayan astrological calendar—the time of transition would indeed take place at dawn on Monday, less than thirty-six hours away.

At which point, Simon would realize the counterfeit we'd given to him.

Lex and the other men had been right. We had to be long gone by then, no matter the risk.

But where were they? Had they even gotten safely into Italy? Had Max actually taken them down the correct tunnels, or had he led them into an ambush? What if they didn't make it?

Not for the first time I wished I still had that ability I'd gotten from the goddess Isis almost two years earlier—the ability to sense where my husband was.

Sometime after our early dinner, after Ana had granted the children a little extra time to stay up and color, Kestrel blinked awake, heavy in my arms. "Dada!"

"Mama," I corrected her gently. "I'm Mama."

It's easy to read more into a baby's expression than could possibly be there, but for a moment her blue eyes seemed impatient. "Dadadadada!"

"Mama," I repeated. "You're Kestrel and that's Lexie and that's Olga and I'm—"

"Dadada!" She began to wriggle, wanted down.

A sudden, startling possibility struck me.

I'd been pregnant when Isis first gave me the ability to sense where Lex was. I'd lost the ability after giving birth to Kestrel, a child conceived in a ritual honoring Isis.

What if...?

"Dadadada!" she insisted, reaching for the wall behind me. That's when I heard the distinct signal, three taps, against the wall.

One one thousand, two one thousand...

"Green light!" I called quickly, for the benefit of the older children. Ana and Olga knew exactly what that meant.

It meant we had less than thirty seconds before the wall came down. Thirty mere seconds during which Simon might recognize something was amiss—and release his deadly gas.

Seven one thousand, eight one thousand...

Herding children before us, we ran for the far side of the bunker.

Chapter 22

"Big boom," warned Ana to the children we sheltered between our bodies and the far wall—just as the force of the actual boom pulled the floor out from under us.

It knocked us into children and the wall, both. But not hard enough to hurt anybody. Nobody flew across the room. No rocks rained down on our heads.

That's why Lex hires experts.

The smaller children began to scream—except Kestrel who, after a funny squeak, kept up her mantra of "Dadadada!" The older children—Laurel, Phillipe and a big-eyed Benny— recovered with slow, stunned silence, looking to the adults to judge our reactions amidst the new turmoil.

"Go with them!" I insisted, echoing Ana's and Olga's shouts. We quickly gathered the children toward the billow of dust resolving itself into a now-missing back wall. Each of us held a baby, Olga's Lexie being the oldest, but that

left us each with one hand free—and, as mothers everywhere know, you can do a lot for children with one hand.
Olga had Benny Adriano by one arm. Ana hauled Phillipe
Fouquet to his feet by the belt. I managed to keep a comforting hand on Laurel's shoulder as I guided her. "They're
here to save us!"

Admittedly, the men in gas masks, anachronistic amidst
the playhouse and toys, looked almost too big and hard to be
good guys. But among them were others, their own masks
hanging down their backs just in case—

"Nick!" exclaimed Phillipe, breaking free of Ana to drag
his sister toward their adopted parents. "Aunt Eve! You'll
never guess what happened!"

Nadia Bishop and Joshua Adriano made it to Olga's side,
surrounding her, Lexie and Bennie in a group hug. Barely had
Robert Fraser appeared through the dust than he was half
gathering, half carrying Ana and baby Mara toward the tunnel
past the rubble.

And Lex—

"Dadada!" trilled Kestrel, even as her father's arms surrounded both of us, hard and sure and alive and *there.* I remembered a week ago, fearing that I couldn't fight properly with a
baby in my arms, wishing Lex had been there to do the fighting
for us. And here he stood, plaster dust in his hair, his eyes suspiciously bright as he pressed his face into Kestrel's neck.
He'd made who-knew-what-kind of devil's bargains to pull this
off, overcome his own instincts to let me come ahead alone.
Now here he stood, fighting for us with everything he had.

"Come on," he insisted then, after barely a breath, and drew
us back toward safety even as the door into the bunker flew
inward and gunfire spat. Lex pushed both of us to the floor
while the mercenaries made short work of the first wave. I

crawled across the debris toward the tunnel with Kes, Lex's body blocking us from further gunfire.

But I couldn't go much farther.

Not yet.

"Christ," my husband breathed, as soon as we'd made it to the safety of a sharp bend in the tunnel, beyond the fallen wall. "Oh, Maggi. Kestrel—"

"Dadada!" exclaimed Kes for him, and I was thrilled to be there to see Lex's face register our baby's confidence in using this name for him. One of his rare smiles lit the tunnel, brighter than the halogen lanterns. I loved them both so much at that moment, it made my chest ache.

And I couldn't stay with them. Not quite yet.

"Take her." I shifted my baby's weight into the arms of the one person I knew, beyond doubt, would protect her as surely as I could. "I'll catch up."

"What? No—Mag!"

"Get her out of here!" I called over my shoulder. Nadia, Joshua and Olga were already hurrying their children to safety, as were the Frasers and the Petters. Lex had no choice.

I didn't stay to see his look of betrayal.

The scene in the bunker was madness. Three of Simon Adriano's guards lay dead. One of the mercenaries had gone down across a plastic play table, the dark wetness of bullet holes tracked across his front. When I saw that horrible, familiar yellow mist sliding into the room from the ventilation ducts, I felt for his pulse and, feeling nothing, fumbled for his mask. It fitted clumsily over my face, but it was better than nothing. Apparently, I wasn't the only one to go back. I saw the small, dark form of Aubrey de Lune vanish through the now-open doorway into the gallery beyond, shadowed a moment later by the taller form of…Max Adriano?

Crap.

I followed and ducked behind a column just in time to avoid another round of gunfire from the far door as Adriano guards flooded into the gallery.

"Clear the line of fire!" shouted one of the mercenaries.

So I dropped to the floor and crawled, from display case to display case, toward my goal. Occasionally I caught glimpses of what else was happening.

Aubrey had reached the vault doorway, pressed against the wall beside it, where the guards rushing in didn't immediately see her. From that vantage point, she managed to grab the arm of one of them, a man who hadn't yet raised his weapon, and to yank aside—

Eric Cabordes. Benny's old bodyguard. The one Ana had called "a good enough guy." From the way they kissed, quick but deep, Aubrey thought he was good enough, too.

But the Adriano guard who came through the door behind him—

"Look out!" I screamed.

Two of the mercenaries behind me opened fire, taking down this newest threat. But not before he'd done his damage.

Not before he'd discharged his weapon right into Max Adriano, who stepped between the lovers and an Adriano guard he'd probably hired himself.

The old man looked ruefully down at the bloom of red across his front before he crumpled.

Now our mercenaries were moving out the round, second door to secure the hallway and the stairs—and, to judge by the gunfire, encountering more resistance. One of them, rushing past me, shouted, "Get the fuck out of here so we can pull back!"

I fully meant to.

But I had one final goal. I loved being a mother, being a wife. But I really did have one more responsibility. I was also a grail-keeper. Not *instead of* being a mother and a wife. But *along with*.

Grabbing a pistol off the floor I straightened and shot the side out of the display case that had taunted me since my arrival. The pane pebbled, then collapsed. And beyond it, on glass-littered velvet as if caught in a freak hail storm, sat the ancient alabaster jar.

"Precious Oils," read the brass plaque beneath it. "Mary Magdalene."

But part of me had already known that.

Eric Cabordes staggered past me with Max Adriano slung over his shoulder in a fireman's carry. Aubrey de Lune raised one curious eyebrow at me as she followed, covering them. And me?

I grabbed the jar, with a sense of absolute rightness—as if it had been waiting for me—and I followed them.

Only once we reached the safety of the tunnels, now devoid of the children and the other escaping Marians, did Eric lay Max Adriano—Myrddin—gently onto the stone floor. That gave us a chance to strip off our humid gas masks and ready ourselves for the final evacuation.

Several halogen lanterns remained, likely left for us. In their unforgiving light, the slim, gray-haired old man, once the terror of Europe, lay white and trembling.

Dying.

I'd once had something of a healing touch—another gift from the goddess Isis—and reached for his wounds, but Myrddin shook his head before I could try. "No," he gasped. "It is time."

Eric was on one knee beside him. "Come on, old man. Let me carry you the rest of the way out. There might be medics."

Myrddin jerked his head in the negative. "It's not enough…can never be enough…"

I said, "Of course it can." But when I reached for him again, it was only to pet his graying hair away from his agonized face. His piercing eyes searched mine. "It's as much as you could give. That's the best we could hope for, right?"

Myrddin's laugh came out as a cough. "Thank you," he gasped, ever polite. "For your honesty."

"Thank you for helping save our children. It means more than you can ever know. It means everything."

I recognized his slow blink as a weak version of a nod.

"Not over," he warned us. "Monday. Dawn. Ultimate… test…" An edge of blood stained the corner of his mouth. "I must trust…the Marians…enough—"

Again he coughed, crying out at the spasm of it—and I wasn't the only one to support his shoulders. My gaze met Aubrey's, over the head of the man who'd murdered everyone she'd held dear.

"Trust that they…will win…" he whispered, and pulled a wry smile. "Without me."

"It won't have been without you," I assured him.

I had the sense that he focused on me only by the sound of my voice. "Natasha…" he gasped. "Forgive…"

Then he was gone. Eric's fingers gently closed his eyes.

"Who's Natasha?" I asked Aubrey in the sudden silence.

"Should I know?" She scooped up one of the lanterns. "If we don't hurry, the bus will leave without us."

Considering that the others had the children, they *should* be willing to leave without us. But it would be a lot easier if they didn't. So the three of us hauled ass. Aubrey led the way, being the only one of us who'd come this way before. Stairs became tunnels became more stairs. I noticed that I wasn't the only one to look over my shoulder, toward where we'd had to leave Myrddin behind.

Not over.

Crap.

We raced for the bus just as it was starting to pull away from the back road outside the Adriano compound—whether the driver was doing that as a "hurry-up," or whether they'd been about to leave, I didn't know and I didn't ask.

It was a touring bus, the kind that charters out, with front and rear doors, large seats, a private toilet. But this one also had mercenaries. Some were already onboard and the others, at a signal from Lex, appeared out of a stand of gnarled olive trees to swing through the rear entrance right behind us. Aubrey and Eric collapsed into seats toward the back. With an apologetic wave to the other relieved faces turned my way, I made my way with the Magdalene jar to where my husband and daughter waited.

Then Joshua Adriano mouthed, *Max?*

Unlike the rest of us, he'd always known Myrddin as Max. He'd probably loved him as Max.

I shook my head in answer, hesitating in the aisle. I should tell him how selflessly his grandfather died.

Joshua nodded, just once, and turned back to his own family. Explanations, it seemed, could come later.

This was a time of reunion. For most of them.

But for the Stuart family…?

Wow. Was Lex ever pissed. The glare he directed at me was second only to the glare he directed at the alabaster jar, which I secured carefully into the net pocket on the seatback ahead of me. What I wanted to do was to carefully wrap it—it was two-thousand years old and, if genuine, priceless. But one priority at a time.

Who would've guessed family time could trump a religious relic?

"I'm sorry," I whispered as I sank into the aisle seat, almost as much to Kestrel, shouting a baby hello from her daddy's lap, as to my husband.

"No, you're not." Lex radiated disapproval.

But you know what? I was so damned glad to be there, to see him and our baby together again, that arguing held no temptation. Actually, the fact that I'd been able to do something he'd resisted soothed a lot of my concerns about marrying such a powerful man. Because I was a powerful woman.

Anyway, I'd have been just as angry at him, had our roles been reversed. That gave me a glimpse of what might help.

I touched his hard arm, where Kes could reach for me with her chubby, damp hand. "I'm sorry for making you feel like this. I'm sorry for not leaving with you right away—I wanted to. I'm sorry I was the only one who could go after the jar. I'm sorry there were people shooting when I did."

He said nothing. And whatever Kestrel was telling us, in her role as moderator, was unintelligible.

"And I'm sorry I fought you on the rescue idea," I admitted. "You were right, Lex. You saved us."

He watched me for a long, conflicted moment, then said, "Hold the baby."

Confused, I took her into my arms—at which point Lex scooped both of us up and over his lap, ending with him in the aisle seat and me and Kes secured between him and the shaded window.

Kes laughed a delighted baby laugh at the clever maneuver. I was tempted to do the same, except for the tremor I'd felt in Lex's strength.

"This way I'll know where you are, for a while anyway,"

he whispered. His feigned nonchalance would have fooled most people. But I knew Lex Stuart. He wouldn't relax for a long time yet. If something had gone wrong in this operation, he would have blamed himself.

So I said, "You did it."

"We lost three men. Four, counting Captain Harris. Five, if Myrrdin died."

I nodded confirmation to that. With him so close, I glimpsed the flash of anguish in his golden eyes before he could fully tamp it down. "Did you force anyone to go on this mission?"

Lex didn't deign to answer that. Of course he hadn't.

"And you paid them well?"

He all but rolled his eyes. Of course he had. I also knew that anyone left behind by the mercenaries' deaths would be well compensated—as well as anybody can be, after losing a loved one.

"Whatever you planned to tell me about Frank's death," I said, about my lost bodyguard, "tell yourself that about these men. We'll live with the guilt together. Was losing four men the worst-case scenario?"

Every child had made it out alive. Across the aisle and behind us, Robert Fraser held his sleeping infant, so small that an arm was free for his wife. Ana's head was on his shoulder, her eyes closed with exhaustion, if not sleep. Ahead of us, Phillipe continued to regale Eve and Nick with his enthusiastic interpretation of everything that had happened over the last week, while Laurel seemed content to let Eve brush and braid her hair. Nadia Bishop and Joshua Adriano sat nearest the forward group of mercenaries. Lexie and Benny were beginning to droop in their laps. Olga kept watch across from them.

After a long moment, during which he fingered Kestrel's

curls, Lex admitted, "No. This was the best-case scenario. Mag—"

Then his arms came around me and Kes both and I let him pin us back against the window shade and just hold us for a while, shivering against us almost imperceptibly. I gave him the privacy of not trying to glimpse his face, half-hidden in my hair and against my shoulder. I know that I shed a few tears against him.

Together. We were all back together, because of him. I'd never considered myself the sort of person who had to be rescued, but thank the goddess I'd married someone who couldn't completely leave that old-fashioned idea behind.

Anyway, I'd rescued him several times in our relationship, too. He was due. If it still made me a little uncomfortable, well… I just had to get over myself.

Eventually he drew back, seemingly puzzled until he caught a glimpse of the unusually silent Kestrel, now asleep in the roomier safety of my lap, her thumb in her mouth. Lex blinked several times, quickly, with a flash of real smile that he transferred from his daughter to me.

Then his eyebrows arched, as if he was really seeing me.

"Where did you get the granny blouse?" he whispered, amused.

Which is when I remembered everything else.

"Crap," I whispered back, before I could stop myself. Luckily, Kes *was* asleep. But it's amazing how quickly the bad language had come back, after only a week without her. "Joshua."

Lex waited for me to clarify.

"I've got to tell Joshua Adriano what happened to his mother."

Chapter 23

"She was supposed to have been in Paris."

None of us mentioned already knowing that, although Joshua had said it more than once. If he'd realized his mother had returned to Italy, he would never have left the compound without trying to find her. The fact that she'd already been dead by then did little to assuage his guilt.

He didn't seem to blame me for my role in disarming her. But a coldness had come over him, to hear that his own father had fired the shot that killed her. I hadn't mentioned everything the poor woman said before that point—nothing about what Max had once done to her, nothing about her accusations to Pauline. I could mention them to Nadia later, sometime in privacy, and she could judge what he needed to know.

In the meantime, Nadia was the person Joshua needed now, not me and not Lex. Already she had her arms around

him, studying his profile with an understanding only a lover—
a soul mate—could give.

But as Lex and I rose to give them privacy, I hesitated.
"Joshua?"

The youngest of the Adriano sons lifted his agonized
gaze to mine.

"I know your mother's maiden name was di Spedalotto.
But—what was her first name? Her real name?" The one that
had belonged to neither her husband nor her father. I'd never
heard anyone use it, not once.

Not even her.

His expression softened. "Her name was Traviata."

I nodded, grateful, and followed Lex—with Kestrel—back
to our seats. At least now I knew what name to use when I
prayed for her poor, lost soul to finally find peace.

We had plenty of time in the bus for prayer. And for sleep.
And then for examining the Magdalene Jar, once dawn
brought us more light, before I would carefully pack it into
several clean diapers for safety.

It felt…holy.

Well, it *should.* Especially if it had really belonged to Mary
Magdalene. The words *Messiah* and *Christos* literally mean
anointed one. And the Magdalene was a keeper of holy oils.

Worth a year's wages, I mused, slowly turning the beautiful jar, admiring the design carved in a band around it…a
time-worn scrollwork that could, if you looked at it right, rep-
resent a circle of women holding hands.

I counted. Twice.

There were seven of them.

"So what's in it?" asked Ana, looking better this morning.
Little Mara still had a faint cough, souvenir of Simon's first
gas attack, but Eve had examined her. Other than a cold, the

infant seemed unharmed. Besides, now Robert was there to share Ana's concerns.

"If the Adrianos labeled it accurately, it's perfumed oil," I said. "Or what used to be. It's probably turned by now."

"Even if it's holy?" teased Eve, who'd come back to see what we were doing.

"I'm sure it was accurately labeled," insisted Aubrey. "The Adrianos were obsessive about that sort of thing."

"It seems to be sealed with wax." I ran my fingers down the curve of the jar's side once more, admiring not just the glow of pure alabaster but the power that shivered through me. *Definitely* holy. "We probably shouldn't open it until we reach the temple."

"Sacred space," agreed Eve.

And the one place, more than any, that we had to reach before dawn the following day. Myrddin had warned us that it wasn't over, despite the rescue. We had to believe him.

I carefully wrapped the jar.

The drive to Lys from Naples would usually take about twelve hours. But instead of the autostrada, we took plenty of back roads, lengthening the journey but lessening the chances of Adriano forces intercepting us.

When I asked Lex why they'd chosen against flying us out—other than Captain Harris's death—he reminded me that they had no way of knowing how long the weather would stay clear. "You're not the only Marian to feel a sense of threat in this lull."

"I'm not a Marian at all. Kestrel is. I'm a grailkeeper."

The glance Lex slid toward me at that was unreadable. But Kestrel's fussiness, probably from the excitement, gave us sufficient distraction. In any case, his decision proved itself when storms began to gather near the French border. By noon the weather crashed down on us like a god—or goddess—slapping flies.

The eye of the storm was over. Mother Earth was no longer waiting. Whatever Simon Adriano meant to do to her ley lines, she seemed determined to wash it away, violently if necessary.

Finally we reached Catrina's farmhouse, although the final, winding drive made the bus tip in a way that had the older children—and some of the adults—staring out the windows in concern. Apparently the driver knew what he was doing.

The enthusiastic welcome from our friends waiting for us had to be cut short—we had to reach the Temple Caves as soon as possible. The time of transition that Max and Simon had gotten from their stolen artifact wasn't until dawn, which—assuming dawn came at all—was some hours off. But neither could we predict what might happen next.

The Adrianos had claimed responsibility for other natural disasters, over the centuries. Earlier earthquakes. Pompeii.

They hadn't had inverted tiles to power those, either.

No, we still needed our mosaic to work her magic on whatever Simon could still throw at us. Worse, if he really wanted either a working mosaic or seven Marians, he knew where to find both.

So as early goddess worshippers had centuries before us, we packed together what belongings we could and took to the shelter of the caves. It was too hard a hike for all but the oldest children, and even they were tired. Most ended up being carried by their fathers. Eric the bodyguard carried Benny Adriano, shoulder to shoulder with Joshua, who held a smaller Lexie in his arms. I kept stealing glances through the sheeting rain at the different family groups around us—and at Lex, who barely let Kestrel's nose and eyes peek out from under his blowing rain poncho. His strength was helping even now. His wealth was why we had our own guards here, stationed through these hills, watching for snipers. Lex was the reason we'd dared rescue Kes in the first place.

Lex had been right, and I'd been wrong. And I wasn't used to that. The me-being-wrong part, I mean. The me needing him so very much, not just because I loved him but for my survival, our baby's survival. How often had I used the words "all-powerful goddess" in invocations and prayers? How long had I believed that, in the end, feminine strength would trump masculine strength?

And now, here we were doing perhaps the hugest piece of goddess work I'd ever seen in modern times—and I was here because of Lex. Not me, keeper of the goddess grails. *My husband* and, through him, my daughter.

But I did have my role.

Our little band of refugees let ourselves in through the locked gates. We checked the caves for intruders and set up air mattresses and sleeping bags near the temple itself. But once the children were dry and tucked in, I dug out the jar and kissed Lex's cheek.

"You need to rest," he murmured, from where he'd leaned back against the wall beside the mattress where Kes slept, her thumb in her mouth. Only occasionally did she sniffle, as if getting Mara's cold.

"You be rested," I compromised, drawing the jar from its clean wrapping. "I need a little more preparation."

He groaned. And I took the jar and a lantern into the temple room.

The underground rhythm of the spring's water feature continued, steady and soothing as a heartbeat to a newborn. The black-featured Madonna smiled down at me, aglow with ancient gems and metals and precious stones, completed except for the small spot between her eyes and the wide patch of negative space near her feet, where Mary Stuart's tiles should have shown the jug. Was it supposed to symbolize the holy ointment of Mary Magdalene, or the jar of Aquarius, the water bearer?

Was there even a connection? Maybe the truth was in the middle.

"Show me," I whispered. "Help me understand."

Kneeling before this representation of the Lady, I fumbled at the lid of the jar. How to get it off without—?

"Ah," interrupted Catrina, from behind me. "You mean to destroy another one."

Just what I didn't need. "The jar wasn't in situ when I found it," I reminded her. "I didn't move it from its historical setting."

"I imagine the Adrianos had a thorough provenance on it, even so. Until now. And yet I am the one thought to be a thief."

Someone else cleared her throat—Aubrey de Lune. Catrina actually smiled at the retired antiquities thief. "But that depends on one's perspective, *n'est ce pas?*"

Aubrey actually smiled back.

"Speaking of perspective," I noted, "with the likelihood of who-knows-what kind of disasters hitting in just a few hours, maybe insight is a tad higher priority than provenance. So if you'd give me some privacy—"

Tru came in. "Hey, a party." To judge by the artist's workbox in her hand, she meant to have one more go at patching the blank spots on the Madonna mosaic. "Where's the booze?"

I stood. "If everyone needs to be in here, I can go meditate somewhere else."

"Let me have it." Catrina extended an imperious hand.

"Why?" So that she could take it from me?

Her eyes narrowed. "I have done more archeological work than you. I believe I am better able to open it."

We held each other's gaze for a long moment.

"As you say," she challenged. "Priorities."

So I offered the jar. She drew an unlikely Swiss Army knife from her pocket and, as I held the jar, she carefully, even lovingly scraped most of the wax sealant away. The alabaster warmed between our hands.

"*Voilà,*" she murmured at last, moving her hands so that I still held the jar. "Now try. Carefully."

As if I would have just whacked it on a rock otherwise? I gently turned the lid. It stuck, just for a moment, then slid open and out, followed by the rich scents of... "Frankincense and myrrh?" I guessed, with a grin.

It hadn't spoiled. After millennia, the oils hadn't turned.

"Yes, with cinnamon," said Ana—which is when I saw, peripherally, that the other Marians had joined us.

"*Cassia,*" corrected Aubrey. "Slightly different from cinnamon leaf. More Asian."

"And something else," murmured Nadia. "Sort of a musky, sleepy smell…"

"Spikenard," I suggested. According to the Gospel of John, the precious anointing oils were spikenard.

Catrina said, "'While the king sitteth at his table, my spikenard sendeth forth the smell thereof.'"

The rest of us stared at her. Of all the people I'd never expected to find quoting the Bible!

"It's something Rhys sometimes says to me," she murmured, and I wondered at just what times, then wished I hadn't.

"It's the Song of Solomon," I clarified, focusing my thoughts.

Apparently, Catrina knew that. "Which some believe is the

source of the Black Madonna. 'I am black, but comely, oh ye daughters of Jerusalem.'"

The sexiest book of the Old Testament had been written centuries before Mary Magdalene—or Jesus—had ever been born. Which answered nothing. "Okay, I've got to have some quiet time with this jar."

"Not to drink from it?" challenged Catrina.

"I was thinking anointing made more sense." I slid a finger into the oily bowl of the jar.

Catrina winced, and for good cause. If this oil had been precious back around 33 A.D., what was it worth *now?* It's not like there was that much of it. The others watched, their expressions reflecting fascination, longing, exhaustion. And on instinct, instead of raising my finger to my own forehead—

I raised it to Catrina's.

She nodded surprised permission. So, beneath the silent acceptance of the Black Madonna, I slid the salve across her forehead.

She closed her eyes, bowed her head…and smiled.

I turned to Ana, who lifted her chin in acceptance, and did the same. Then Aubrey. Eve. Tru. Nadia.

Nobody spoke, though they exchanged encouraging looks. Their exhaustion seemed to recede, their spirits seemed to rise. And I tried really hard not to feel disappointment. So it wasn't a goddess grail—no big deal. If this was all the ointment did, it would be enough.

Then Catrina took the jar from me, slid a finger into the oil. I let her silently smear some of the fragrant ointment between my brows, and—

Voices. Too many voices, some soft-spoken, some ringing with passion, all of them powerful beyond comprehension.

I dropped with a groan of…pain? Sort of. Not quite. It felt

as if I'd flown into a zillion pieces. But I recognized the impact of my knees on stone.

"Maggi!" I sensed more than saw Eve come to my side, but I raised a hand to keep her away. Instead, I fumbled for the jar. Catrina kept a firm hold on it as she tipped it toward me, allowing me to scoop more oil. I rubbed the oil between my hands, turned toward the mosaic and drew them down my face, down my neck, into my shirt, popping buttons, uncaring as I spread it over my chest, the tops of my breasts. The perfume wafted around my head.

And the voices dragged me under, as surely as the River Cher at full flood. But I didn't drown. Instead, I just…*knew.*

Everyone, everything fit together like the pieces of a mosaic, each piece of vital importance—Isis. Sophia. Inanna. Diana. Juno. Aphrodite. Hekate. Astarte. Kuan Yin. Morrigan. Demeter. Persephone. Shekinah. And, yes—Allah and Jehovah and Vishnu and Christ. Each of them. All of them. Every time someone better understood any of the faces of God—which included Goddess—they strengthened a whole that was greater than the sum of its parts. And that whole, beyond its individual facets, beyond the cultures and names, was…

Love.

Oversimplification, sure. I sensed far more than that. I caught compassion, forgiveness, integrity, kindness. But if I focused on the whole, instead of the pieces, it really did come down to love. The vicious love of a protective mother, attacking anything that threatened. The selfless love of a martyr, letting go, letting God. The hot lust of sexual love. The pain of filial love, holding parents' hands as they slowly vanish. No one kind usurped the other. But all of it…

Love beyond comprehension. Sentient love.

"Maggi!" Then Lex was there, kneeling beside me, gathering me into his arms, and I was back in my body and being lifted by his. Eve may have been content to hold my wrist, monitor my pulse. Not my mate. I was the priestess, prone to visions. He was the warrior, prone to action.

I smiled into his concern, my head on his shoulder as I blinked back to full reality. "It's okay," I assured him. "I love you."

He looked even more worried. I should say it more often.

"It was a Goddess thing," I assured him. "Or a God thing. *Same* thing, this time. If this really was the Magdalene's oil, her beliefs didn't contradict Christ's ministry. Not my understanding of it, anyway."

"That's a relief," said Rhys, who'd apparently followed Lex in. When Catrina arched an eyebrow at him, he didn't back down. "It *is*."

"But it didn't contradict the idea that the Black Madonna was an ancient mother deity, either. In fact—"

"Stuart!" called someone impatiently—and from the way Nadia took off, that someone was Joshua. "Come *on!*"

At Lex's moment of hesitation, I wriggled free of his hold. Luckily, my legs managed to support me and to keep pace with him as he strode after the call. "What is it, Lex? Who's with—"

But as we left the main temple, I saw that Olga was sitting between the mattress with Lexie and Benny asleep on it, and the mattress with Kestrel. She made it easier to keep walking.

"One of the guards called for us," Lex explained, lengthening his stride to catch up with Josh and Nadia. Nick followed, fully armed, along with Eve. The others stayed with the children.

"Apparently," said Nick, "we've got company."

Welcome to Monday.

Chapter 24

I slowed when Joshua, with his head start, came to an abrupt halt at the mouth of the cave. While my throat didn't clench in full-out warning, it hurt to swallow. So I wasn't quite as surprised as the others when I could finally see who stood in the pounding rain, surrounded by our guards, on the other side of the barred entrance.

We didn't have just any company.

We had Simon Adriano.

He'd raised his hands, but with an attitude of complete control. Four men had machine guns pointed at him. To judge by the rumpled state of his trench coat, he'd already been searched—and none too gently.

Somehow, on our territory and in our power and soaking wet, somehow he looked more dangerous than ever.

"Sir," the head guard greeted Lex. "He said you wouldn't want him cuffed."

"He lied." Lex slanted a concerned glance toward Joshua. He needn't have worried.

"We should kill him where he stands," spat Joshua, while a guard wrestled Simon's arms behind him for the cuffs.

"Son—" began Simon.

"You're already dead to me." Joshua turned away, strode back into the darkness of the cave. "I am not sure you were ever alive."

He and Nadia didn't go far. They were as curious as the rest of us. But they gave Simon no hope of using them for sympathy. So his sharp gaze settled on me.

"Mrs. Stuart. Not the best behaved of houseguests."

"Try 'prisoner,'" challenged Lex.

I thought that, rather than a pissing contest, it might be better to figure out why he was here. "Hello, Simon. Don't you have an appointment to wreak death and destruction on innocent heads in a few hours?"

Hopefully, without the real mosaic he could only work injury and damage.

"Did you think so massive a shift could come down to the flip of a switch, the pull of a lever?" Simon's smile condescended. "It has already begun. It began before you came to me. I've fed the Earth illness, power outages, earthquakes and storms and despair for over a year. The destruction scheduled to burst along the ley lines and into France, Switzerland, Germany, Belgium…it can no longer be stopped. Even with a flawed mosaic—and yes, I did discover your little fraud—I believe Europe will have reason to pay attention…especially when you agree to dismantle your own mosaic."

That was on par with saying, *We're about to crash. Unfasten your seat belt.*

"Or," I said, "no."

Simon shook his head. "But if you refuse, I will not share the location of the antiserum for my newest strain of the Spanish flu. The one with which I infected the hostages, as of Saturday morning."

Nobody interrupted now.

"I fear you missed out on that, Mrs. Stuart, but even should you not catch it—and it's quite virulent—I imagine you'll suffer beautifully just from watching your baby die."

Nick surged forward, but Lex extended a single hand to stop him. "It's a bluff."

Behind us, I heard Eve turn and race back into the caves to check on the children. If anybody would recognize a new epidemic, it would be the fabled Flu Hunter.

"Not all gasses," Simon reminded us, "are visible."

I looked over my shoulder in the direction Eve had gone, increasingly afraid. We'd commented earlier today about how fussy our daughters were. Baby Mara still had her cough. Kestrel had developed sniffles. Even Laurel and Phillipe had complained of being tired. We'd assumed it was the stress of the day, but it could be…it *could!*

Nadia spun and, grabbing a stunned Joshua's hand, followed after Eve.

I hesitated only a moment longer. "Lex…?"

"We won't kill him yet," my husband assured me, with a coolness that couldn't hide his desire to do just that. "Just in case."

And since the bad guy was cuffed and held at gunpoint, and Lex and Nick were more than competent to keep him that way?

I did the same thing the other mothers had done. The same thing mothers always do.

I went to my child.

The adults and half the children were already awake. Eve

was using a stethoscope to hear Lexie Bishop breathe, when
I arrived—and the blankness to her hazel stare clearly gave
no comfort to the child's parents. She moved on to Benny,
who buried his face into his father's neck in grumpy protest.
Then she came to Kestrel, who slept in my arms right through
the examination.

"I should have looked closer," Eve murmured to herself.
"I should have seen…"

It was all I could do not to nudge Kes to consciousness,
just to reassure myself that my baby *could* wake up. *She's
always been a heavy sleeper,* I reminded myself. *She was
overexcited today.*

But I couldn't quite drown out another, uglier voice: *If
you'd let Lex rescue the hostages earlier, this wouldn't have
happened.* Saturday morning, he said.

I laid my cheek on Kestrel's red curls and inhaled her, my
breath catching.

"Aunt Eve, what's wrong?" Ten-year-old Laurel rubbed
her eyes. "Why does it matter that my throat hurts?"

Eve must have sensed all our gazes, heavy with fear. "They
are coming down with something," she admitted, too steadily
for real comfort. "And it's not dissimilar to last year's epidemic."

Laurel gasped. She and her brother had lost their mother,
Eve's sister, in that outbreak.

"And last year's epidemic?" I'd read the articles in the
news magazines, seen the footage of temporary morgues in
the Swiss village where only a quarantine by the European
Center for Disease Prevention and Control had kept the
outbreak from turning into a modern-day Bubonic Plague.

"It had a much higher mortality rate than the Spanish Flu
of 1918," Eve admitted matter-of-factly, and, I thought,
equally horrified. "Especially among females. People were

dying within twenty-four hours of falling ill. We developed an antiviral medication for it, but if this strain has been too severely altered, it's anybody's guess."

"But you can heal them, *n'est-ce pas?*" That was Catrina, standing beyond the cluster of parents and children. "As you healed Nick, Eve. As you healed me."

"I—" Eve's eyes shone, as close to panic as I'd ever expected to see her. "The energy isn't here. The ley lines. When I 'walk into' people, to heal them, I draw on the positive power of healthy ley lines. But it's gone."

"They can't be *gone,*" protested Nadia. "Ley lines are eternal."

At the same time Tru said, "Oh, crap."

Apparently, she saw whatever Eve did. Or worse, she saw its absence.

"The lines are still here," insisted Eve. "The channels. But the energy in them is receding. Like the ocean draws back, before—"

"Before a tidal wave," whispered Ana.

It has already begun, Simon had said.

Tru's eyes widened. "You mean, it could come back at us all at once?"

"And I can't access it," agreed Eve, her voice hollow. "I can't even heal."

"Da," murmured Kes, turning her sleepy head vaguely in the direction of the cave entrance—which was a ten-minute walk away.

I said, "Company."

Sure enough, Nick and Lex—and two of our armed mercenaries—appeared, dragging Simon Adriano between them. They stopped at a safe distance, just near enough for me to see that Simon wasn't just wet with water now. Blood ran from his mouth, his nose—a blood that matched the smears on Lex's knuckles as well as Nick's.

And Simon still held his head up, as if despite his swollen face, he was still in charge. Considering what he'd just done, maybe he was. To be here, he also had to be desperate.

I was glad of that, deep inside. I wanted him desperate.

"We thought all the parents deserved to make this decision," Lex explained, his voice echoing against stone. "And we didn't want anyone to have to leave the children."

His eyes found mine, found Kes in my arms, and he must have read my concern. Even his tamped-down fury vanished behind a complete mask.

I moved toward Simon like a sleepwalker, only remembering I had Kestrel in my arms when Lex stepped forward and took her from me. Our baby made a happy grunt before curling into her daddy's chest, her chubby legs drawn up.

I stared at the man, the *thing,* who'd valued destruction so thoroughly that he'd done all of this to us, and to his own family, and—as of morning—countless others.

And I spat at him.

Simon jerked back, between his captors' grips, and I saw a real emotion flare into his gaze. *Disdain.*

As if I were a bug who'd happened to sting him, a vexation, nothing more. That is what we Marians had always been, would always be to his type. What *women* were. Pets, when we were useful. But absolutely nothing when we were not.

No. He really had nothing in common with Lex.

"I shall see the mosaic now." He ignored me like just such a bug. "I mean to watch as you ladies destroy it."

Tru folded her arms, approaching with several others from where they'd left the children with Eve, with Rhys. "Has anyone ever mentioned that you're *insane?*"

"As are you, if you believe I would leave such things to chance. When Dr. St. Giles interfered before, our men escaped with a canister of the virus. What use would I have for it, but to ensure my moment? I did have an antiserum made up this time. I left it in Marseilles, not three hours' drive from here. If you know exactly where to look, you have time to fetch it back before any of your precious offspring start to die. That is, if you leave very, very soon."

"In return for the mosaic's destruction," I clarified.

"Otherwise, I say nothing."

"And you die." That was Ana, leaving her baby with Robert.

"Along with the location of the antiserum. Remember that I have dedicated my life to this goal. I have lost sons." He looked toward Joshua as he said that, then shifted his glare to Lex. "Apparently since your departure my assets have been frozen and my business reputation…sullied. What do I have left? If you should actually stop me? Mutually assured destruction provides as good a consolation prize as any. However—" His chin dipped, as if he meant to check his watch. In handcuffs, he had to count on memory. "I believe we've barely an hour before the world must accept her change. So you'd best begin dismantling your little arts-and-crafts project. *Now.*"

"We may not be able to get to Marseilles," noted Nick. I hated that we were even considering this. "Roads may be down. There could be fires, floods."

"Your lot have proven annoyingly adept until now." Simon looked from one of us to the next. "At the point that the transition begins, the offer is rescinded. You will simply have to take my word about the antiserum."

"Sure," I said. "Because you're so damned trustworthy."

I had his attention again. "No, Magdalene. Because you, all of you, are *so damned needy.*"

A new voice interrupted us. "Needy? Is that all you see?"

"Mama!" Benny Adriano tore himself from his father's arms and raced past stalagmites and columns toward our latest intruder. "Mama!"

Pauline Adriano looked half-drowned, her arm in the tight grasp of Eric Cabordes. She began to take a quick back step from her son, as she had in the bunker. Then perhaps she saw her once-chic pantsuit sticking to her skinny frame, her necklace dripping water into her cleavage. Her shoulders fell in acceptance. Her hand even lifted toward Benny's head, but she dropped it before it touched.

Benny grinned from her to Eric, completely missing the bigger picture. But he was only five.

"Grand Central Station," murmured Tru, behind me.

"She says she followed the duke," Eric explained. "I thought she—"

"Impossible," dismissed Simon. "She does not have it in her to track anybody, much less not be seen doing it."

"I only followed you to the caves. I came ahead this far." Pauline wiped a wet hand across her wet eyes. "I left after you killed your wife. You didn't even hesitate, Simon! You didn't—"

"If you came ahead," I challenged, "why did you come here?"

Her doe eyes met and left mine, then found and veered away from her ex-husband, then from Nadia. She finally found Tru. Pauline's voice quavered. "I didn't know where else to go."

Without her child. I tried to tell myself that not everybody can be strong. But mothers should be, damn it. They *should* be.

It was Nadia, not Joshua, who filled her in. "Simon says he infected the children with a virus, Pauline. He says he'll trade us for the antiserum."

Pauline's eyes widened. This time she did touch Benny's head. "But he...there is no antiserum."

I backed into Lex, eliciting a squeak from Kestrel. No. As awful as the idea of dismantling the mosaic was, the idea that there wasn't even an antidote—

High mortality rate. Especially females. People dying...

"You know nothing!" hissed Simon.

Pauline shook her head. "I do! I have been listening. I have tried to be part of your life, of your future for so long, and I have paid attention. I was there when you told Caleb to be careful, that this time there could be no cure, no vaccine."

"Perhaps I lied to Caleb."

"But you would not even go to the labs, even two weeks ago, for concern that—"

Simon lunged at her, as if to silence her by force. She cringed back. The guards on each arm stopped him quickly enough.

"There is no antiserum," repeated Pauline, eyes welling with tears. "Because you never loved anyone enough to need one. Not even me. And now..." Her gaze dropped to Benny, then lifted to her ex-husband. "I'm sorry, Joshua. You deserved more."

No antiserum. I turned on Simon. "Tell me you didn't really infect the hostages." As if I could trust anything he said. But this couldn't be right, be real. The world couldn't be so cruel. And the one person with the power to not let it be was...him.

Power can be incredibly attractive. But power abused...

Simon only smiled. Ana appeared beside me, covered a cough with her hand. She looked awful. "No," she rasped. "It's real. He infected us."

Meaning, he'd probably killed her. Killed Olga. *Killed our babies.*

Miserable, lingering, plaguelike deaths.

And something broke in me. Something like…restraint.

I was closest. I got to him first, had him by the collar. "Let go," I warned the mercenaries to either side of him. I didn't recognize my own voice.

"Ma'am," protested one, while the other looked over my shoulder toward Lex.

"Not him!" My words tore from my throat, like an animal straining for the capacity of language. "Me! *I'm* telling you—let the son of a bitch go, or get caught in the crossfire!"

Whether Lex nodded his okay or not, the guards backed quickly away.

"Magdalene," murmured Simon, as if we were friends, as if I were doing him a favor. But the doubled-up fists I swung across his jaw, like a volleyball swing, cracked on impact. The force of it shot up my arms, but I embraced the hurt. It meant I was still alive. It meant I could hurt him, too.

Simon grunted as his head snapped to the side. Then he spat out a tooth. "Mrs. Stu—"

Olga kicked him, hard in the solar plexus, knocking him onto the rock floor, cuffed hands and all. "Me," she snarled. "You killed me. And my Lexie. *My Scarlet!*"

Her— Scarlet had been hers? Olga suddenly made more sense.

Simon began to crab backward, awkward on his elbows, pushing with his feet. Ana Fraser caught him by the hair and dragged him up, as if some sense of honor would not allow her to hit a man while he was down. Before Simon could catch a breath, she drove a fist into his gut. He staggered backward, into the cave wall—at which point Aubrey, the smallest of us, was on him, slamming his head against rock.

"Matthew!" she growled. "Mama, Therese, Nicole—" and more, unintelligible names. She beat him with her fists, her knees, her kicks. Even as he fell again, she kept kicking him. Damned if I wasn't about to join her when, with some desperate surge of survival instinct, Simon recovered his feet and staggered down the closest passageway.

Did someone scream at us to wait? We didn't hear, were beyond language as we tore after him as one. Me and Ana and Aubrey. Olga and Nadia. I think Catrina and Tru trailed after us. I didn't look, couldn't care. We were predatory, deadly and utterly, instinctively brutal.

We were women, to our most primitive cores. Protecting our young, even if all that was left was to avenge them.

He had hurt our families, *our babies.*

He had to—

And he did. Die. One moment he was just ahead, strobed by darkness and careening lantern light, evading us through sheer desperation. His breath came out in moans, and he was starting to limp, and *we had him.*

The next, with a primal scream of horror, Simon vanished.

Right into one of the many stone shafts that littered the branches of this cave complex. As if Mother Earth herself had swallowed him. His scream stopped with an unearthly thud, followed by…*nothing.* No moan. No breath. Someone grabbed my belt from behind, as if I would launch myself after him. Who knows—maybe I would have. I wasn't thinking, wasn't caring. I wanted to claw his flesh apart with my bare hands.

Other hands caught Aubrey back and Ana. Twisting free, of Catrina I think, I crawled forward and peered over the edge of the inky pit. What light we had came from behind. Tru had brought the lantern.

Aubrey appeared beside me then, also searching for the blood scent of our enemy, but we still could see nothing below, hear nothing below. When I caught her gaze, she smiled. I almost smiled back, except for the sense of horror lingering at the edge of my mind. Not horror over this death. This felt absolutely right—as right as bedding my husband, as right as holding my baby.

My baby.

The sense of horror washed forward, and I understood again.

"Light," I commanded, embracing my language skills because maybe, just maybe, thinking could hold the worst of it at bay, just for a few breaths more. Someone passed the lantern forward. Ana, standing between Aubrey's and my prone bodies, leaned forward and shone it down the pit.

Thirty feet? More?

It wasn't the first time I'd seen a man twisted like that.

He'd gotten off far too easily.

We walked back as silently as we'd pursued Simon, but far more slowly. Killing him, hurting him, had not been our last hope. Not logically. But maternal instinct is as illogical as it can be vicious. It had been our last possible *action*, the last possible goal. Now, now…

Our babies might still die. And no amount of punching, kicking or flesh tearing would stop it.

Our men, as we reached them, looked almost…scared. And why not? Men think they're the most violent sex, when in fact they're only the quickest to violence. Men fight for dominance, fight for honor. Men strike out at pain and launch themselves at threats. But women?

Usually women fight—physically, bodily *fight*—for one reason only. To kill.

That's why we do it so rarely.

Lex came forward first. Braver yet? He carried Kestrel with him. He knew that, despite the blood on my hands, I wouldn't hurt her. The way my baby's sleepy face brightened at the sight of me, the way she began to babble, "Mamama!" shattered my heart. The last of my strength deserted me, and I began to crumple—

But Lex caught me. The arm not holding Kestrel held me to him, tight. I buried my face between the two of them, my doomed family…

And I sobbed.

And Lex did what he does when he is wholly broken.

He did nothing.

Chapter 25

That didn't last long, for either of us.

Eventually I turned my head on Lex's shoulder and, as I watched the other stunned couples over the top of Kestrel's red curls, I slowly gathered myself. Not two hours ago, I'd been communing with Goddess—or God—with Deity, in any case.

I'd been reminded of forces far greater than us, and far more capable. Maybe I couldn't reverse what Simon Adriano had done to the hostages. But maybe Someone Else could.

Even as my mind began seeking possibilities, Lex drew a deep breath and shifted Kes into my arms. "I'm calling in Care Flight. We'll get everyone the best doctors, the best hospital. They'll have the best chance of survival in Europe."

No matter what favors he might end up owing, or to whom he'd owe them. Anything for the family. Goddess, I loved him.

"In the meantime, we keep giving them water." This was Eve, moving among the children, now her patients. "The ley lines aren't the only game in town, damn it. I've administered antiviral medications, which will help. Once they develop fevers, we'll treat those, as well. But the sooner we can get everyone to a hospital, the better."

Catrina said, "In less than an hour, the hospitals of Europe may be very, very—Magdalene, where are you going?"

"You'll see." And I ducked with Kestrel into the altar room where, after I'd had my vision, Catrina had left the alabaster jar sitting at the feet of the Madonna mosaic. Kes coughed and reached her pudgy hands toward the pretty tile Lady. I returned with the jar. "While the rest of you are working out the medical and logistical issues, let's not forget the obvious. Father Pritchard, if you could help?"

Rhys looked up from where he knelt over young Phillipe, his lips moving in fervent prayer. He didn't even frown at being called "Father."

"You take God," I suggested, accepting Catrina's help to pour half the remaining oil into the bowl of the alabaster lid. "And I'll take Goddess."

If they really were two names for the same being, all the better.

"But I'm not—" he protested. "The church—"

"I thought you said that ordination was permanent?" Apparently there was no such thing as an ex-priest…only one who no longer had a job with the church.

"It is, but—" He glanced at Catrina, seemed to commune silently with her, then made a decision. "I can try. Let's cover both bases, shall we?"

"A baseball metaphor?" I teased.

His blue eyes crinkled. "Cricket." But even as he said that, he dipped his thumb in the oil and drew a small cross on Kestrel's forehead. *"In nomine Patris et Filii et Spiritus Sancti."*

In the name of the Father and of the Son and of the Holy Spirit. As soon as he finished a brief prayer of healing, I used oil from the jar itself to draw a small circle on my baby's chest and whispered, "Mother of all things, protect and heal you."

I no longer needed a specific name—Isis or Demeter or Mary—to understand the deity to whom I prayed. This Black Madonna was all of them, all faces in one face, all colors mixed into one shiny blackness. She was everything, the All-Mother. And as with any mother, She would recognize Her children's needs and, if possible, answer.

So it went—the children first, then the exposed adults, then the rest of us. Even a weeping, solitary Pauline. Nobody tried to distance themselves from the infected hostages. A surge of gratitude and respect soothed the worst of my desperation.

For all the Simons in this world, there were good people, too. Amazing people. Maybe there were enough of us to make a difference.

Almost out of oil, Rhys and I anointed each other. The last of it we used on Lex and Joshua as they strode back from the front of the cave, where they'd gone for better cell-phone reception.

"They have to wait for a break in the storm," Lex bit out, silencing himself only a moment for Rhys to anoint him. Then he continued, "They say it will be at least an hour or two. Maybe we should try the bus."

"Not yet." I'd all but finished the oil in the jar, but had Kes on my hip, and she'd been helping. So I handed Lex the jar, shifted our baby higher and guided her reading, oily hand in a circle on her daddy's chest. "Mother of all things, protect and guide this man, our champion."

Lex's golden eyes flicked from me to Kestrel and back, as if he only now saw the likelihood that his daughter might follow

in her mother's Goddess-worshipping, grailkeeping footsteps.
Either that, or he was remembering the last time I'd anointed
him in the name of a goddess. That time, the goddess had been
Isis, the oil had been edible and the result had been Kestrel.

I gained comfort from that memory as I took the jar back.

"Why not yet?" Nick ruffled Laurel's dark curls as the ten-
year-old tried to look brave. "The sooner we get these children
to a hospital—"

It was Eve who gently answered him. "Because these are
not the only children in danger."

Maybe it's true, what they say about women being better
multitaskers. To judge by their expressions, some of the men
had either forgotten about, or at least dismissed, the pending
time of transition.

"If nothing else," noted Catrina smoothly, "consider this
an attempt at freeing up the hospitals to focus on us."

Tru shook her head. "Assuming that the mosaic's any good
without all those missing tiles. If it works like a sieve with a
hole in it, it's better than nothing. But if it's like a computer
chip, with some of the connections gone, it's useless."

The missing tiles, of all those collected worldwide. The
Mary Stuart tiles. *Alabaster.*

My heartbeat sped. Was it possible…?

I carried the Magdalene Jar and Kes into the altar room.
As the others followed, I knelt before the Black Madonna.
The All-Mother. *Please, Lady. Please let me be right.*

And, on the stone at her feet—I smashed the jar.

Kestrel's mouth made an *O*. Catrina actually screamed.
She lunged at me. Rhys had to physically drag her back.
Stymied, she launched into a flood of rapid French that I
could understand, but choose not to translate. Young Laurel's
eyes widened, and she clamped her hands over her brother

Phillipe's ears. Trusting Rhys to handle Cat, I began to lift the different pieces up to the mosaic, one-handed, careful to keep them out of Kestrel's petulant reach. And just as I'd thought…

Yes…

Tru crouched beside me and touched a broken fragment of jar, as if sensing something deep inside it—and grinned. "The jar and the tiles must have come from the same quarry. This is *exactly* the right kind of alabaster. I'll go get the adhesive."

Tru seemed to take forever, arranging and mounting each piece of alabaster, occasionally breaking a larger chunk so that it would better fit. She kept stopping to spread her hand on the results and nod, or shake her head and move a piece. But eventually she finished the Black Madonna's white jar. The jar of one of Her greatest priestesses. The jar of Aquarius. When she was done, we stood back and gazed at the result.

Centuries after She'd been scattered, the Black Madonna's daughters had rebuilt Her. All except for that one, final hole in the Lady's forehead, where a pendant should have dangled.

"Considering everything," said Nadia hopefully, "I suppose missing only one piece isn't so very terrible."

Someone cleared her throat. Stepping forward to join us Pauline Adriano, doe eyes swollen from weeping, lifted a chain over her head. "Is…is this the one you need?"

Nadia's eyes widened.

Tru caught her breath, then snatched the necklace. Its gemstone spun on its chain, glinting red, then green, then amber in the shifting light of various lanterns. "Alexandrite?" She smacked her forehead with her hand. "*That's* why it changed colors in the different versions of the Madonna!"

Pauline had descended from the Marians, too.

"But isn't Alexandrite a relatively young gemstone?" asked Ana, then shook her head in understanding. "Of course.

Just because it wasn't *officially* discovered until Tsar Alexander doesn't mean it didn't exist."

Tru was already applying adhesive to the spot above the Madonna's nose. After slipping the pendant from its chain and carefully removing the metal finding, she pressed this last piece firmly into place. Her eyes closed in satisfaction.

At that moment, a sense of absolute completion came over me. Several of the Marians gasped softly. Kestrel squealed her delight. And faintly, almost inaudibly…the room began to hum.

The energy settled around us, like the warmth of sunshine.

Or a mother's hug.

Yes. This might actually work.

"It's almost time," announced Nadia, checking her watch. "To fully activate the mosaic we need seven Marians, right? Holding hands?"

Remembering the design on the jar, I nodded. "I think so." And they began to organize themselves for their end game.

Suddenly exhausted, I turned into Lex's waiting arms, let him take Kes from me, let him hold me. They'd been available quite a bit lately, him and his arms. I'd never meant to need him this much. I still wasn't sure how I felt about it—about my own dependence, now that we had a daughter who needed him, too. But either way, he'd been there. "Thank you," I whispered.

Lex's eyebrows rose. "For…?"

Where to start? "For being here. For getting the gemstones. For the guards. For not ruining Simon until everyone was safe. For coming up with the rescue plan. If I hadn't fought it so hard—" But my throat closed against revisiting the awful consequences of my actions. I leaned my forehead against Kes. We could have rescued her earlier. She wouldn't have been infected by Simon's engineered virus.

"Wait, Maggi—"

"No. You were right, and I was wrong. I'm sorry. Both of you. So…"

"No." He cupped my face with his free hand. "We were both right. The rescue *should* have been a last resort. If we'd rushed it, before you went back, hostages could have been hurt in the blast. Simon might have been more guarded. We wouldn't have had Myrddin to guide us in. It worked out…" He swallowed, hard. Because it had worked out with Kestrel contracting a deadly virus. "It worked out the best we could manage. The only one who owes me an apology—owes all of us an apology—is that son of a bitch Adriano."

Who wouldn't be apologizing to anyone.

I shrugged. He scowled, moved his hand to grip my shoulder. "Don't start doubting yourself, goddess. I need you right now."

Emotionally, maybe. But otherwise? "If we save Kestrel, it will be through your money. Your connections."

"As if any amount of money could make me feel as safe as my faith in you?"

Around the mosaic, the Marians were discussing from which direction Simon's blast of destructive energy would come and who should stand on that side. Just in case.

"I should probably tell you something," admitted Lex quietly, moving Kestrel's fingers from his mouth.

Oh, crap. I looked at all these women, descended from ancient priestesses, just as I was…but from different ancient priestesses. From Marians. "Your timing sucks."

Now it was Lex who shrugged. "I told you about my… during the bone-marrow transplant. How I died on the table and saw…things."

"Your near-death experience," I clarified.

"But I didn't tell you everything. I—" His jaw set, but he seemed to make the decision. "I saw even back then that the one person I could trust, could always trust, was you."

The very next time I'd met him, after his remission, he'd asked me on our first date. "You went out with me because of a vision?"

Lex nodded. I felt conflicted. He'd been following some *instructions?* "I thought you just wanted…me."

He blinked, then understood. "No! That is, I don't remember everything that happened, but nothing, nobody *told me* to do anything. I just…*knew,* Maggi. In that moment I saw everything so clearly. Right and wrong. Good and evil. And *you.* You'd already stood up for me at school. You were strong enough to stand against me, too. It's as if everyone who would ever be in my life were lights, some brighter than others, but you were so bright I could barely look at you. I knew that whatever else I did in my life wouldn't mean a damned thing unless I could do it with you.

"I've forgotten a lot of it since then. The good and evil and right and wrong business—that's still a challenge sometimes, without the instructions right in front of me. But never, *never* have I seriously doubted you. So please don't doubt yourself." His breath caught. "It scares me when you doubt yourself."

I gazed up at him, and I…got it. Men aren't necessarily stronger than women. Women aren't always stronger than men. But couples—loving, secure couples—could be stronger than either. Man *and* woman, like my recent vision of Deity. If Lex and I were going to save Kestrel, it would be because of us both.

I kissed him. He kissed me back, so strong yet so needy

himself. Then Kes yanked on my hair, and I broke away with an "ow," and Lex smiled into my eyes, so very much in love with me that I could hardly breathe in the echo of his love.

"Magdalene!" I think Catrina took some vicious pleasure in interrupting us.

I looked over to realize that this wasn't the first time they'd tried to get my attention when Tru asked, "Are you in or out?"

"Me?" I looked at Olga, who was holding Lexie. At Pauline Adriano, hanging back, still uncertain of her welcome. I looked at Laurel Fouquet, clinging tightly to Nick Petter, and even at Kestrel—not that I meant to volunteer Kestrel.

"I can do it," offered Olga, starting to pass Lexie over to Joshua, who had to let go of Benny's hand to take his daughter.

I protested. "No, I just meant—it needs to be seven *Marians*."

They looked at me blankly.

"And I'm not a Marian." Only Kestrel. Through Lex.

The other women exchanged uncertain glances. Then Ana rolled her eyes amiably. "Of course you're a Marian."

"But—"

"Maggi," Eve assured me. "Several of us have no proof of Marian lineage. But I'm not the only one who can just *sense* Marians. And I've come to trust my senses. You're one of us."

Which frankly? Was a bit too coincidental for me. Not that I might be of lost Marian descent, since I did come from a long line of powerful women and goddess worshippers. But that I would marry a man with Marian descent, and end up consulting with a group of women from Marian descent just in time for the Marians to reunite against an age-old threat.

Still, I could figure out the missing links later. If there was a later in which I cared. For now I trusted their senses, too. So with a final kiss on Kestrel's warm forehead, and a different kind of kiss for a conflicted-looking Lex, I stepped forward and took Nadia's hand on one side of me and Catrina's on the other.

Power, washed through me. Clockwise. From one woman to the next. And I understood.

The key to the seventh Marian was *people*. People conduct energy as much as metals do—that's why you shouldn't touch someone in contact with a live wire. Probably all being women, all being Marians, maybe even having exactly seven of us fine-tune our mingling life force to whatever ingredient this process needed. Like using the exact right alabaster. By forming a human ring around the mosaic, we became part of the ancient energy grid. Just in time.

Something quickly became different, not just in us but around us. *Changing*. The caverns seemed to groan under the force of that change, as if in labor pains of stone and dirt. An anticipatory hush became rumble became roar became the scream of tectonic plates and tearing rock against hard place. The ground beneath our feet vibrated. Sand sifted from the ceiling, then bits of stone hailed down.

The earth wept, crumbling gravellike tears.

I turned my head, squinting to see Lex still standing, his body curled protectively over Kestrel but his gaze, his focus, on me. He still wanted to save me. And no way in hell was I letting go of the hands of my sisters.

I shook my head.

With a last, steady look, Lex joined the others herding the children under the altar, adults forming human shields around them, against whatever roared toward us.

"Oh, God," whispered Eve, staring upward as if at a rushing wave. "It's all so…black."

Then the Adrianos' fury, launched by their corruption of this every-other-millennium time of transition, broke over us.

Chapter 26

Tru and Catrina had taken the posts between the mosaic and the rush of Simon Adriano's blast. The women without children. Sacrificing more than any of us.

Their bodies arched against the dark force. Catrina's hand tightened painfully around mine, and I gripped her just as hard, unwilling to let go. *No!*

Dust and debris clouded out our halogen lanterns, blinding us. And then—

Then, that horrible, destructive force—surging through the ley lines with the seeming energy of a tsunami—slammed over us and the mosaic. Devouring us. Ending us. Until…

The Madonna flickered, then glowed, every tile backlit with power beyond description. She came alive, and I heard a muffled cry from my own throat—a cry of joy. Of reunion, with everything to which I'd dedicated my adult life.

Motherhood. Sisterhood. Goddess. *Yes.*

Then? Stillness.

The power scattered into a rainbow of beautiful, harmless light. Shafts of illumination radiated out from the Madonna and upward, downward, everywhere. Like a great sun. Like a supernova. As it washed through the last, sifting bits of sand around us it created bright, winking sparks, like stars or fairies. Power—*Her* power—embraced the world, healing, loving. And here we stood, saturated, at the hub.

In the radiance I thought I saw glimpses of familiar and not-so-familiar faces. Faces from the distant future—could that beautiful, ginger-haired woman be an adult Kestrel? And who were the others, boy and girl, gazing at me with such love? Faces from the recent past—Max Adriano, finally at peace. For a moment I saw his hand on the shoulder of his daughter-in-law, Traviata, who looked calm, secure in herself at last. So the afterlife knows forgiveness. They vanished.

"Elise," breathed Ana, across the circle from me.

"M-Matthew?" whispered Aubrey. "Ma Ma?"

From beyond our circle, I heard Olga cry out in joy, pressing her hands to her mouth, at a vibrant young woman, identical to Nadia except for her brilliant red hair. Catrina's fingers dug into my hand with similar, heartfelt recognition. The illusory woman threw herself, laughing, into the arms of a large, stunned, tawny-haired man—who wept.

"How do you do, Scarlet Rubashka," I whispered, barely giving the greeting voice. "It's good to finally meet you."

She waved vigorously before vanishing.

Everything became peace. Everything became joy. Everything…began again. And as the intensity finally ebbed back to a hum, spent, leaving the temple feeling cleansed and renewed—we began to breathe.

It was over.

Slowly unlocking our hands from those of our sisters, we drew apart. We went to our families—Catrina to Rhys, Aubrey to Eric, Tru to the waiting arms of Griffin, and the rest of us to our husbands and children. The men seemed shaken, even Lex. The babies laughed, highly entertained. Kestrel, whom Lex immediately placed in my arms, felt cool and real and wiggly. We could get her to a hospital now. We could do everything within our power to save these children—and our power, we'd realized, was pretty damned impressive.

"My throat feels better, Aunt Eve," announced Laurel, her ten-year-old voice somehow piercing the exchanges of love and reunion and relief. "It doesn't hurt anymore."

I spun toward them, unable to speak—but Eve, catching my gaze with her own sudden hope, seemed to understand exactly what I wanted. "My bag," she told Nick, who ran for it. But her flush of pleasure said she was already aware of both the healing energy in the ley lines—and the absence of the virus.

A handful of disposable thermometer strips later, Eve lowered her penlight, let her stethoscope fall to her chest and struggled to maintain her clinical objectivity. "They aren't sick."

"We sure aren't," agreed Ana, more cheerful than I'd seen her since the gas attack, and she tickled her baby. Mara squealed her delight, all traces of a cough gone.

Maybe because of my previous experience with Isis, Egyptian goddess of medicine, I was one of the first to fully catch on. I turned, handed Kestrel to Lex, and began to unbutton his shirt.

"Um," he said. "Maggi?"

But for once I wasn't just after a view of his incredible

chest. I pulled the shirt down over his solid shoulder, ripped the white bandage off his upper arm. Where there had been a bullet wound, I now found smooth, healthy flesh.

Lex's eyes flared, for a split second, before he'd schooled his face back into simple acknowledgment. But I could read the smile in his satisfaction. He kissed Kestrel's cheek. "Look at that, baby. We're both all better."

His eyes shone suspiciously before he kissed me. And we, the three of us, were whole.

Others began to inspect their wounds—Nick Petter trying out his once-bad leg, Pauline pressing a marveling hand to her side, Catrina flashing her shirt open at Rhys with a throaty laugh. Then we were all laughing, grinning, high-fiving each other. Robert whispered something to Ana, who threw her arms around him.

Miracles. All miracles. But when you fool around with Divinity, sometimes, if you're very lucky, you get those.

Unable to form words, I carried Kes to the altar to get the marble cup—the Marian Chalice—and filled it from the still-beating water feature. Its rhythm seemed all the more natural, in the almost inaudible rush of clean ley-line energy through the mosaic, through the caverns. I carried it and my child to the mosaic and knelt, once again, at the feet of the Black Madonna. I raised the cup to Her, my throat too tight to even manage a thank-you. I prayed that She could read the silent gratitude exuding from every cell in my body as I then put the cup to my lips to drink, in honor of Her.

"This will be difficult," says the dark priestess, Sarah. She grips the shoulder of a younger Marian, who holds some kind of bundle for travel. It almost feels like a ceremony, something done with many women. The

Marians are setting out to find the materials that will eventually become the tiles, the mosaic, that will save modern-day Europe from catastrophe. "The journey could take more than one lifetime."

"Then may the Lady bless me with daughters, to continue Her quest."

They embrace, and the younger priestess turns to her own adventures. Just before leaving the temple, she looks over her shoulder and says, "Goodbye, Mother."

She is pale and Nordic blond. She cannot be Sarah's biological daughter.

Alone now, Sarah slowly circles the large column in the midst of the altar room, her dusky fingers brushing it as if sensing, confirming her choice of location for the mosaic. Then she hears something and looks up with welcome. "Hello, Mother."

The echo is too obvious. The use of the honorific, "Mother," is no sign that Sarah is Mary Magdalene's daughter.

Nor is it proof that she is not.

It is, however, as great a sign of respect as ever it has been.

"You have done well." The old priestess's eyes glow at Sarah with pride. "Your foresight may save the world."

"It may buy us time, little more." Sarah seems haunted. "If our daughters' daughters cannot stand firm, or if they forget, or if they are overrun…"

"Trust them," insists her elder. "Trust them, as I trust you."

"Oh, Magdalene—"

But the vision faded, and my eyes opened.

"Hey, Maggi," teased Tru after a moment, seeing that I was done. "Don't bogart the holy chalice." I passed it to her. I shifted Kestrel's weight and slowly stood, making way for the other Marians to pay their respects, and tried to completely understand this last vision.

I was right? The older priestess was, indeed, the Magdalene—at the least, *a* Magdalene, and to judge by previous visions, a Mary.

I really wished I could have gotten a little more information about whether Sarah was her daughter—and, yes, whether she and Jesus really had been together. But then I looked at the other women around me, historians, scientists, agents. And it occurred to me, far later than it should have occurred to a woman big on female empowerment, that not a one of us defined ourselves by our mate or our lack thereof.

Whom we married—or chose not to marry—was our business. Our children were a responsibility for which we would die.

Yet that was not all we were, and never would be.

I would not try to define Mary Magdalene by anything except who she was, what I knew she'd done as an apostle and priestess. But still, catching the Black Madonna's gentle gaze, I had to suddenly grin.

It occurred to me that there was no proof the child in her arms was a boy, either.

Who was the Black Madonna? Mother? Child? Both?

She was all of us.

Epilogue

And so we left the Temple Caves and stepped into the clear, blue and pink skies—the dawning of the Age of Aquarius. And the dawning after that. And the one after that. We started watching the news again, watching the great cities of Europe begin to dry out, to repair and rebuild. By the fourth day, even the women who'd been at this the longest were getting used to the idea that this particular danger had been averted.

We noticed a few other things, too. Remember how coincidental I found it that I just happened to be a Marian?

"I'm noticing them everywhere," admitted Eve, coming home with her family after a morning at the weekly market to stock up on supplies for all of us visitors. Aubrey and Eric had slipped away to wherever Aubrey goes—after we took a group picture of the lot of us, children included, for her mantel. Pauline Adriano had left for her family's home in Rome, agreeing—*offering!*—to sign custody of Benny to

Joshua, which seemed refreshingly sane of her. The rest of us did have jobs to recover, and residences to check—it wasn't unusual to walk into Catrina and Rhys's living room and find four people on their laptops, or step outside and run into two or three folks on cell phones. But it was hard to leave, as if the miracle of what had happened, and what had been averted, would fade like a tenuous memory.

It wouldn't. Ana and Robert were already planning to build a house—with guest additions—nearer the cave entrance, to help us all keep watch on the Temple. But in the meantime, Lex and I would stay to Friday. We needed our own cusp between worlds.

"Noticing what everywhere?" asked Catrina, chopping an onion. Somehow, she and I had ended up fixing food in the kitchen at the same time, along with Ana. Tru and Griffin were off at the caves. Nadia was out in the orchard with Lex, Joshua, and the children. I'd already figured out that within the Catrina/Rhys dynamic, Rhys did the bulk of the cooking. But he was British, and so was his food, so occasionally Catrina stepped in and proved herself far more capable than you'd think.

"Marians."

That caught our attention. Catrina, Ana and I all turned to our epidemiologist friend.

"Everywhere?" repeated Ana, putting down a lemon zester.

"Selling pastries. Pushing strollers. Herding goats. Marians." Eve shrugged.

"Perhaps it is a calling," Catrina suggested. Like me, she'd found no definitive proof of direct descent from other Marians. "Perhaps all women are awakening to the possibilities."

"That could be part of it," hedged Eve. "But what I've usually sensed is physical, something in the blood. Maybe it's just…gaining strength, now."

I shrugged. "Bloodlines expand, right? I'm sure some die out, but we've all seen family trees. Narrow at the top, wide at the bottom."

It's something that had always bothered me about the single-royal-bloodline theory—which I've researched. Heavily. For very personal reasons. While I could certainly imagine important men charting the oldest son of the oldest son of kings, all the way from Sumerian times through the House of David and Merovingian royalty and into secrecy, the blood couldn't be everything. Because how many of those oldest sons had brothers? Sisters? Cousins? Once you discounted seniority, just how many people could claim similar lineage?

"So by now, more women are of Marian descent than are not," agreed Ana cheerfully. So maybe we weren't special just because of descent. We were special because of what we'd done with it. Because we'd answered this particular call.

There would be other calls for other women.

"Scientists have used mitochondrial DNA—found only in women—to trace European genetics to one common ancestor and seven distinct lineages or haplogroups." That, no surprise, came from Eve. "The common ancestor is called Mitochondrial Eve, and the seven supposed clan mothers are called her 'daughters,' although there's no proof that they lived at the same time, and some may have descended from…"

For a moment, I couldn't even hear her. *Like my old family stories about the queen who sends her daughters out with their sacred cups.* I would definitely talk to Eve some more about this theory.

"So we truly are sisters?" Catrina looked at me with less than familial welcome. "*All* of us?"

"'Fraid so," laughed Eve.

I threw a piece of apple at Catrina. Like a sister might.

Her eyes narrowed. "I am no longer injured," she warned.

"Calm down, sis. I'm letting you keep Rhys, aren't I?"

Then I had to run. *Fast.* But I really was teasing. I'd never seen Rhys so happy as these past few days. It infused his walk, his eyes, the way he would casually touch her or would laugh when she not-so-casually touched him.

Who would have imagined?

I lost Catrina in the orchard, which is where I came across Lex and Nadia, keeping watch on Benny, Lexie and Kestrel. Kes could walk with the help of Daddy's finger. For a few minutes I leaned against a tree trunk and just watched them, as if I'd stumbled onto a photo shoot. Lex and Nadia wore jeans and sweaters with casual elegance. They chatted with old familiarity. Tentatively, like poking a sore tooth with my tongue, I wondered if they would have looked like this had they married each other. If Lex hadn't gotten leukemia, and had an NDE and envisioned *me.*

They really did love each other. But somehow, even as an overexcited Benny knocked Nadia backward a step and Lex reached out to catch her, the only word that came to mind for that love was, again: *sister.*

And, might I say, thank Goddess.

"I'm not worried," said Joshua Adriano gently, behind me. I looked up at him and shook my head in agreement. I'd reconnected with the Goddess. I'd remembered how good I was at these kinds of adventures, though I hoped to keep Kestrel out of my future quests. And between my vision of Mary Magdalene—*trust them, as I trust you*—and the reawakening of Marians everywhere, how could I not have confidence in the future?

For womankind and, by default, for me and my daughter?

A few trees away Lex carefully withdrew his finger from

Kes's grip. She swayed on her feet, all by herself, before plopping onto her well-padded butt. She blinked her surprise, then laughed. He scooped her up and grinned back at her.

Then, as Joshua and I headed over to our families among the apple orchard, Lex grinned pure welcome at me.

And all was well.

* * * * *

Happily ever after is just the beginning…

Turn the page for a sneak preview of
DANCING ON SUNDAY AFTERNOONS
by
Linda Cardillo

Harlequin Everlasting—Every great love
has a story to tell. ™
A brand-new line from Harlequin Books
launching this February!

PROLOGUE

Giulia D'Orazio
1983

I had two husbands—Paolo and Salvatore.

Salvatore and I were married for thirty-two years. I still live in the house he bought for us; I still sleep in our bed. All around me are the signs of our life together. My bedroom window looks out over the garden he planted. In the middle of the city, he coaxed tomatoes, peppers, zucchini—even grapes for his wine—out of the ground. On weekends, he used to drive up to his cousin's farm in Waterbury and bring back manure. In the winter, he wrapped the peach tree and the fig tree with rags and black rubber hoses against the cold, his massive, coarse hands gentling those trees as if they were his fragile-skinned babies. My neighbor, Dominic Grazza, does that for me now. My boys have no time for the garden.

In the front of the house, Salvatore planted roses. The roses I take care of myself. They are giant, cream-colored, fragrant. In the afternoons, I like to sit out on the porch with my coffee, protected from the eyes of the neighborhood by that curtain of flowers.

Salvatore died in this house thirty-five years ago. In the last months, he lay on the sofa in the parlor so he could be in the middle of everything. Except for the two oldest boys, all the children were still at home and we ate together every evening. Salvatore could see the dining room table from the sofa, and he could hear everything that was said. "I'm not dead, yet," he told me. "I want to know what's going on."

When my first grandchild, Cara, was born, we brought her to him, and he held her on his chest, stroking her tiny head. Sometimes they fell asleep together.

Over on the radiator cover in the corner of the parlor is the portrait Salvatore and I had taken on our twenty-fifth anniversary. This brooch I'm wearing today, with the diamonds—I'm wearing it in the photograph also—Salvatore gave it to me that day. Upstairs on my dresser is a jewelry box filled with necklaces and bracelets and earrings. All from Salvatore.

I am surrounded by the things Salvatore gave me, or did for me. But, God forgive me, as I lie alone now in my bed, it is Paolo I remember.

Paolo left me nothing. Nothing, that is, that my family, especially my sisters, thought had any value. No house. No diamonds. Not even a photograph.

But after he was gone, and I could catch my breath from the pain, I knew that I still had something. In the middle of the night, I sat alone and held them in my hands, reading the words over and over until I heard his voice in my head. I had Paolo's letters.

* * * * *

Be sure to look for
DANCING ON SUNDAY AFTERNOONS
available January 30, 2007.
And look, too, for our other Everlasting title available,
FALL FROM GRACE
by Kristi Gold.

FALL FROM GRACE is a deeply emotional story
of what a long-term love really means.
As Jack and Anne Morgan discover,
marriage vows can be broken—
but they can be mended, too.
And the memories of their marriage
have an unexpected power to bring back
a love that never really left....

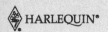

EVERLASTING LOVE™

Every great love has a story to tell™

Save $1.⁰⁰ off

the purchase of
any Harlequin
Everlasting Love novel

Coupon valid from January 1, 2007
until April 30, 2007.

Valid at retail outlets in the U.S. only.
Limit one coupon per customer.

5 65373 00076 2   (8100) 0 11302

HEUSCPN0407

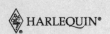

EVERLASTING LOVE™

Every great love has a story to tell™

Fall from Grace

Kristi Gold

Save $1.⁰⁰ off

the purchase of
any Harlequin
Everlasting Love novel

Coupon valid from January 1, 2007
until April 30, 2007.

Valid at retail outlets in Canada only.
Limit one coupon per customer.

52607370

HECDNCPN0407

REQUEST YOUR FREE BOOKS!

2 FREE NOVELS PLUS 2 FREE GIFTS!

◆ HARLEQUIN®
INTRIGUE®

Breathtaking Romantic Suspense

YES! Please send me 2 FREE Harlequin Intrigue® novels and my 2 FREE gifts. After receiving them, if I don't wish to receive any more books, I can return the shipping statement marked "cancel." If I don't cancel, I will receive 6 brand-new novels every month and be billed just $4.24 per book in the U.S., or $4.99 per book in Canada, plus 25¢ shipping and handling per book and applicable taxes, if any*. That's a savings of close to 15% off the cover price! I understand that accepting the 2 free books and gifts places me under no obligation to buy anything. I can always return a shipment and cancel at any time. Even if I never buy another book from Harlequin, the two free books and gifts are mine to keep forever.

182 HDN EEZ7 382 HDN EEZK

Name	(PLEASE PRINT)	
Address		Apt.
City	State/Prov.	Zip/Postal Code

Signature (if under 18, a parent or guardian must sign)

Mail to Harlequin Reader Service®:

IN U.S.A.
P.O. Box 1867
Buffalo, NY
14240-1867

IN CANADA
P.O. Box 609
Fort Erie, Ontario
L2A 5X3

Not valid to current Harlequin Intrigue subscribers.

Want to try two free books from another line?
Call 1-800-873-8635 or visit www.morefreebooks.com.

* Terms and prices subject to change without notice. NY residents add applicable sales tax. Canadian residents will be charged applicable provincial taxes and GST. This offer is limited to one order per household. All orders subject to approval. Credit or debit balances in a customer's account(s) may be offset by any other outstanding balance owed by or to the customer. Please allow 4 to 6 weeks for delivery.

HI06

HARLEQUIN

Super Romance

Is it really possible to find true love
when you're single...with kids?

Introducing an exciting new five-book miniseries,

SINGLES...WITH KIDS

When Margo almost loses her bistro...and custody of
her children...she realizes a real family is about more
than owning a pretty house and being a perfect mother.
And then there's the new man in her life, Robert...
Like the other single parents in her support group, she
has to make sure he wants the whole package.

Starting in February 2007 with

LOVE AND THE SINGLE MOM

by C.J. Carmichael

(Harlequin Superromance #1398)

ALSO WATCH FOR:

THE SISTER SWITCH Pamela Ford (#1404, on sale March 2007)
ALL-AMERICAN FATHER Anna DeStefano (#1410, on sale April 2007)
THE BEST-KEPT SECRET Melinda Curtis (#1416, on sale May 2007)
BLAME IT ON THE DOG Amy Frazier (#1422, on sale June 2007)

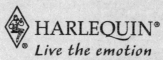

HARLEQUIN®
Live the emotion